HAUNTED CHRISTMAS

A Reverend Paltoquet
Supernatural Murder Mystery

by

Pat Herbert

OTHER NOVELS IN THE
REVEREND PALTOQUET MYSTERY SERIES:

The Bockhampton Road Murder
The Possession of November Jones
The Witches of Wandsworth
So Long at the Fair
The Man Who Was Death
The Dark Side of the Mirror
Sleeping With the Dead
The Corpse Wore Red
Seeing Double

THE BARNEY CARMICHAEL
CRIME SERIES

Getting Away With Murder
The Murder in Weeping Lane
The Mop and Bucket Murders

Also by Pat Herbert:

Death Comes Gift Wrapped

Bergen, Norway, March 1948

The snow glistened white beneath the pale, full moon. Any creature, be it human or animal, making its way through the wooded landscape would be silhouetted clearly against its rays, which was a disadvantage to one small lone figure that cold March night. The trees were sparse and, although they afforded some shelter, there were many gaps where hiding was impossible. But the figure the moon highlighted couldn't afford to be seen.

Little Halle Dahl knew he had to keep running. This was the only chance he had of staying alive. His mother had told him this, and he knew she was right. His ten-year-old legs were strong, but they were weakening now. But if he stopped he was dead. The man behind him had a gun; he had watched him point it at his mother as she lay on the bed, her clothes in disarray. He had pushed little Halle out of the way as he made his way up the stairs to the boy's mother's bedroom. He knew his way for he had been there many times before.

And now the man was following him, pointing that same weapon at his back. He had heard the explosion and felt the bullet whizz past his ear. The man was very close now. Then he saw the tall tree in front of him. Summoning up what was left of his strength, he began to climb up into the spindly branches. The man wouldn't see him there, he prayed. As he climbed, the man stopped directly beneath the same tree. Of course, thought little Halle, his footprints had stopped here too.

The snow had given him away. The man knew just exactly where he was.

He heard the fatal shot ring out as he tumbled out of the tree. The man was running away, as little Halle's life's blood ebbed out of him, making a crimson river on the white snow.

London, March 1948

Reverend Bernard Paltoquet was sitting in his new home in the London borough of Wandsworth, surrounded by all his worldly goods. Being a frugal man, they weren't many. He gazed about the cosy vicarage living room where his housekeeper, a rotund body called Mrs Harper, had just installed him.

She had welcomed the new vicar of the St Stephen's parish brusquely, but not unkindly. She was used to vicars, having served two before Bernard. The previous incumbent had recently died in harness, as it were, in the pulpit. His heart had given out during one of his long-winded sermons. She had surveyed the new vicar on his arrival with a critical eye: he was a lot younger than the last one, which was a blessing, even if he was a bit green about the gills. But knocking vicars into shape was something she was used to, and this young man would present no problems, she was sure.

Bernard had already inspected his church just a few yards down the road and had been dismayed by its dilapidation and air of neglect. Much needed doing to make it habitable. At least a half-ton of lead was missing from the roof, and several panes in the stained-glass windows had been broken. It was a daunting task for any vicar, but for Bernard, in his first incumbency, it seemed almost insurmountable. The early spring weather, being still frosty, didn't help matters. It made the interior very cold and unwelcoming, but at least the vicarage itself was warm. He toasted himself by the fire, wondering how he was going to afford all the improvements needed to entice the congregation to flock to his sermons.

"The chain in the toilet doesn't work unless you yank it."

He was brought back to the present by this bald statement from Mrs Harper, who was standing in the doorway with her hands on her ample hips.

Another problem to worry about, but Bernard just smiled. "Never mind, Mrs Harper, just call a plumber, please." Simple.

"A plumber? Do you know 'ow much they charge these days?"

"Probably a lot?" he hazarded.

"You can say that again with knobs on. I'll ask my friend Ada to ask 'er 'ubby to come and have a look at it, if you like."

"Is he a plumber?"

"Not so's you'd notice it."

"Er, then what good do you think he'll be?"

She shrugged. "'E's 'andy. And 'e's cheap."

"I see. Well, whatever you think best, Mrs Harper. Thank you."

Bernard was already bored with the vicarage's sanitary arrangements or lack thereof and just wanted to be left in peace. The difficulties with the lavatory chain were hardly his domain. No doubt this Ada's husband would be able to fix it. Mrs Harper retired with a sniff, while he continued to speculate on what he would do to make the lives of his parishioners a little better.

The war had been over for just under three years. Although rationing was still very much in evidence, bananas and oranges had begun appearing in the shops, and the queues which accompanied these happy events were getting shorter as the fruit became more available. Life was getting back to normal, even though it was still a trial to many. Bernard tried to be optimistic, although his natural position on most things was to err on the pessimistic side. However, there was no time to dwell on the negatives, he told himself. Things needed doing, and spring was here, if struggling a bit, so it wasn't all bad news.

He was a slightly-built man, with a mass of brown curly hair, friendly brown eyes and an open, fresh face. He had left Leeds after qualifying at the university, with high hopes for a future full of good works. He had no wife to accompany him so Mrs Harper, landed on (correction, given to) him by the Archdeacon, was to 'do' for him until such time as he installed a Mrs Paltoquet.

Mrs Harper, on first acquaintance, was almost as daunting as the sad state of his church and apparently now the lavatory, and Bernard was already in awe of her. Being a naturally timid man, her abrupt manner alarmed him. She had spoken to him as if he was a naughty child who had just broken her best china. And it seemed she blamed him for the broken lavatory chain, which seemed unfair as he hadn't even had the chance to use it.

He was sad for a moment as his thoughts turned to Sophie. Where had she gone? he wondered. One minute they were planning to marry, the next she had walked out of his life, apparently forever. The note she had left him had held no clue. He could only suppose she had just fallen out of love with him; but they had been so very much in love, he couldn't see how her feelings could have changed so suddenly.

Still, the past was the past, there was no use in dwelling on it, he supposed.

Another newcomer to Wandsworth was Doctor Robert MacTavish, having arrived a little under a month ago, and he was sitting in his new surgery with the same mixture of hope and trepidation as the new vicar just a few streets away. A Scotsman by birth, MacTavish had lived south of the border since he was a small child, so any trace of a Scottish accent had long since disappeared. He could, when occasion demanded, however, turn on a soothing Glaswegian brogue, but he used it sparingly and mainly on the fairer sex. A tall, bonny man, with a shock of sandy hair, now slightly receding, he was used to the adulation of his female patients, whose blind faith in his skill and knowledge he found flattering as well as touching.

He had previously shared a small practice in a village just outside Gloucester and was looking forward to the challenge that a busy South London practice would offer. He had no doubt the work would be harder than he was used to, but he was ready for it. Come epidemics or plagues of locusts, he was ready for them.

The new National Health Service was due to be introduced in a few months' time, so the young doctor would have no more pleading poverty and unpaid bills to deal with. That part of his workload would be easier and, now that he had his living quarters over his surgery, he wouldn't have to cycle to and fro in all weathers. The first thing he planned to do, now that he was in London, was buy a small second-hand car to make his life even easier, especially when called out in the middle of the night to a woman in labour.

Like Bernard, he was a bachelor, and therefore in need of a housekeeper to see to his meals and do the general chores. He had selected a young woman from the various applicants sent to him by the nearby domestic bureau. Lucy Carter seemed capable and willing, and was quite pretty, which didn't hurt. Living only minutes from his surgery there would be no excuse for her to be late, either.

She was an amply proportioned lady in her late twenties or possibly early thirties. Gently-spoken and polite, she had been delighted to be offered the position as a GP's housekeeper, which she saw as a pleasant change from the old curmudgeon she had looked after until his very welcome death the previous month. And she had soon proved herself indispensable to Robbie. When he climbed the stairs at the end of his working day, the whisky decanter and glass were set at the ready, his supper was warming in the oven, and the fire in the living room was freshly banked.

Robbie's love life was uncomplicated, not to say non-existent. Having no lost love to moon over, he was able to make a fresh start where affairs of the heart were concerned. If he had left a pining female behind in Gloucestershire, it didn't appear to worry him unduly, being a man who subscribed to the adage that there were many more fish in the sea. He was in the prime of life, being in his mid-thirties and handsome, and in a profession that so many women revered. So it was unlikely he would go short of female company for very long.

He sat at his desk after the last patient had left that morning and took a tally of his good fortune. He had a new practice, a comfortable home to go with it and a delightful housekeeper who looked after him with efficiency and goodwill. Things didn't get much better than this, and it was spring. The war was over, and you could get a proper egg sometimes. What more could anyone want?

Mrs Harper stood outside her friend Ada Appleyard's front door, impatiently tapping her foot. She had rung the bell three times, and no one had come to answer it. Typical, she thought. If she had told her once, she'd told her a hundred times to turn her hearing aid on. What was the point of it, if she didn't use it? She supposed the stupid woman worried it would run the battery down.

Then she saw the front room curtain move. She's seen me, all right, thought Mrs Harper. Why doesn't she open the door? As this thought crossed her mind, and she was preparing to ring a fourth time, the door opened slowly, and Mrs Appleyard's head peeped round it.

"Oh, it's you, Nance. I thought you was the tally man."

"Do I look like the tally man? 'E's got a moustache and no 'air, as well as being at least a foot taller than me."

"Well, you can't be too careful, Nance. He's been round three times this week, already, and we've got nothing to give 'im till Dick gets paid on Friday. They think we're made of money, them people."

Nancy Harper sympathised with her old friend. "Yes, I know what you mean. When I bought a carpet from them, they wouldn't leave me alone till I'd paid for the bloomin' thing. If I missed a week, they were down on me like a ton of bricks. I wouldn't 'ave minded, but by the time I'd finished paying for it, it needed renewing."

Ada laughed. She was always pleased to see her old friend, and today especially was a good day, as the new vicar had just arrived, and she was eager to hear all about him.

"Come in, love," she said, wiping her wet hands on her apron. "I was about to take a break, anyway. I 'ate washdays. I swear there's always more sheets than we've got beds in this 'ouse."

Five minutes later, the two women were seated in the parlour by the fire, waiting for the tea to brew. The hearth gave off a warm glow, a pleasant antidote to the wintry March weather outside.

"So, Nance, what brings you out on a day like this?" Ada asked, stirring the tea, and rocking the pot back and forth to encourage it to mash properly.

"Well, me and the vicar were wondering if Dick could come and look at the toilet," she replied.

"You want my Dick to come and look at your toilet?" Ada repeated, pouring the now very strong brown liquid into the china cups on the small occasional table in front of them. "Why?" It seemed a strange request.

"Oh, Ada, don't be daft. What I mean is, can 'e see if 'e can do anything as the chain don't work properly. You 'ave to give it a yank before it'll flush. I don't want the new vicar to 'ave to put up with things like that. 'E'll wonder what sort of a place 'e's come to."

Ada's ears pricked up at the words 'new vicar'. The last old duffer had sent her to sleep in her pew regularly each Sunday, so the new one could only be an improvement.

"Yes, I see," she said, offering Mrs Harper a Garibaldi biscuit. "You don't want 'im getting upset before 'e's even preached 'is first sermon." She replaced the lid of the biscuit tin before her visitor could help herself to another one. "But my Dick's not a plumber, you know," she pointed out.

"'E's an odd job man, though, ain't 'e?"

"I suppose that'd be what you'd call 'im," Ada agreed. "But 'e's getting a bit past it, these days."

"Well, it can't 'urt for 'im to come and 'ave a look at it, can it?"

"No, all right. I'll ask 'im to come over when he 'as the chance, shall I?"

"Thanks, ducks."

"Come on, Nance, you know I'm dying to know," said Ada in a confidential tone, reopening the biscuit tin as an inducement. "What's the new vicar like?"

"Well, 'e's got an unpronounceable name, for a start," said Mrs Harper slowly, holding out her cup for a refill and taking another Garibaldi at the same time.

"What do you mean? Is 'e foreign?" asked Ada as she replenished her friend's cup.

"Well, 'e don't talk 'foreign', but 'e's definitely got a funny name."

"What is it, then?" asked Ada, beginning to lose patience with her friend. "Get on with it, can't you?"

"Oh, all right. Keep your frock on," grumbled Mrs Harper. "I don't know 'ow it's spelt, but it's pronounced Pal – toe –kway."

"You what? What sort of name is that when it's at 'ome?"

Mrs Harper shrugged. "Apparently it's French."

"French? 'E's a bloody frog?" Mrs Appleyard looked as shocked as if Nancy had told her he was a German.

"No, no. 'E's as English as you and me. Bit 'oity-toity, like, but nice enough. 'E's very young and quite nice looking. I think 'e'll cause a bit of a stir among the ladies."

"Oh, that sounds better. What's 'is Christian name?"

"Bernard."

"Bernard? Well, that's English enough, at least. Is 'e going to be easy to get on with, do you think?"

"Oh yes, I think so. 'E probably wants to make changes – don't they all? But I'll soon knock that out of 'im."

"Never known you to fail yet, Nance," grinned Ada.

"I should think you 'aven't, Ada Appleyard," sniffed Mrs Harper. "I should think you 'aven't."

While Nancy and Ada were indulging in parish gossip, the main subject of it had decided to spend the day getting to know his new environs. The best way to do that, Bernard thought, was to travel on the upper decks of the local buses, looking about him as he went. So, putting aside the problem of the faulty lavatory chain, which he had found impossible to work, he set off at eleven o'clock, taking a number 37 from outside the Town Hall all the way to Peckham. From there he took another bus to Camberwell, then to Brixton, Clapham, ending up at Battersea for the final leg of the journey back to Wandsworth.

It had been an instructive day. He'd had lunch in a little cafe in Brixton before climbing up the stairs of a bus going to Clapham Common. He had enjoyed the views of the spacious greens and well laid out streets which looked pleasantly regal, despite a smattering of bomb sites and half-demolished buildings. It would take many years before all traces of bomb damage would be swept away, he imagined.

His journey almost at an end at six o'clock that evening, he joined a busy rush hour bus queue in Battersea, feeling pleasantly tired. It was still fairly light, although the threatening rain had long ago obliterated the sun. Bernard turned up his coat collar and stared impatiently down the street for his homeward bus.

"These buses are very unpredictable, don't you find?" came a voice next to him. He turned to see a little man standing beside him and was immediately struck by his appearance. Not only had he seemingly arrived out of nowhere, Bernard had never seen anyone so odd-looking outside of a book of Grimm's Fairy Tales. He was extremely short, almost a midget, very thin, of indeterminate age, with a greyish-green complexion and short tufts of black hair dotted sparsely all over his disproportionately large head. But his eyes were the oddest feature of all, sometimes looking green, sometimes amber and, most alarmingly, sometimes bright red. The man's easy, conversational manner seemed at variance with his appearance, and did nothing to dispel Bernard's unease at, what seemed to him, to be some sort of apparition.

He didn't want to be impolite and ignore the man, however. After all, the poor chap couldn't help looking the way he did. "Yes, indeed," Bernard replied. "I have been travelling on buses all day and now I'm quite ready to go home. I've been waiting a good twenty minutes already for this one."

"Dear, dear, as long as that?" asked the man, giving a funny little jerk with his elbows. "I can't get behind with my schedule."

"Your schedule?" asked Bernard, too tired to wonder what such an odd little man would want with a schedule.

"Yes, I have a strict schedule to adhere to, you know, and I must say I hadn't bargained for waiting for buses. I hadn't factored it in. Are they always so late?"

"I can't really say," Bernard replied, "I've only just moved here from Yorkshire. Mind you, buses were non-existent there."

"I see. Hmm." The little man seemed confused. "Right, anyway. It is a pleasant enough evening to wait, despite the clouds. It isn't as cold as it was yesterday."

"No, indeed," agreed Bernard. "Perhaps spring is coming after all."

"Let's hope so, but I don't suppose it need bother you anymore."

Bernard looked at him in puzzlement. "Why do you say that?" he asked, staring anxiously down the street for his bus yet again.

Their innocuous conversation had suddenly taken a strange turn, and Bernard wasn't sure if the man was all there. Still, he admonished himself, one mustn't judge people until one knows them better. But he really didn't want to get to know this man better at all.

"No, not anymore," repeated the man. "According to my schedule, that is."

"What sort of schedule is it, if you don't mind me asking?" asked Bernard, his tiredness now forgotten.

"Oh, nothing to bother your head about, Mr Paltoquet," said the man, giving another funny jerk with his elbows. "My name's Diabol, by the way."

"How on earth do you know my name?" Bernard was now thoroughly disorientated. The man was beginning to seriously frighten him.

"Yes, that's right," said the man, ignoring his question. "Diabol by name and diabolical by nature." He laughed. It wasn't pleasant. "The schedule tells all, my dear fellow," he replied, tapping his nose with his index finger. "It is the fount of all my knowledge. Mind you, I must admit, your dog collar has thrown me, rather."

"My dog collar? What's my dog collar got to do with anything?" This man was definitely unhinged, what his late father would have called 'a rum cove'.

"Well, I don't usually play host to men of the cloth. They're usually waited on by the people from the other place. Upstairs."

"The 'other place'? 'Upstairs'? Forgive me, but are you actually sane at all?"

"But I thought you would be expecting me. Maybe not at this particular bus stop, perhaps. My schedule isn't usually wrong, although it's not the first time it's let me down. My schedule – "

"Stop going on about your schedule!" yelled Bernard. "If this is some kind of a joke, it's gone a bit too far, so I would appreciate it if you would leave me alone."

"But, my dear sir, I can't. The schedule – "

Bernard was sorely tempted to grab him by the throat and shake the 'schedule' out of him, through the top of his head, if need be. However, the man suddenly looked very confused and apologetic.

"Your name *is* Paltoquet, isn't it?" he asked.

"Yes, you know it is."

"*Michael* Paltoquet?"

"No, *Bernard* Paltoquet."

"Oh dear, there's been some dreadful mistake. Lucifer is always employing young people to do the administration. They've usually just arrived downstairs, after falling off their motorbikes or coming off worst in gang fights. And, of course, there is a rather large contingency of dead Nazis to allocate jobs to now. They're all at sixes and sevens, if you ask me."

"I think maybe you should seek professional help," advised Bernard, although he thought a psychiatrist, no matter how experienced, would have his job cut out with this one. "Now, will you please go away? Go to the end of the queue. I think you're just talking to me so that you can get on the bus quicker."

"No, that was not my purpose. And I realise now that I'm talking to the wrong person. Sorry to have bothered you."

Bernard looked once more for a sign of a bus as the man said this, then turned to address him. There was no one there. He must have gone at quite a lick to have disappeared so quickly, thought Bernard. As he was thinking this, he saw the bus coming towards him and he realised that, all the while he had been talking to the funny little man who called himself Diabol, he hadn't heard any background noises or seen any other people or traffic. Everything had just gone away somehow, and now it was all back with a vengeance. People's voices seemed too loud and the hooting of the traffic was practically splitting his eardrums. He thought he was about to faint as the bus pulled up. His legs felt so wobbly, he decided not to attempt the upper deck and was relieved to take the last seat inside on his final journey home.

∞

Stepping off the bus, Bernard's legs practically gave way beneath him, and the thought of walking the distance from the bus stop to the vicarage seemed impossible at that moment. Looking across the road, he saw a welcome sight – the Bricklayer's Arms, fully lit up and inviting. He managed to negotiate his way through the rush hour traffic towards the saloon bar door, stepping inside with relief. What greeted him was almost as daunting as trying to walk home. It was the usual sights and sounds to be found in any pub but, to Bernard, the noise was deafening. There was a jangling piano competing with a group of men who were singing a well-known ballad of the day at the tops of their voices. They were also very out of tune.

Realising it had been a bad idea, after all, he turned to leave but was prevented from doing so by a tall, sandy-haired individual entering at the same time as he was trying to exit.

"Excuse me!" exclaimed Robbie MacTavish, as Bernard practically fell into his arms. "Are you all right, man?"

Bernard remained upright with difficulty. "I'm very sorry, I feel quite faint. I think I need to get some air."

"Nonsense, you need a double whisky inside you." Robbie could see the young and very pale vicar was about to demur. "Trust me, I'm a doctor," he said.

"You are?" murmured Bernard, as Robbie helped him to a seat in a corner alcove away from the general hubbub.

"Yes, I am and my diagnosis for your ailment, my friend, is whisky. It never fails."

Leaving Bernard to gratefully ensconce himself in the alcove, Robbie went to the bar and ordered the drinks. Returning with two double whiskies, he watched with concern as the pale young man tentatively sipped it. He was obviously unused to strong liquor.

"Get it down you, man," he ordered. "It needs to be polished off in one go to do you the most good."

"I see – right." Summoning up his courage, Bernard did as he was bid. Swallowing the whisky, he managed to choke on it, and coughed and spluttered into his handkerchief for a good five minutes.

"Not used to it, eh?" Robbie observed, patting him on the back.

Bernard nodded, as he began to control his coughing fit and wipe his streaming eyes. "No, I'm afraid I'm not."

Robbie laughed. "Never mind. It looks as if it's done you good already. The colour has come back to your cheeks."

Bernard politely refrained from pointing out that the colour in his cheeks was probably more likely due to his coughing fit rather than the efficacies of the whisky. "Er, it's strong stuff, that's for sure," he hedged. "Anyway, thank you for your assistance this evening. My name is Bernard Paltoquet, by the way. How do you do?" He held out his hand to the doctor who shook it heartily.

"Robbie MacTavish to you," he said. "I've just set up in practice in the neighbourhood."

"What a coincidence! So have I – as vicar, I mean."

"I think I got that," winked the doctor, looking at his give-away dog collar. "Anyway, man, what on earth was the matter just now? You looked as if you'd seen a ghost."

"Funny you should say that because ..." Bernard stopped. Should he relate his experience at the Battersea bus stop? he wondered. Wouldn't his new friend think he was completely mad?

"Go on," encouraged the doctor. "Oh, wait, before you do, let me get us another couple of drinks." He made to get up, but Bernard stopped him.

"Not for me, thanks. I feel quite drunk, as it is. Anyway, it's my turn."

"Nonsense!" insisted Robbie, pushing him back into his seat. "My treat, I insist. What about a soft drink instead? Orange juice or something?"

"Er, well, an orange juice would be most welcome," Bernard replied. If only to take away the taste of the whisky, he thought. "Thank you."

While Robbie was at the bar, Bernard continued to debate with himself whether to tell him what had happened. The man knew something had, because of the state he had been in when he entered the pub. Yes, he decided. He'd tell him and let him draw his own conclusions.

Robbie listened to his story without interruption. He lit his pipe and sucked on it, all the while giving Bernard his full attention.

"Well, what do you think? Am I going mad? Was it all just a figment of my imagination?" Bernard asked, picking up his orange juice with a shaky hand.

Robbie didn't speak for a moment. "No, not at all. Why would you make up a story like that? As a man of the cloth, I'm sure you don't make a habit of lying." He grinned at him. "There are more things in heaven and earth etcetera, don't they say?"

"Well, William Shakespeare did once, I believe," said Bernard with a hint of mockery. "In *Hamlet*, wasn't it?"

Robbie's grin widened. "Probably, man. English literature wasn't my strong suit at school."

"Sorry. I didn't mean to be pedantic. Anyway, what do you think, really?"

"I think it might have been *Macbeth*." They both laughed.

They concentrated on their drinks for a moment, then Robbie continued, "It may interest you to know that I'm very interested in the occult and that sort of thing. I've read lots of books on the subject, and there are many cited cases of people having just the kind of experience you've had."

"Really? What, like seeing someone who wasn't really there and having a conversation with him and all that?"

"Well maybe not quite that. But I'd be interested in your take on the matter. Who do you think this strange man was? Diabol? That sounds like a devil's name."

Bernard ruminated for a few seconds before replying. "Hmm, I know, but he didn't seem particularly frightening. Just odd."

"So, what do you think he wanted with you?"

Bernard paused before replying. Then he told Robbie about the name mix up and what he dared not think would have happened if Diabol had really come for him.

"Do you mean he was going to, well, take you back with him?" Robbie looked less sanguine now.

"I know it sounds far-fetched, but I suppose that's the only conclusion to draw." He paused again and watched Robbie's reaction.

"So, you're saying that you would have died and been carried off to Hell or whatever they call it. The other place? Down below? Fire and brimstone?"

"Well, in the Christian church we believe there is a Heaven and a Hell. Although, not literally. But, yes, that's what it amounted to. It was just lucky for me my name's Bernard and not Michael."

"Two things strike me here," said Robbie.

"Which are?"

"One, you, being a vicar would hardly be a candidate for the 'other place'."

"One would hope so," interrupted Bernard with a grin.

"Yes, all right, man. Don't interrupt. Two, your name. It's strange enough. I certainly have never heard of it. So it amazes me that there's at least two of you knocking about."

Bernard laughed at this. "Yes, well. There you are."

"I hope he didn't find this Michael," observed Robbie. "He's not a relation of yours, is he?"

"Not to my knowledge. So, you really believe me?" Bernard was both surprised and delighted. He liked this bluff doctor very much already.

"I do. And I'll let you into a little secret," he said in a confidential tone, leaning towards him. "I'm a bit psychic, too."

"But I never said I was psychic," protested Bernard.

"But you are, man. You are."

Bergen, March 1948

Birgitta peeped through the crack in the cupboard door but could see nothing out of the ordinary. The kitchen seemed deserted, what she could see of it, and there was no sign of any disturbance. Her brother had instructed her to stay there, but she didn't know for how long. He had told her to get in the cupboard when that man arrived carrying the gun. The man was a friend of her mother's, but she had never liked or trusted him. He was big and stocky with dark hair and a thick moustache. He was very ugly and had slobbery lips. She particularly didn't like his slobbery lips.

When she had heard raised voices coming from her mother's bedroom, she had become frightened. Halle had told her not to worry, they were always arguing. But not like this. Their voices had got louder and louder, and Halle had then told her he would go and see what was happening. He, too, had become frightened and that's when he had told her to hide in the kitchen cupboard, just in case. In case of what? she had wondered but had obeyed all the same.

Then she had heard a shot being fired, her mother's screams, and Halle running down the stairs. She had heard him run out of the house, slamming the door. She had then heard the big man's footsteps run down the stairs and the front door slam again. Then all had become quiet. She had continued to hide in the cupboard, too scared to come out, even though she was on her own now. But she had been terrified the big man would return and find her.

She had no idea how long she had been in the cupboard. What had happened to her mother and little brother? The house was eerily silent. She needed to answer the call of nature now, and she started to cry as she felt pins and needles creep up her legs. But she mustn't move, not until Halle came back, she told herself. She waited a few more minutes, then decided. She wasn't going to pee her pants. Her mother would be very cross with her. Finally, she stepped cautiously out of the cupboard.

When she had relieved herself, she proceeded slowly towards her mother's bedroom door. She stood outside for a moment, afraid to call to her. She couldn't hear any sounds from inside. Pushing it gently, she heard its familiar creak, as she saw her mother's body slumped across the bed. Her clothes had been ripped off and there was a dark red stain in the middle of her breasts. Birgitta's tears made clean rivulets down her dirt-smeared face, as she tried to cover her mother's nakedness with the tattered garments.

"Mummy?" she said softly. "Are you awake?" No answer.

She stroked her hair and then her face, which looked quite calm and still. She tried not to look at the stain now oozing through the dress she had covered her with, but she was an intelligent little girl. She knew that she had been shot by the big man with the gun; the man who had come to see them on many occasions before.

He had worked on the farm and she recalled how her mother had seemed pleased with him.

She couldn't understand why her mother didn't wake up and tell her it was all a mistake. The blood wasn't blood at all. Maybe she had spilt some paint on herself. Maybe she and the big man had played a game that had been rough and got out of hand. But the blood was real. Her fingers were wet with it and it was still warm. There was no mistake about that.

Birgitta tried shaking her mother awake knowing, as she did so, that it was no use. She would never open her eyes again. Her mother was gone from her forever; she wasn't there anymore. Only her dead, useless body that would no longer hold her when she cried or tickle her to make her laugh. She sat there, stroking the dead woman's matted hair, sobbing her heart out. It was dark outside now. She felt lonely and afraid.

She began to wonder where her brother was. Where had he run off to? Had the man followed him and caught him? Maybe Halle was dead too? She couldn't bear to think that. She had to find out what had happened to him.

She thought about her dead father. Killed by a Nazi storm trooper. It was then that things had started to go wrong. Her bereaved mother had struggled to keep their little farm going but, without her husband, she had found it impossible. She had tried to get one of the lads from the next village to come and help out, but he turned out to be a disaster. He never arrived in time to milk their two cows and complained of backache after planting only half a row of potatoes. Then another lad had come who had been much better, but he had received his call up papers after only two weeks.

Then that slobbery-lipped man had arrived on the scene. He seemed all right at first. He had brought her mother armfuls of flowers practically every other day and had even given her a doll and Halle a kite. He had made himself useful about the farm too, for which they had all been grateful. When their mother had asked him why he hadn't been called up, he had whispered something about a medical condition. Birgitta and Halle had wondered about this, but they supposed it was all right. Anyway, he was too useful to bother about this too much. Their mother had told them it was all right and not to worry. So they hadn't.

But then he started making demands on their mother. At first, it was to do with his meals. She had given him breakfast every morning, but he was soon having all his meals with them. As they hadn't been able to pay for his services, this had seemed reasonable enough, but then he had wanted to move in on a permanent basis. That was when their mother had put her foot down, and when the arguments had started. Gradually he had begun hanging around all night, long after she had given him his evening meal. But she hadn't given in to him. Not then.

But one day, she and Halle returned from school to find the kitchen deserted. There was no sign of their tea. They had started to panic, running through the house and up the stairs, calling out for their mother. Her bedroom door had been locked, and they had heard muffled sounds on the other side of it.

She had come out onto the landing and taken them in her arms. She had told them not to worry, she would be down in a moment to cook their tea. Then they had heard *his* voice. All low and gruff, telling them to run off and play and not to disturb their mother.

When she had finally come down the stairs, they could see she had been crying and there was a bruise under her right eye. Birgitta hadn't been fooled when her mother had told her everything was all right. How could it be all right with that bruise? She had walked into an open cupboard door and it had hurt, that was why she had been crying, her mother had assured her.

The man was evil, no matter what her mother told her to the contrary. He had forced her to do unspeakable things with him, even if she hadn't been sure exactly what. Halle hadn't seemed bothered, though. He even said he liked him. But that was because he sometimes played football with him and helped him fly the kite.

So, the man had finally moved in with them, and Birgitta had had to accept him. And now it was too late. Her mother was dead and, very probably, her brother too. She must get help.

She left the farmhouse wrapped in her warm winter coat. She was a sensible child. There had been no fresh fall of snow, and she could see the small footprints of her brother and the much larger ones of the man very clearly. She could see them by the light of the full moon as she followed them into the dark, forbidding forest. She saw the big prints getting closer to the small ones, and fear took her in its grip. Where were they? Where was her little brother?

On and on she went, through the tall fir trees until she reached a tree beneath which both sets of footprints stopped. The snow here had been disturbed by what looked like some kind of a sled or, she realised with fright, possibly a body? Her eyes tracked the source of this disturbance and rested on a large mound of snow at the other side of the tree. She knelt down and started to scrabble at the piled up snow.

Then she saw the little hand and knew it was her brother's. She scrabbled frantically until his face was uncovered. His eyes were wide-open and completely still. His mouth was also open, filled with the cold, unforgiving snow. Her tears fell on his eyes as she gently closed them.

Then she heard a noise behind her and spun round. She collapsed into the soft snow and, as the bullet pierced her heart, the last thing she saw was the feet and legs of the man who had ruined all their lives.

~

Baldur Hanssen glanced fearfully around him as the moon shone down on his large, brawny figure.

Beside him, under the big fir tree, was the body of a little girl. He had lost all sense of reason. He had shot and killed her little brother and buried him here under the snow, and now he had killed her too. He sank down on his knees in despair.

He hadn't meant it to be like this. He had awoken that morning full of hope. He had planned to ask Marianne to marry him, taking to his heart not only her but her children too. He had been particularly fond of Halle; he was a dear little soul. Birgitta, however, had always seemed suspicious of him, but he had been determined to make her like him too. He had been prepared for fatherhood, as well as matrimony. But it had all gone disastrously wrong.

Marianne had turned down his proposal in disgust. She had said he was too ugly! She had slept with him because she had needed his help on the farm, and that had been the only reason. She had used him. How could she? If it hadn't been for him, they would have starved. After the Nazis had taken her husband and killed him, she had struggled to survive, she had told him. It was only when he had turned up to help, that things had improved for her and her children. She should have been grateful to him, not disgusted by him.

He had found out only that morning just how much she had despised him all these months. Nothing had mattered then. He had been glad he had taken the gun that day, while he had been alone in the Dahl family kitchen making himself a hot drink. He had wandered around, looking into drawers and cupboards, looking for anything to take. He had seen it as his right, for Marianne never paid him for his work. He had found the gun behind the packets of oats and nuts and other grains in the larder. It was a small, brown paper parcel, but he had known what it was before he had even opened it.

He could still hear her bitter words. "I wouldn't marry you if you were the last man on earth." They had rung in his ears as he'd grabbed her by the shoulders and started to shake her. She had tried to scream, but he had put his hand over her mouth. He had the gun in his hand before he had known what he was doing. It had all been a blur. But then he'd realised what he'd done. He had killed the only woman he had ever loved. He had never meant to do it, never in this world.

As he'd held her lifeless body, he had heard a noise behind him and turned to see the small figure of Halle run from the room. He'd had to chase him. He'd had no choice. He couldn't let him tell the police. Then little Birgitta had followed him here. She, too, had to die.

As he knelt there in the snow, he thought how only that morning he had been full of hope and happiness. He had envisaged that, by this time tonight, he would be the proud future head of a fully-formed family but, in reality, he had become Death. All his hopes had died with the family he had so mercilessly killed.

ও

Baldur knew he had to get rid of the bodies. The snow was beginning to fall again which was welcome, but would it be enough to cover them? He knew that, at this time of year, there weren't many people rambling about the woods. It was generally too cold. And, if the snow kept falling, all traces of little Halle and Birgitta would soon disappear, he hoped forever.

But could he rely on that? No, he needed to make sure. He pulled some leaves from the tree above him and covered the bodies roughly. That should be enough for now, he thought. Enough while he went back to the farm and fetched a spade.

Returning about half an hour later, Baldur couldn't find the spot at first. He had been sure he had hidden the bodies just here. For one awful moment he thought they'd already been discovered, although he knew that was unlikely. It was three o'clock in the morning and, apart from the wan light from the pale, full moon, it would surely have been impossible for anyone to have spotted the mound where the bodies were. Not unless they were looking for them. And that, too, was very unlikely. Time was on his side, at least.

He was glad he had had the foresight to bring a torch as well as a spade, because he would never have found them otherwise. He was relieved to discover them exactly where he'd left them, but well covered with the fresh snow which was falling heavily now. He shivered, wishing he'd also fetched his coat when he collected the spade and torch. Still, the spadework would keep him warm, and in minutes he was sweating profusely as he dug deeper and deeper past the soft, fresh snow into the hard, frost-bitten ground. It was back-breaking work, but he deserved to suffer, he thought. Murder was something he never thought he would be capable of, but now he had killed not one, but three human beings. It wasn't real. It was a nightmare.

The big man kept digging, tears rolling down his big, slobbery face, the harsh moon his only witness. When he had dug down as far as he could, he placed the little bodies gently into the hole. He patted the earth flat with the spade and covered the spot with leaves. The snow had stopped falling and the pale moon had gone behind a cloud. It was very dark in the forest and, if it wasn't for his torch, he wouldn't have been able to see anything at all.

But at least one problem was dealt with. The children were well and truly buried; no one would ever find them there. The next problem was the gun. He didn't want to part with it but knew that he had to. If it were ever found on him or in his lodgings, all would be lost. He was safe enough as long as he got rid of the evidence.

He was a loner, always had been, and had always liked it that way until he'd met Marianne. Now, he would go back to his anonymous life, speaking to no one from one day's end to the next. There was nothing to connect him to the Dahl farm, no one ever knew he'd gone there. He had never told anyone. The only people who knew wouldn't be able to testify. The police wouldn't have a clue who he was, or where to find him.

He wiped the gun clean of fingerprints and wrapped it in his handkerchief. Now, he thought, where should he put it so that it would be easy to find when the dust had settled? Mustn't make it too easy for the police, of course, but he had to be able to locate it himself when the time was right.

He looked around him. As he did so, he thought he heard a rustle of movement behind him. He spun round and stared into the unbroken darkness. There was nothing there, just his fevered imagination. Calm down, he told himself. He mustn't get distracted. He must find somewhere to hide the gun.

The forest was just fir tree after fir tree, nothing to distinguish the spot he was standing on from any other spot as far as he could see. He could bury it here, of course, but would he be able to find it again? No, he thought, not a chance.

He scratched his head as the moon came out from behind a cloud, illuminating an old tree stump about ten yards away. It was the only one in that spot. He thought he'd be able to find that again, so he dug a hole and placed the weapon carefully in it. Once he had covered it over, he heaved a sigh of relief.

All done. There was no more to do. All that was left for him was to return to his lodgings and keep a low profile. He would soon find some casual labouring work and pick up where he'd left off before he'd met Marianne. No one would be any the wiser.

London, April 1948

It was Saturday morning, nearly two weeks after Bernard's disturbing experience at the Battersea bus stop. He and Robbie were firm friends already, drawn together by their shared circumstances. Robbie had even dropped round to the vicarage the previous evening for supper and a game of chess. It was likely to become a habit, as a second invitation had already been issued to the good doctor to come to supper again soon. Whenever he liked, in fact.

This morning, however, Bernard was alone, agonising over the wording of his first sermon. He didn't want to give his congregation something too heavy to start with; he wanted to make a good impression. He chewed the end of his pen in deep thought. It wasn't easy for him, as he had never been at his best with the written word. However, he was rising to the occasion, and the ideas were at last beginning to flow.

Then he heard the doorbell ring and, a few moments later, heard Mrs Harper and someone she called Dick talking outside his study. He popped his head out of the door.

"Is everything all right, Mrs Harper?" he asked. He saw she was accompanied by a stolid, red-faced man carrying a bag of tools and scratching his head.

"Yes, Vicar. It's only Dick," she replied.

"Dick?"

"That's right. My friend Ada's 'ubby. I told you about 'im. 'E's come to 'ave a butcher's at the lav."

Bernard sighed and returned to his desk. 'Butcher's', indeed. He was quickly learning cockney rhyming slang, courtesy of Mrs Harper. Still, he was glad that someone was at least *looking* at that wretched lavatory chain, having spent his first few days in the vicarage waging war on it and praying for his waste matter to disappear. He just hoped this Dick knew what he was doing.

Meanwhile, Dick Appleyard was dutifully having a 'butcher's' at the toilet, accompanied by Mrs Harper who stood beside him with her arms folded. She watched with impatience as he pulled the chain to no avail.

"I told you, Dick, you 'ave to yank it. Like this." And Mrs Harper demonstrated.

Dick rubbed his chin. "Hmm, I see," he said. "Probably it's your ball cock."

"Is it?" said Mrs Harper. "So, what does that mean, exactly?"

"It needs adjusting."

"Can you do it then?" was the not unreasonable question. "Only the Reverend ain't been able to flush it properly since 'e got 'ere."

"Blimey," said Dick, although apparently unperturbed by the vicar's embarrassment. "That's a nuisance. I can 'ave a go, if you like?"

39

His lack of confidence wasn't reassuring. "Do you know what you're doing, Dick?" she asked. "I thought you was good at this sort of thing."

"Well, I'm not your actual plumber ..."

"No, I know that. But can you adjust the what's it, like you just said?"

"I should think so. Leave it to me."

Mrs Harper, although unconvinced of his competence, left him to it. As she descended the stairs, Dick called after her. "I take two sugars in my tea. Ta."

She huffed crossly but went into the kitchen to put the kettle on. It was time for the vicar's elevenses, anyway. She knew he was busy writing his sermon for the following morning, and she was looking forward to it. It would be a nice change from that old duffer, Reverend Smallpiece. His sermons had been interminable. She only hoped Bernard didn't go in for epics. If he did, she decided, he wouldn't get any chocolate biscuits with his morning coffee in future.

Meanwhile, Bernard continued with his sermon. Since the interruption by the good Dick Appleyard, he had managed to fill six sides of foolscap with his trusty Parker. Five minutes later, he put the cap on his pen with a sigh of satisfaction. If that didn't impress them, nothing would, he thought. Now, where's Mrs Aitch with that coffee?

❧

As Bernard surveyed his congregation the next morning, he couldn't suppress a feeling of disappointment. Far from the big turnout he had expected, there was just a couple of rows of females of various, ages, sizes and hats. There were only two men in the whole church as far as he could see, and one of them was asleep or dead, he couldn't decide which and didn't much care.

The good Mistresses Harper and Appleyard were sitting in the front pew, looking eagerly up at him. He smiled down at them, grateful for their support. As everyone stood to sing the first hymn, *God Is Love*, one of his favourites, the door opened with a loud clatter, and he saw Robbie slip quietly into one of the pews at the back. He was grateful for this welcome addition to the spear side, as his friend had only confessed to him the night before that he 'wasn't much of a churchgoer'.

When the rousing hymn, which was accompanied on the organ by a battle-axe in a hairnet, had finished, the congregation sat down and awaited his pearls of wisdom. As he looked down on the people below, he smiled, cleared his throat and began.

He couldn't understand it. He had thought his words of wisdom would be seized upon with eagerness and gratitude but, as he read on, he heard a muffled whisper start along the first row of ladies, beginning with Mrs Appleyard, who had a dark frown on her face.

Undeterred, however, he carried on. After all, what he was saying was innocuous enough. Surely, they couldn't be taking offence? But the angry buzz was getting louder and louder as his voice became less confident and softer and softer. Somehow, he managed to get to the end of his sermon amid the continued buzz of annoyance. He gathered the pages together and stepped down from the pulpit, avoiding the eyes that he could feel burning into him with disapproval.

As his flock (which was more of a straggle) left the church, he shook each one by the hand. They were polite, but distant, and not one of them congratulated him on his sermon. When it was Mrs Appleyard's turn to shake his hand, she gave him a severe stare. "Thank you, Vicar," she said politely enough. "I just 'ope the dinner ain't ruined, that's all." She stalked down the path, with Mrs Harper following in her wake in full sail.

Robbie stood beside him when the last person had left the church. "Well, dear boy, that could have gone better."

The understatement of the year, thought Bernard. "Have you any idea what I did to offend them?" he asked him, as they returned together into the church.

The battle-axe at the organ was folding up her sheet music and looking through her pince nez at Bernard as he collected the hymn books.

"Thank you, Mrs er..." he said. He had been introduced to her earlier that morning, but he had never been good at remembering names. "Your organ playing was very rousing indeed." If a trifle out of tune and time, he added to himself uncharitably. There was no denying it. He wasn't in the best of moods this morning.

Her only response was a sniff, a habit that many of the ladies in Bernard's compass seemed to be fond of. The enormity of her sniff was only surpassed by Mrs Harper's. She stomped out of the church, clutching her hymn music sheets.

"She didn't look too pleased with you, either," observed Robbie with a grin.

Bernard scratched his head in puzzlement. "Come on, Robbie, what's the matter with them all? I could hear them fidgeting and muttering all the while I was reading my sermon."

"I think it might be something to do with the *length* of it," said Robbie. "I mean, you did go on a bit, dear boy. I expect the womenfolk were worried about the roast beef getting burnt."

"Oh dear," Bernard sighed. "I never thought of that. I just didn't want to sell them short. I so wanted to make a good impression at my first service."

"Well, you made an impression, all right, Bernie," said Robbie, clapping him on the shoulder. "Only I don't think it was the one you were after. Anyway, why not come and have a swift one at the Bricklayer's? We've got time."

But Bernard, looking at his watch, shook his head. He didn't want to risk Mrs Harper's further disapproval by being late for his Sunday dinner. Besides, he was looking forward to it and, if there was one thing he could say for his curmudgeonly housekeeper, she was an excellent cook. "I'd better not. I seem to be in the doghouse, as it is," he said.

"I see your problem, old boy," said Robbie. "I suppose I'd better get back as well, as Lucy will have my dinner on the table in about half an hour."

They were strolling slowly out of the church. "Maybe see you this evening?" suggested Bernard, as they stopped outside the vicarage.

"I'd like that," said Robbie. Then he noticed a worried frown on his friend's face.

"Well, I won't come, if you don't want me to," he said.

"Of course I want you to, Robbie," said Bernard impatiently. "I wouldn't have asked you otherwise. It's just that – well, would you make sure you go to the toilet before you come?"

Robbie's eyebrows almost hit his hairline (and it was receding). "What?"

"Oh, sorry, that sounds weird, I know."

"You can say that again."

"It's just that the plumbing, you know – "

"Oh, yes. You mentioned something about the faulty chain. I still don't see why you're so upset about it. I don't mind things like that, Bernie."

"No, I know. It's just that we had a chap look at it yesterday morning – a friend of Mrs Aitch's. And, well, whatever he did has made it worse. Now the toilet won't flush at all, and this morning I yanked it so hard, the chain actually broke off in my hands."

Robbie roared with laughter. "You'd better get a proper plumber in," he advised.

"Well, I wanted to do that in the first place," said Bernard, "but Mrs Harper said he'd cost too much."

"Aye, they're not cheap – plumbers. But, come on, just a quick one. It's only half past twelve. We've got time. And I've got some good news that I rather wanted to share with you."

"Good news? I could do with some, after this morning's fiasco. Okay, just a very quick one, then."

So, the two men carried on past the vicarage towards the pub, watched by an irate Mrs Harper who was looking out of the front room window at them. "That's the dinner ruined," she muttered. "First the lav, then the sermon, now the dinner. Bloody man! No consideration, and him a vicar, too!"

≈

Five minutes later, the two men were seated with their drinks in the Bricklayer's Arms. Bernard had risked a half of shandy, which Robbie put down in front of him with distaste, handling the glass as if contained liquid plutonium.

"How can you drink that stuff, Bernie?" he asked, sipping his double whisky.

"Well, sherry's my usual tipple, as you know. But I had a shandy once before and remembered that it was quite nice. Like lemonade, really."

"That's because it *is* lemonade, man, mostly."

"Yes, I suppose I'm just not fond of alcohol," Bernard was apologetic.

"Never mind," said Robbie. "With me as your friend, you'll soon learn to like it."

Bernard wasn't sure if this was a threat or a promise, but he simply smiled as he sipped his shandy.

"Anyway, Bernie, what I really wanted to tell you is I've won a competition."

"A competition? Oh, congratulations!" Bernard raised his glass to him. "What sort of competition?"

"Oh, one of those put them in order of preference things they're always running in the *News of the World*."

"Oh, yes, I saw Mrs Harper doing one of those the other day. It looked quite difficult. It was a row of young ladies in identical pleated skirts, or so they seemed to me. There didn't seem to be any actual correct answer, either. So, I don't know how these things are judged."

"I don't know and don't care," declared Robbie. "All I know is I won. And guess what I won?"

He swigged more of his fast-diminishing whisky and looked at Bernard with a crooked grin that seemed to be spreading like a Cheshire cat's.

"Golly, I don't know. A book? Some money?"

"Guess again."

"Oh, tell me, Robbie. Don't be so annoying."

"A tour of ten European countries, that's all." Robbie slammed his hand down on the table, shaking the glasses. "What do you say to that?"

"Wow!" was what Bernard said to that. "That's marvellous! You're a very lucky man."

"Yes, I am, aren't I? But you're lucky too," Robbie's grin was as wide as it would go now.

"Me? How?"

"Because it's a trip for *two*. Takes in France, Spain, Portugal, Sweden, Norway ..."

"You mean, you want me to come with you?" Bernard was completely taken aback.

"Of course that's what I mean."

"But you hardly know me! Haven't you got other friends or relatives you'd rather invite?"

"Not really. You're the closest friend I've got now. And I can hardly take my housekeeper – it wouldn't be right..."

Bernard smiled. It certainly wouldn't, he thought. "Well, that's wonderful – for me, I mean. When is it booked for?"

"Er, sometime towards the end of May, I think. I haven't got the details with me. What d'you say? Are you game?"

"Well, I'd love to come, but I've only just taken up my incumbency here. I don't think the Archdeacon will be too pleased if I ask for a holiday so soon."

"But it's a once in a lifetime opportunity, man! And you're entitled to a holiday. Surely he'll understand and get someone to cover for you? It's not as if your congregation is that big – sorry – but it's true. They could all be accommodated at St Margaret's while you're away, couldn't they?"

Bernard thought fast. Yes, it *was* a chance in a million, there was no denying that. He had done a bit of foreign travel during his summer vacations while at university, but only to Belgium and France. There was a whole world out there that he hadn't even touched upon.

"Okay," he said, after a moment. "I'd love to come with you, Robbie. Let me see what the Archdeacon has to say first, though. If he agrees, then you're on. Who are you getting to cover for you, by the way?"

"Ah! For me it's easy. My predecessor, old Dr Winfield, will be more than happy to oblige. To tell you the truth, I don't think he was ready to retire, but he kept making mistakes, so he was gently 'forced' to go, if you know what I mean."

"But surely he won't be suitable if he makes mistakes?" Bernard was a little shocked that Robbie considered leaving his patients in the hands of an old duffer like that.

"Oh, there's no real harm he can do. Most of my patients will be happy to wait until I get back anyway. If there's a real emergency, he'll be given strict instructions to refer them to the hospital without delay. No need to worry."

"If you say so, Robbie," said Bernard doubtfully.

Robbie drew out a letter and showed it to him. "Here, Bernie. These are all the places we'll be visiting."

It was the trip of a lifetime for both of them, and they began deciding which sights they would visit in the short time that had been allotted to each country, according to the itinerary given in Robbie's letter. It was Bernard who suddenly remembered the Sunday dinners waiting for them. So lost had they both been in mapping out their coming tour, that neither man had noticed the rumblings in their stomachs which, they now feared, would match the angry rumblings of Lucy Carter and Nancy Harper. With one accord, they finished their drinks and left the pub with somewhat more speed than they had entered it.

ॐ

"Thank you, Mrs Harper, this looks delicious."

"It's spoiled, that's what it is," stated Mrs Harper, standing over Bernard, with her arms folded.

"Not at all," said Bernard, sampling the dried-up beef. "It's perfect."

"Get away with you," she said, unmollified. "Your dinner 'as been sitting in the oven for over 'alf an hour. I tell you now, I don't like cooking good food just to see it ruined by selfish people who'd rather go to the pub."

Bernard knew she was right and was suitably chastened as he chewed his way through his unappetising meal. But as soon as she left the room, his spirits lifted. It was a shame about the roast beef, but nothing could dampen his good mood now. The day hadn't turned out so badly after all. So what if his sermon had been too long? That was easily remedied.

He was going on a tour of Europe with his new friend, Robbie MacTavish, and life was good again.

When he had finished his dinner (the apple pie had been compensation as it hadn't been ruined like the main course), he retired to his study and, sitting by the fire, lit his pipe and began to dream of exotic places and warm sun. He started to plan his wardrobe for the trip; how many suits to take, how many shirts, how many shorts. And, most importantly, how many changes of underwear. The list was quite long he realised, and he wondered if his small leather suitcase would hold all he would need. Oh well, he'd better ask Robbie's advice about what to take. Robbie, to Bernard's way of thinking, was a man of the world and an expert in such matters.

As his thoughts turned back to that morning's service, he had an idea. He went to the study door and called down to his housekeeper. "Mrs Harper? Are you busy? Can I see you for a moment?"

"I'm up to my elbows in soap and water, Reverend," she called back. "The washing up don't do itself, you know."

Everything that woman said to him seemed like a rebuke. Bernard swallowed hard. Just who was the boss around here? He tried again.

"It'll only take a few minutes. Please."

"When I've finished. Not before." The 'boss around here' was obviously Mrs Harper.

"Oh, all right then. When you've finished. Thanks."

Bernard sat back down by the fire and relit his pipe, puffing it in silent rage. He would have to lay down some ground rules with that woman before too long, otherwise she would walk all over him. However, when she finally deigned to put in an appearance, she brought with her a tea tray piled high with home-made scones dripping with butter. At the sight of the butter, Bernard melted. This woman was really an angel in curlers and apron. Just how did she manage to keep the vicarage larder so well stocked with rationing still going on? She must have used up the butter ration on one scone alone.

She poured his tea and smiled at him. It was as if she knew what he was thinking, and her look told him it was better not to ask.

"Er, Mrs Harper?" he began, licking the melted butter from his fingers.

She interrupted him quickly. "Well, what do you want that was so urgent?" she asked.

"I'm sorry to be a nuisance, it's just that I was very disappointed with the turn-out this morning, and I wondered if you could shed any light on the reason why?"

"Did you, now?" she said blandly.

"Yes. You see, I expected more people, seeing as it was my first service here. I just thought they would be curious, if nothing else."

"Well," she said, considering Bernard's question carefully. "It's been a while since we 'ad a vicar at St Stephen's. I expect they're still going to St Margaret's."

"Oh, I see. I wish I knew how to bring them back, Mrs Aitch." He bit into another scone, and the butter dripped down his chin and onto his jumper.

Mrs Harper smiled, handing him a napkin to wipe it with. "There might be a way," she said.

"Please," said Bernard. "Anything. Tell me."

Mrs Harper drew herself up to her full height (which didn't take long as she was only four foot eleven inches) and gave one of her sniffs. "Well, you know I carry a lot of weight around 'ere, don't you?" She paused to let the full import of this remark sink in.

Bernard thought, rather impolitely, that the amount of weight she carried was obvious, even to the partially sighted. "I'm sure you do, Mrs Aitch," he said, smiling at her. She looked rather comical, standing on her dignity like that.

"I could get your congregation back without much persuading only, on the strength of this morning's performance, I don't think I will."

Well, that put him in his place, he thought. "Sorry about that. I suppose it was too long, wasn't it?"

"We could 'ave done without all the text quoting," she pointed out. "You'd do well to remember we 'ave to get the dinner on of a Sunday morning."

"Yes, I realise that. It won't happen again. Do I get another chance, Mrs Aitch?" he wheedled.

Bernard was rewarded with a smile. "I'll get you some more scones. And, Reverend?"

"Yes?"

"I think I can guarantee a much bigger attendance in the future."

"Oh, thank you!" He was fast realising that his dumpy little housekeeper was worth her weight in gold. If she could spread the word and get people to come to his services, then she was obviously of some standing in the community. He was lucky to have her, that was for sure. He just had to be careful how he handled her. He sat back in his comfortable armchair and sipped his scalding tea with relish.

❧

Mrs Harper was as good as her word, and St Stephen's church was almost full to capacity the following Sunday. If there had been any marshalling of troops or coercing, there was no evidence of it. The people gathered looked happy to be there and, as he ascended the pulpit, they were all smiling at him. Some of the younger women were even fluttering their lashes with a look of pure adoration in the eyes underneath them. He was gratified by this, if a little wary.

When it came to his sermon, he had made sure it didn't last longer than fifteen minutes. He had also made sure that he didn't come across too heavily. He didn't want to tell them to 'go and sin no more' or threaten them with fire and brimstone if they behaved badly. Instead, he told them that God wanted them to be happy, to enjoy themselves. Especially now. After the austerity of the war years, they deserved it. He smiled as he finished and was glad to see that his audience was still smiling too.

The hymns had also gone down well, particularly the one about the 'green hill faraway'. In fact, Mrs Lavinia Pettigrew, a sweet old lady wearing an elaborate feathery hat and boa, came up and addressed him after the service on that very subject.

"I did enjoy singing that again, Vicar," she said, shaking him by the hand. "It's one of my favourites. Since I was a girl."

Bernard smiled pleasantly at the frail little woman who reached no higher than his waist. She must be ninety, if she's a day, he thought. "I'm glad, dear," he replied. "It is one of mine too. So uplifting."

"Indeed," she said. "But, tell me, Vicar, I've always wanted to know. Why is the green hill in the hymn described as not having a city wall? I mean, green hills generally don't have city walls around them, do they? It's never made sense to me, that hasn't."

Bernard smiled. He enjoyed imparting knowledge on a subject he felt sure about. "That is a common misconception. It is not the green hill that doesn't have a city wall. The green hill is *outside* the city wall. It is just phrased ambiguously." He hoped he didn't sound too patronising.

Mrs Pettigrew looked up at him with a malicious look in her eye. "That's what you think, is it?"

"It's the correct interpretation. Yes."

She walked off, and Bernard could almost swear he heard her mutter 'bollocks' under her breath as she went. He couldn't resist an inward chuckle, sensing she must be the local 'character' (one of them anyway), as he turned to shake hands with the rest of his departing congregation. It was taking a lot longer this morning than it did last Sunday.

When they had all gone, a frown marred his boyish looks. They were pleased with him and most of them had told him they would be back next week. Some had even said they would be at the mid-week evening service, too. But what would they think of him when he gallivanted off on holiday after only two months?

Robbie appeared beside him at the church door. "Penny for them," he said.

"What? Oh, I was just wondering what will happen when I go on holiday. I don't want to lose my congregation for good."

"Don't worry," said his friend, "They like you. They'll soon be back."

"I hope you're right," said Bernard, not wholly convinced. "Maybe I shouldn't go, after all?"

"Don't be silly, man. We're going to have a great time. Do you really want to sacrifice such an opportunity?"

"No, of course I don't. But – "

"No more buts. It's settled," said Robbie with determination, as they made their way through the churchyard to the main road. The early spring sunshine was warm today, and daffodils added splashes of colour everywhere. Everything was looking green and beautiful.

"If you say so," said Bernard.

He didn't have the heart to argue. It would just have to be all right, he told himself, but he wasn't looking forward to his interview with the Archdeacon. From what he had seen of him, he didn't look the sort of man to bend easily. He had seemed to Bernard like something out of Anthony Trollope, a sort of male version of Mrs Proudie.

"Now, don't worry, Bernie," Robbie told him, as they parted company at the vicarage gate. "You just tell the old fossil you're going and that's an end of it."

It was all right for him, thought Bernard crossly, as he let himself in. The smell of Mrs Harper's roast lamb wafted towards him as he hung up his outdoor coat.

"So, the old buzzard is keeping you in suspense, is he?" said Robbie.

He and Bernard were sitting in the vicarage study, the chess board between them. He picked up his Queen's pawn and put it down again in the same place.

"Yes, I'm afraid so," replied Bernard, beginning to grow impatient waiting for his friend to make a move. It was at least ten minutes, by his reckoning, since his own opening gambit, and the night wasn't getting any younger.

"When will he let you know?"

"He said in a week's time."

The Archdeacon was keeping him in suspense, just like Robbie was doing now. He watched his friend's hands move to the various pieces on the board, hover over them, then move away.

Finally, Robbie moved his Queen's pawn and it remained moved. Bernard followed this up almost immediately with a tactical move that he had been planning while waiting for his opponent to take his turn.

"What will you do if he says you can't go?" asked Robbie as he stared at the board.

"I don't know. I suppose I won't be able to come with you."

"That'll be tragic, man," exclaimed his friend. "You must come. I don't want to go alone."

"There must be someone else you can ask? A girlfriend, perhaps?"

"Not anyone special," he replied, fingering his Queen's pawn again. "Anyway, women always complicate things. Sleeping arrangements, for example."

Bernard nodded sagely. "That's true. Let's hope it won't come to that. I don't like the Archdeacon much. He's a funny little man. Bald as a coot. And, as for his housekeeper – she's a strange bird. Looks too old, for a start. Bent double, poor thing. But I must say she produced the tea quickly enough."

Robbie laughed. "These housekeepers are a sturdy bunch, aren't they?"

"You can say that again," grinned Bernard, thinking of Mrs Harper. "Are you packed yet, by the way?"

"Packed?" Robbie stared at him. "I haven't even thought about packing. It's ages yet."

"I know, but we'll need to take quite a lot of clothes to make sure we're wearing the right thing in the various countries. I mean it'll probably be hot in Spain, but still quite cold in Sweden, won't it?"

"True, true. But I believe in travelling light myself. Just one set of warm stuff and one set of light stuff. Several pairs of underpants and a toothbrush, that'll do me," said Robbie.

"And don't forget your passport, of course," smiled Bernard, tapping his pipe on the fender.

"Checkmate!" said Robbie suddenly.

Bernard looked at the board in horror. He should have seen that coming. "Well done," he said with a reluctant smile. He began collecting the pieces. Chess was too hard. He preferred draughts, much less complicated. "Would you like a nightcap before you go?"

As it turned out, Bernard didn't have to wait a week for the Archdeacon's answer. He finally heard his fate a mere two days after he had made his request. If, and it was a big if, Bernard could arrange to send his congregation to St Margaret's for the duration of his

European holiday, then the Archdeacon would (reluctantly, mind) grant him leave of absence. As St Stephen's needed repairs to its roof, it would probably be in order to close it for the duration of his holiday for these to be carried out.

Bernard was cock-a-hoop. The Archdeacon wasn't such a bad old stick, after all, he thought. Permission had been granted unto him from on high and all it now involved was arranging for his congregation to go to St Margaret's while he was away. Mrs Harper's help would be invaluable in this matter, and ...

Then he realised. He had omitted to mention his holiday plans to her. Doubtless she would be offended that he hadn't deemed it necessary to ask *her* permission, never mind the Archdeacon. This was a stumbling block he hadn't envisaged. Even if he could placate her for this oversight, which wasn't at all a foregone conclusion, he was sure she wouldn't help him unless he got down on his bended knees to her. It would shift the balance of power in the vicarage forever, if he did this. No, he wouldn't stoop so literally low. After all, who was Mrs Harper? Not God Almighty, and Bernard was in a position to know this for certain.

As he predicted, she was none too pleased when he finally got up the courage to broach the subject with her.

"What are they? Bloomin' yo-yos?"

"I'm sorry, Mrs Harper. I do see your point. But I really don't think it would be much of a hardship for them to go back to St Margaret's for a couple of weeks."

"Don't you?" she sniffed.

"No. Anyway, Mrs Aitch," said Bernard cajolingly, "is there any chance that you could work your magic and tell them the reason? You know most of them, and I'm sure they'll understand when you explain it to them."

"It ain't going to be easy," she said. "Not easy at all. When they see the sign on the church door saying you was gone on 'oliday, they might just not come back. That's all I'm saying."

"I realise that, but could you do your best? You can persuade them, I know you can."

"Well, I suppose I can, but you won't be Mr Popular, I can tell you that. Deserting them to go on 'oliday is bad enough, but to go somewhere foreign just about puts the tin lid on it. I can 'ear them now. 'What's wrong with a boarding 'ouse in Clacton?' That's what they'll say."

"Will they, Mrs Harper?" Did he have an entire congregation of xenophobes? he wondered. He very much doubted it.

"Yes, they will. And another thing. All that foreign food will play 'avoc with your digestion. You won't find cooking like mine where you're going."

Bernard had to agree that he probably wouldn't. He wasn't particularly looking forward to a diet of frogs' legs and paella and had secretly planned to find room in his case for a couple of tins of baked beans.

60

"I know, Mrs Harper, I know. But it's a free holiday, and Robbie has been kind enough to ask me – so I can't really say no. And besides, I don't want to. He's my friend and we get on so well. The holiday's sure to be something to look back on over the years with pleasure. I'll take lots of photos. Maybe I'll give a slide display when I get back. How about that?"

Mrs Harper sniffed again as if to say 'big deal'. "That'll be something to look forward to," she said with hardly any trace of sarcasm. "Now, if it's all right with you, can I get on with my dusting?"

"Of course, Mrs Aitch, thanks."

Bernard breathed a sigh of relief as she closed the study door behind her. He was glad he'd got that over. She could huff and puff as much as she liked, but he had won out in the end. She'd make sure his congregation understood, he felt sure, although he'd make it a priority to let them know himself in good time, too. It wouldn't do not to mention it to them, as they might never come back from St Margaret's at all. That would be a disaster. He might be chucked out altogether and never get another incumbency. He felt sure he wasn't the Archdeacon's favourite person, as it was.

Still, he couldn't worry about that now. He couldn't wait to tell Robbie that their trip was well and truly on.

❧

"So, it's all sorted, eh?"

"Yes, I think so. I wasn't sure how my parishioners would take it if I deserted them so soon, but Mrs Harper has agreed to help, thank goodness."

They were seated at their now customary table in the Bricklayer's Arms. The lunchtime rush had just begun, and Robbie had persuaded Bernard to have a whisky with him. But, while the good doctor sipped his with pleasure, the young vicar was struggling. It was no good. He still hadn't got the hang of it.

"Aye, that's good news, Bernie."

"Yes, it is. I thought I'd have to wait a whole week for the Archdeacon to get back to me. But the roof repairs swung it, I think."

"Well, they certainly need doing," said Robbie, finishing his drink. He also finished Bernard's and then stood up. "I'll get you a sherry," he grinned.

Bernard returned to the vicarage at one o'clock on the dot. The last thing he needed to do today was antagonise her by being late for his dinner. He smelt the steak and kidney pie as he hung his coat on the hall stand and smiled. Although he was very much looking forward to his foreign trip, he knew he would be more than thankful to return to Mrs Harper's cooking, if not her carping.

Bergen, May 1948

Baldur Hanssen had slipped quietly back into working life. Luckily, he was able to turn his hand to most things not requiring too much brainwork and had got a job as a fitter and welder at one of the local factories. With the money he made from that, he had been able to quit his lodgings and rent a cheap apartment on the outskirts of Bergen, as far away from the Dahl farm as he could get. Thus, he passed his days in comfortable anonymity, almost forgetting that awful day in late March when he had turned into a killer.

Keeping as low a profile as a man looking like he did could, he worked hard and did a good job. He was respected by his workmates for his skill and efficiency, if not particularly liked. The work was sporadic, but it kept him out of trouble. Nobody took the least bit of notice of him, and that's how he liked it.

When Marianne Dahl's body was finally found, the police came to the factory asking if anyone knew anything about the man who had helped out on her farm. Everyone in the building had been questioned, including himself. He had felt the butterflies in his stomach as he saw an officer of the law approaching his factory bench, but he was ready for him.

"We're sorry to bother you, sir," the man had said, respectfully, "but do you know anyone who could have been helping out on the Dahl farm recently?"

He had shrugged and carried on with his welding. The man had been satisfied simply with that and left him alone. It was that easy. He hadn't even actually lied. All he'd done was shrug. He wondered if the police were really bothered and was almost indignant that they weren't trying harder to find Marianne's killer or the children. For all the police knew, they could still be alive.

And, as the weeks wore on, the police seemed to be making no headway at all. There had been no breakthrough, according to the papers. Well, he grinned to himself, of course, there hadn't; otherwise, he'd be in a prison cell by now. He began to relax more and more. He was safe.

Bergen, June 1948

Bernard and Robbie's European trip was into its final leg: Norway. They had seen the sights in many countries and, despite the bomb damage in most of them, they had been amazed and delighted by what they had seen: the Eiffel Tower, the Leaning Tower of Pisa, the Colosseum in Rome, the Acropolis in Athens. This last caused Bernard to quip: those wicked Nazis have a lot to answer for, ruining a lovely building like that.

Now here they were in the land of snow and Christmas trees and fjords. After the heat and sun of Spain and Portugal, the delights of provincial France and the beauty of Rome and Athens, this final country was, to the two friends, a bit of a let-down. There wasn't so much to see, although the scenery was austerely beautiful.

They would be staying one night in Bergen in a small hotel that was sparse but adequate, similar to the other hotels in which they had stayed thus far. Travel had proved quite arduous for the two intrepid sightseers; some journeys being more comfortable than others. Most of their travelling had been done by train, although coaches featured occasionally. These latter contraptions were usually rattling and extremely uncomfortable, as well as inducing varying degrees of nausea and back pain, depending on the heat and condition of the roads.

But, on the whole, their holiday had been a great success. Robbie had brought his box Brownie camera and had taken many photographs. Bernard was looking forward to seeing these when they got back. Unfortunately, he had forgotten to pack his own camera, despite his promise to give a slide show to his parishioners on his return. No doubt Mrs Harper would be dreadfully disappointed, he had remarked to Robbie, but Robbie had only grinned.

Now that they were in the last country of their visit, the two men were feeling a bit anti-climactic. They couldn't quite quell their feeling of disappointment that their journey was soon to end. However, they decided to make the best of their last day 'sur le continent' and set out after breakfast to explore the nearby forests. It was a lovely warm day in early June; the sun was beating down from a cloudless, vivid blue sky, and their hearts were uplifted.

They stopped for lunch by a small lake. The hotel had provided them with packs of cheese and spam sandwiches, plus a flask of tea and some enigmatic-looking fruit. "Here, have a tot of whisky in that tea, man," said Robbie as his friend screwed up his nose in distaste. Thermos tea was never a success, Bernard had complained, accepting the offer doubtfully. To his surprise, it improved the taste immeasurably.

As they sat and munched their unappetising sandwiches, they watched the diving birds over the lake, marvelling at their colourful plumage. They were a beautiful sight. The two men were enjoying the peaceful scene, something only a couple of years ago would have been unthinkable. It was true, though. The war was well and truly over.

They remained where they were for a while, enjoying their last chance of leisure before they returned home. Then, reluctantly, they packed the remains of their lunch into their rucksacks and continued their trek through the Norwegian forest. Everywhere was a mass of green in varying shades of that colour, seared through with the azure of the sky. They were in awe of everything around them. And how quiet it was, too; nothing to be heard but the rustle of the breeze, the chirruping of the birds, and the buzz of the insects.

Suddenly, Robbie halted in his stride and seemed to be listening for something. He turned to his friend. "Did you hear that?" he asked.

"Hear what?" Bernard strained to listen. All he could hear was the breeze and the birds; nothing else.

"I thought I heard someone crying. It sounded like a child," said Robbie.

"No, I didn't hear anything. Must have been a bird."

"Nonsense, man," said Robbie testily. "I know the difference between the sound of a bird and a child crying."

"Sorry," said Bernard meekly. "But I didn't hear a thing."

"There it is again!" said Robbie. "It came from that tree over there." He ran towards it, closely followed by his friend.

Then Robbie turned a deathly white face to Bernard. "Can't you see them?" he asked.

"See who?" Bernard began to think his friend had caught a touch of the sun. "It's just a tree. That's all I can see. A particularly nice variety of Norwegian spruce. It'd make a great Christmas tree for the church hall."

"There's two little children sitting under it. Surely you can see them? They look very sad. They're trying to tell me something, but it's in Norwegian."

Bernard put down his backpack and scratched his head. "There's no one there, Robbie. Maybe it's the sun. It can do funny things to people if they're not used to it."

"I can see them as clearly as I can see you," Robbie insisted. "Pretty blond, blue-eyed children, not much older than eight or nine. The little girl looks about five. They are both in distress. Why can't you see them?"

"I'm sorry, Robbie, but I can't." Bernard shook his head sadly.

Suddenly Robbie collapsed on the ground by the tree. "They've gone," he whispered. "They just vanished before my eyes."

Bernard was surer than ever that Robbie had sunstroke but decided not to venture that opinion again for fear of getting his head bitten off.

"Okay, Robbie, we'd best be getting back now, anyway. The day's almost over. The sun's going down."

It was true. It was growing dusk very quickly, and the two friends knew they had to get out of the forest before it grew too dark to see their way back.

Back in the hotel, over their supper, Bernard broached the subject of Robbie's 'vision' of that afternoon. He didn't want to upset his friend, but he was worried in case he needed treatment for his heat stroke, or whatever it was.

"Er, what do you really think it was you saw this afternoon?" he asked, playing with a very raw-looking piece of fish on his plate. The Norwegian cuisine left a lot to be desired.

"I saw them, I tell you. Two little children. They were very unhappy little souls. Then they disappeared."

Bernard had never seen his hale and hearty friend looking so despondent, almost frightened by his experience.

"Don't you think that maybe ..."

Robbie eyed him with suspicion. "I know what you're going to say, but I'm not mad – I really saw them!" He slammed his fist on the dining table, causing other diners to look up in alarm. A knife clattered onto the floor.

"Sshh!" hissed Bernard. "People are looking." He bent to retrieve the knife.

"I don't care! I know what I saw."

The two men continued to plough through their unappetising dinner in silence. As they left the dining room, Bernard suggested a nightcap, something he knew Robbie was hardly likely to turn down. But his friend still wore a worried frown. "I can't understand what I saw, Bernie," he said, as they made their way through to the bar. "I only know I saw it."

As they ordered their drinks, Robbie glanced at the newspaper on the counter. It was a Norwegian paper, of course, so not a word of it made any sense to him. But the grainy photographs of the two small children did. They were pictures of the children he had seen that afternoon under the Christmas tree in the forest.

He grabbed the paper and stuffed it in his pocket before Bernard had a chance to see it. When they got back up to their room, he took it out and studied the children's pictures more carefully. There was also a photograph of a very pretty woman, possibly their mother.

Bernard, who was cleaning his teeth in preparation for bed, came over and peered over his shoulder. What on earth could his friend find so absorbing in a Norwegian newspaper? he wondered.

"Do you see those two children there, Bernie?" Robbie asked him.

Bernard nodded, as he gargled and spat in the sink. "What about them?" He put his toothbrush carefully into his sponge bag. He'd already left one behind in a Spanish hotel and didn't want to risk losing another.

"Well, they're the children I saw today in the forest, or I'm a Chinaman. Something bad has happened to them."

Bernard was speechless for a moment. He began thinking fast. Could this mean that Robbie had seen the *ghosts* of these children? It seemed the only possible explanation. He remembered now what his friend had told him on the day they had first met: that he was psychic. If Robbie was speaking the truth, and he had no reason to doubt him, then it looked very much like some awful disaster had befallen these children. Otherwise, why else would their pictures be on the front page of a newspaper? It was always bad news there.

"We need to find out what it says, Robbie," said Bernard calmly, "before we start jumping to conclusions."

"You're right. Maybe the hotel manager will oblige?"

"That's a good idea. But he'll probably be off duty by now. It's gone eleven. Let's ask him in the morning, before we leave."

Robbie folded up the newspaper carefully and put it in his suitcase. "All right," he agreed. "But you do know what all this means, don't you?"

Bernard eyed his friend carefully. "You mean you think you saw and heard their ghosts?"

"That's exactly what I mean. I told you I was psychic, didn't I?"

Bernard swallowed hard. He had never been a believer in the occult or rather had never *wanted* to believe in it. Ghostly visitations and the like filled him with horror. He liked a good ghost story like anyone else, but he was a man of the cloth and his only belief, or faith, was in God. He believed in a force for evil, that went without saying. There were demons as well as

71

angels. It was the stuff of his religion. But seeing apparitions of children in dark forests. No, that only happened in fairy tales.

Bernard slept fitfully that night, an indecipherable newspaper headline featuring heavily in his dream-filled slumber. When he woke with a start, he could hear Robbie snoring. Nothing, it seemed, could keep his friend awake. Not even the possibility that two dead children were, in some way, haunting him.

The next morning dawned dazzlingly bright. The sun poured in through the shutters of their bare little room as the two friends finished their packing and prepared to go down to breakfast.

"Have you got the newspaper?" Bernard asked, as they left the room.

"Here," he replied, "in my jacket." Robbie tapped his breast pocket. "Now, we'll know the truth, eh, Bernie?"

"I suppose so," said his friend, secretly worried where all this was going to lead them.

After their breakfast of cold meats, flabby cheese and bread, they approached the hotel manager, who was on duty at reception.

"Ah, gentlemen," he greeted them cheerfully. "You're checking out today, yes?"

"That's right," said Robbie. "We're just going up to our room to get our cases. But, before we do, would you please do me a favour?"

"A favour?" The man didn't seem to understand what Robbie meant.

"I mean, would you translate something for me? From Norwegian into English?"

"By all means," said the polite young man, "my pleasure, sir."

Robbie took the newspaper out of his breast pocket and unfolded it carefully, laying it flat on the counter before him. Suddenly the look on the man's face changed; instead of his previous pleasant smile, there was a dark frown furrowing his brow.

"We would like to know what this is all about. Just who is this young woman and these two pretty children? And why are they on the front page?" Robbie pointed to the photos, while the man glanced cursorily at them.

He coughed politely. "Er, it is hard to translate directly from our language to yours, sir," he began. "But, basically, it is about this widow whose children were saved from drowning in the lake."

Robbie stared at him in disbelief. "You mean to tell me that this major headline in your national newspaper is just about two children being saved from drowning? I thought they had been murdered."

"Murdered? Oh, dear me, no. They were saved from drowning, as I said." The man began to shuffle his feet nervously.

"But why such a big headline, man?" persisted Robbie. "It's a nice story, but not the stuff of major news, surely?"

"Oh, we here in Norway pride ourselves on being crime-free. We have no 'murders', as you put it, to report. We are a peaceful, law-abiding nation." And with that, the man turned towards another hotel guest, cutting off any further chance of interrogation by Robbie.

"Well I never," said Bernard, as they made their way up to their room. "He seemed quite put out, didn't he?"

"Hmm," Robbie muttered, turning the key in the lock. "Very put out, I'd say."

As they gathered their things together, Bernard smiled encouragingly at him. "Anyway, at least we know that those children you thought you saw can't be ghosts."

Robbie glared at him as he snapped his case shut. "What on earth are you talking about? The man was lying, it was obvious."

"But why would he do that?" asked Bernard, puzzled.

"Could be any number of reasons," muttered Robbie, taking a last look around the room. "Have you packed everything? Got your toothbrush?"

Bernard smiled. "Yes, thanks. I don't think I've forgotten anything this time."

As they boarded the coach that was to take them to the port for onward ferrying back to London, Robbie turned to his friend.

"I'm not giving up on this, you know, man," he said. "I know someone who can give me the *real* translation of this newspaper article."

"You do?" Bernard sighed. His friend was like a dog with a bone. He'd been told that the children had been the subject of a rescue from drowning, but he didn't believe it or, rather, didn't *want* to believe it. Why on earth would that hotel manager have lied? It didn't make sense to him at all.

"Yes. I know a professor of linguistics. I met him at university," said Robbie. "Carl Oppenheimer – he's an American. But he speaks dozens of languages. If he can't translate this, then no one can."

"I see," said Bernard. "So, when this friend tells you what is says, and he says it's about a rescue not a murder, will you believe *him*?"

"Naturally," said Robbie, seating himself at the back of the coach, squashing up to make room for his companion. "But he won't tell me that, Bernie, I know he won't."

Bergen, June 1948

Torrad Heglund looked at his wife in horror. She returned the same look and exploded into hollow sobs. Edda Heglund was a woman in her late sixties, who looked at least twenty years older, bent double as she was with osteoporosis. Her husband, also in his late sixties, looked about fifty. They were an ill-matched couple as they sat together opposite the Politimester, the Chief of Police, in Bergen police station.

The Politimester, who wasn't the most tactful of men, had broken the news of their daughter's death almost brutally. Edda Heglund had clutched at her eyes as if she wanted to tear them from their sockets. Her husband had tried to pull her hands away, but she turned them on him, pummelling his chest so hard, he had trouble catching his breath.

When she had calmed down slightly, the Politimester coughed and continued. "It would seem," he said, eyeing them carefully, "that Mrs Dahl had been dead for some time." He paused and watched their reaction carefully. "Did you not keep in regular touch with your daughter? A widow with two small children?" If there was a note of censure in his tone, Torrad chose to ignore it.

"We did as much as we could," he said. "But we had lost touch since she took up with some man, some *peasant*," he spat the last word. "We told her we didn't want anything to do with her if she continued to see him."

"Do you know who this man is?" The Politimester leaned back in his chair, eyeing them now with palpable dislike. They were obviously prudes as well as snobs.

"No, we had no idea. Only that he was some working man from the next village, although I think he was more of a drifter. The kind of person who didn't belong anywhere."

"So, are you saying that your daughter took up with him?"

"She told us he was only helping out on the farm, but we knew she was sleeping with him from what Halle and Birgitta told us. They said he never went home, so we drew our own conclusions."

"Halle and Birgitta are your missing grandchildren?" It was more or less a rhetorical question, but it didn't do to skimp on the facts. Not in a case of cold-blooded murder.

"That's right. Then, when Marianne realised they were telling us things she didn't want us to know, she stopped bringing them to stay with us."

"So, you've had no contact with your daughter or grandchildren for – how long?"

Torrad shrugged. "Not since last Christmas," he said.

His wife broke in at this point. "What are you doing about finding our grandchildren, Politimester?" she demanded, still sobbing.

"We are doing all we can," he told her. "We have a search team out scouring the area all around your daughter's farm. We have organised posters to be put up at strategic points in the city and outside and appeals for information have been published in the national newspapers and on the wireless. I'm sure we will find them soon."

Torrad could see, by the man's expression, that he wasn't hopeful. Halle and Birgitta had been missing since their mother's death over two months ago. What hope was there of finding them now?

As they left the police station, the grieving couple were met with a barrage of flash bulbs as reporters, anxious for a story, fired questions at them. Torrad pushed a particularly annoying reporter down the station steps as he ushered his wife into the waiting police car. The news of the terrible murder was all over the city; a city that was usually serene and pleasant was now turned upside down. The populace was baying for blood, and anyone's would do. Someone had to pay. But there was no one. Marianne's mystery man had gone to ground. No one knew who he was or where to begin looking for him.

Edinburgh, June 1948

Professor Carl Oppenheimer had just finished his final lecture of the day and was enjoying an early evening sherry before supper in halls. The American scholar had taken up a full-time teaching post at Edinburgh University, after gaining his Master's Degree in Linguistics. He wasn't really sure that this was where he wanted his life to go, but it would do for now. Brooklyn-born and bred, he had no intention of returning to that hell-hole but, on the other hand, university life in an austere post-war Britain was something he hadn't envisaged for himself, either.

As he was contemplating his life and wondering what to do with it, the telephone bell rang. "Hello?" he said.

"Hello?" came the echo.

"Who is it? Can I help you?" the Professor asked. The voice on the other end of the line seemed very far away. Tasmania, at a guess.

"Is that you, Carl?"

"Yeah, that's me. Who wants to know?"

"It's me, Carl. Robbie MacTavish. Remember? I always promised to look you up, and now I am."

"Well hi, old buddy!" exclaimed Carl, genuinely pleased to hear a voice from his distant past. "How are you? Long time, no hear. How long's it been?"

"A good few years. Too long. How have you been keeping?"

"Oh fine, fine. I'm teaching here now, on a sort of semi-permanent basis while I decide where I want to settle and what I want to do with the rest of my life. That kinda thing."

"Good for you. Are you enjoying it?"

"Some. But I need a change. Perhaps I should do some travelling before I fossilise here."

Carl could hear his friend laugh at the other end of the long-distance line, but it was very faint. "Hey, buddy, I can hardly hear you. This line's none too good. Where are you calling from? Timbuktu?"

Robbie spoke up. "No, not quite that far. London."

"Gee, London! Now I haven't been there in a while. Say, can we meet?"

"That's just what I was about to suggest. Can you get away? Come down here for a bit? I'd come up to you, but I can't leave my practice at the moment. Having been away for two weeks, my patients will lynch me if I take any more time off."

"You been travelling, man? Gee, I envy you."

"Well, that's sort of the reason I've got in touch, Carl. I've been to Norway, among other places, and I need your linguistic skills to help me translate a newspaper article that's in Norwegian. It's one of your languages, isn't it?"

"Sure is. How interesting. What's the angle?"

"Angle? Oh, you mean, why?"

"Yeah, why. Why do you need me to translate this newspaper article?"

Carl could hear his friend cough nervously down the ever-fading line.

"It's a long story. Can you come down soon?"

"You try and stop me. Just give me your address, and I'll be on my way. I'll cancel my lectures for the next few days. Nobody comes to them anyway."

This wasn't strictly true, however. Never mind, he could sort something out before he went. No problem. This call from his old university pal seemed like the answer to his prayers. He couldn't wait.

London, June 1948

It was cold for June, feeling more like early April, as Robbie paced up and down the platform at King's Cross station, two days after his telephone conversation with his friend, Professor Oppenheimer. The train from Edinburgh was due in two minutes, at six-fifteen a.m. precisely, and he couldn't wait to see him again.

He hadn't told Bernard about Carl's impending visit, sensing that he might be a bit jealous of his earlier friendship. He was also aware that Bernard still didn't entirely believe that Robbie had seen the ghosts of two children under a fir tree in Bergen. He would probably have been annoyed, or at the very least, sceptical, of the lengths Robbie was prepared to go to prove him wrong.

Whether or not Bernard would approve of Robbie's American friend, especially the reason for his visit, didn't matter. When he got confirmation of what was in that newspaper story, then he could tell Bernard he'd told him so and, hopefully, they could heal the slight rift that had developed between them.

Why the hotelier had lied about the article was a puzzle, of course. Maybe the man was worried about the effect it would have on his trade. Robbie thought it would have the opposite effect, himself. Tourists would flock to the place, if he was any judge of human nature.

He saw his old friend's head poking out of the train window as it puffed its way into the station. Carl waved at his friend and Robbie rushed up to open the door for him as the train slowed to a halt.

"Hi ya, old pal!" greeted his friend. Robbie's hand was outstretched to him, but he handed him his suitcase before realising he was meant to shake it instead. He thumped him on the back. "Sorry," he said, taking his case back. "I forgot about your quaint old English custom of shaking hands. You're looking great, by the way."

"You too," said Robbie, looking into his friend's fresh, open face and round, clear blue eyes which made him look younger than his years. However, the medical man in Robbie noted a certain pallor in his cheeks, and he had lost quite a bit of weight since he'd last seen him. Still, that was to be expected. There weren't many overweight people knocking about these days. The lack of proper food during the lean years of the war had seen to that. He also noticed dark circles under Carl's eyes and wondered if he had been overdoing it.

"It's so good to see you again, Robbie," said Carl affectionately. "I missed you."

"Me too. Come on, I've got a taxi waiting."

"Wow! A taxi! You must be doing well," observed Carl, as he followed his friend out of the station.

"Oh, I'm doing all right, I suppose," said Robbie, smiling. "But I don't go about in taxis every day of the week." The fare had made a bigger dent in his finances than he had bargained for, but he was collecting his little second-hand car from the dealer in a few days, so he would be able to drive his friend back to the station, at least.

"Gee! Thanks, pal," smiled Carl.

"Well, I can't have you struggling with your luggage on the blasted tube."

Once Carl was settled into the spare room and given breakfast by Lucy Carter, Robbie left him to attend to his morning surgery, promising his friend a pub lunch and an interesting story about his Norwegian holiday.

∽

Lucy was pleased to have another man to look after, especially an American. She had had some fun with the Yanks during the war, and had even become engaged to one of them, a man with the impossible name of Hiram B. Finkelman the Third. He was from Oklahoma and had promised her an exciting, open-air life on his ranch when the war was over. But he was killed in the D-Day landings, and that was that.

She had been heartbroken for a time, but she wasn't the only one to have lost a sweetheart to the war. It had been almost the norm to see the telegraph boy cycling down the street, the occupants of the houses praying he would pass them by for another day. Now she had two men to fuss over, so things weren't so bad. You got over everything in the end, she supposed.

And Carl was happy to be left in the charge of Robbie's rather plump but pretty housekeeper. He had begun flirting with her outrageously from the first moment he met her.

"Hi there, Lucy. My, my, you're a sight for sore eyes. Robbie's a lucky man."

Although she had been pleased that he obviously found her attractive, she didn't let him see how she felt. She soon let him know she wasn't to be trifled with. He was charming and handsome, there was no denying that, but she had her dignity and pride. Besides, he would probably only stay for a few days and be off, she knew not where.

It would, however, be nice while it lasted, she thought.

Bernard had slowly begun to wonder what had happened to Robbie since their return from holiday. They had been back for almost a week. Thankfully, his Sunday service had been very well attended, and any misgivings he'd had that his congregation would give him the cold shoulder were dispelled. He had been disheartened, however, when he realised Robbie wasn't there. He was missing their evenings together, too.

He and Robbie had become inseparable very quickly, maybe too quickly, thought Bernard. There was no denying that their European holiday had been a great success, serving to cement their friendship even further. Except for the last leg of their trip; that's when things started to go wrong This ghost business had driven a wedge between them, and Bernard didn't know how to overcome it.

It was now Friday evening, a fine drizzle was falling, and he was at a loose end. One of many loose ends, lately. Then he had an idea. Why not go to the pub? Hopefully, Robbie would be there winding down after his evening surgery, and they could pick up where they'd left off. Feeling much better, he put on his raincoat and called out to Mrs Harper that he was 'going for a walk'. He decided not to tell her his destination, as he knew her opinion of men who drank. She allowed him his glass of sweet sherry of an evening, but that was where it stopped.

The Bricklayer's Arms was full, being the end of the working week. Punters were feeling rich with bulging pay packets already starting to burn holes in their pockets. There was the familiar out-of-tune jangle of the piano, although Bernard still wasn't sure if it was the instrument or the player that was at fault. The man who usually tickled the ivories was called Sam, but nobody ever asked him to 'play it again'.

Almost immediately, he spotted Robbie, but who was that with him? His friend was seated at their usual table with a strange man, and they were talking animatedly. He felt completely excluded. So that was it, he thought. No wonder he hadn't been by or near all week. Robbie had found another friend. Oh, for God's sake, he chided himself, stop behaving like a nine-year-old schoolboy. The man's entitled to have other friends if he wants to!

But Bernard was hurt by Robbie's defection all the same, and nearly walked back out of the pub. But just as he had decided to do so, Robbie looked up and caught his eye. He gave him a friendly wave and beckoned him over.

"Hi, Bernie," Robbie greeted him as Bernard made his way through the crowds to their table. "Come and sit down. Let me introduce you. This is my university friend, Professor Carl Oppenheimer. He's down from Edinburgh for a few days." He turned to Carl. "This is my good friend, Bernard Paltoquet, Carl. As you can see from his collar, he's a vicar."

Carl shook Bernard's hand and gave him a warm smile. "Hi there, Bernie," he said, dispensing with any formalities that Bernard thought appropriate on first acquaintance. 'Bernie' indeed. He was shocked at hearing the man's transatlantic accent. How on earth did Robbie know a Yank?

"Glad to know you," Carl said. "Sit down and I'll get you a beer."

"No – no thank you," said Bernard, now quite determined not to stay. "I need to get back to write my sermon for Sunday. I haven't written a word yet."

Robbie eyed him suspiciously. "But haven't you only just come in, man?" he asked. "Surely you can stay for one drink?"

"No, no. I don't want to intrude. I only looked in to see if you were here," he said. "I thought you might be in need of company, but I see you don't."

"Please sit down and don't be a silly arse," Robbie said impatiently.

That was the last straw. How dare he make a fool of him in front of that Yank? Bernard gave him a meaningful glare and began fighting his way back through the crowds to the door. As he reached it, he felt a firm hand on his shoulder.

"Stop acting like a child," said Robbie, "and come and join us."

"No, Robbie, you don't want me interfering." Bernard was aware how stupid he sounded, He was also aware of dozens of pairs of eyes on them now. He could hear sniggering, too.

"Now look what you've done," said Robbie. "They think we're a couple of fairies! Wait there while I tell Carl what I'm up to."

Two minutes later, both men were outside the pub heading back towards the vicarage in silence.

"What goes on?" asked Robbie, breaking it at last.

Bernard didn't reply but quickened his pace instead. After a few more yards, Robbie tried again. "What's up, man? Why are you behaving like this? Carl must think you're mad."

"I don't care what Carl thinks. Who is he, anyway?"

"He's an old student friend of mine from Edinburgh. He's a professor of linguistics. I think I mentioned him to you before."

Bernard suddenly twigged. So, this Carl Oppenheimer was the man Robbie told him could translate the Norwegian newspaper article about the two children. He stopped in his tracks.

"Oh, I see," he said. "I didn't realise."

"I didn't tell you he'd arrived because I knew you weren't too keen on me following up this thing," said Robbie. "I was waiting to get Carl's translation of the newspaper article before I told you any more. If, the hotelier had been right, and it was a rescue, then I knew you'd be pleased. But, if it wasn't, and it was about something much more sinister, then I wanted to be sure before I broke it to you."

"So, have you asked him to translate the article?" asked Bernard. He was wishing with all his heart that they had missed out Norway altogether. Then they'd still be friends, enjoying each other's company of an evening, and this Carl Oppenheimer would still be in Edinburgh.

If Robbie was really psychic, then he supposed he would have to believe him. But hadn't he told him that he was psychic, too? If that was true, then why hadn't he seen the children as well?

"Not yet. I haven't given it to him yet," he heard Robbie saying. "I haven't got it with me. I thought I'd sound him out first. Give him all the gen and see if he's as sceptical as you are. Not that it matters, as long as he translates that article."

They were now at the vicarage, and Bernard had his hand on the front gate. "Are you coming in for a toddy? Or maybe a game of chess? We haven't had a game for ages and I'm getting rusty."

"Yes, sorry, Bernie. I've missed our games too, but I need to get back to my guest tonight. He's only here for a few days and I want that translation. We'll resume our chess when he's gone back. Okay?"

"Okay," said Bernard reluctantly.

A feeling of isolation and loneliness descended on him as he entered the vicarage and hung up his coat. He also realised that, despite going to the pub, he hadn't even had a drink. Then he heard Mrs Harper's voice from the kitchen.

"Would you like a slice of chocolate cake, Vicar? It's just come out of the oven."

London, July 1948

A qualified plumber had finally been called to the vicarage after Dick Appleyard's various attempts at fixing the lavatory chain and adjusting the ball cock had failed miserably.

Bernard had put his foot down in the end, realising, despite reassurances from Mrs Harper, that the man didn't know what he was doing. "I don't care how much it costs, Mrs Aitch. Just get a proper plumber in – now!"

He wasn't prepared to argue with her any further. It was embarrassing when any visitors wanted to use the facilities, and there had been several occasions when he'd had to refuse a parishioner the use of them. One man had accused him of being un-Christian, which had cut him to the quick. It had been the last straw. He would find the money, somehow. If not, the Archdeacon would just have to stump up.

"Your cistern's knackered," said a doleful sounding voice from the doorway of his study. The tall, glum figure of Gilbert Hardcastle loomed, his sleeves rolled up, the remains of the lavatory chain dangling from his large, hairy hands.

"I see," said Bernard, wondering if that was what qualified plumbers usually said. Didn't they usually dress it up in more technical jargon? Maybe this man was cheaper than the rest. Mrs Harper had been determined he shouldn't spend a fortune, even though he was past caring. He just wanted it fixed for good and all. "So, what do you suggest should be done?"

"You need to replace it," said Gilbert.

"Yes, well, I suppose you're right? Can nothing be done to repair it?"

"It's not worth it, mate," said Gilbert. "It'd be cheaper to get a completely new cistern – I know where I can get one cheap," he added, tapping the side of his nose.

Bernard had no idea what that particular gesture meant, but he suspected it was something not altogether 'kosher'.

Just then, Mrs Harper put in an appearance. "What are you doing in here, Gilbert?" she asked crossly. "You're not supposed to bother the vicar. Anything you need to say, you say to me. I told you."

"Oh, right," said Gilbert, somewhat abashed. "Well, I was just telling the reverend here that his cistern's knackered."

"We don't need you to tell us that," declared Mrs Harper. "We need you to tell us what you're going to do about it." She folded her arms at him.

"It's all right, Mrs Harper," interposed Bernard. "He was just telling me that he could get us a new one at a discounted price."

"Oh, 'e did, did 'e?" She turned to Gilbert. "Now, you look here, Gilbert 'Ardcastle, you get back up them stairs and fix the one we've got. And none of your flannel. I know what you're up to. You plumbers are all alike. But you're not diddling the vicar while I've still got breath in my body."

Bernard was quite touched by her concern, even if he felt it was really none of her business what he spent his money on. "Thank you, Mrs Harper," he said. "But I am quite capable of sorting this out."

Far from backing down at this rebuke, she went on. "You 'eard what the vicar said, Gilbert. 'E's telling you to fix the one we've got."

Had he been saying that? Bernard wondered.

"Okay, okay," Gilbert muttered, "I'll do what I can. But it'll only be a patch-up job. You'll need to get it replaced before it's too much older."

"We'll see about that," said Mrs Harper, "You just do your job and let's not 'ave so much of it."

Bernard listened to the pair trudging up the stairs and smiled. No wonder Hitler couldn't get a foothold in this country, he smiled to himself, with women like Mrs Harper to contend with.

❧

It was the following evening when Robbie decided to pay Bernard a long-awaited visit. Mrs Harper ushered him into his study with an air of disapproval.

"The wanderer returns," she announced.

"There was no need to show me up, Mrs Harper," said Robbie with a grin. "I know my way."

"I thought you might 'ave forgotten after all this time," she said with meaning.

"It's all right, Mrs Harper," said Bernard, his eyes looking at the ceiling. "Thank you."

She departed with a sniff.

"Come on in and sit down," Bernard said. "It's good to see you. Has your friend gone back to Scotland?"

Robbie smiled and came and sat by the unlit fireplace. Although it was midsummer, there was still a definite chill in the air. He took out a flask from his jacket pocket, took a swig and returned it from whence it came. He looked nervous now, as if he'd needed the whisky for Dutch courage.

"Yes, Bernie, Carl's gone back – for a while," he said.

"A while?" asked Bernard. "You mean he's coming back?"

"He will be, yes."

Bernard eyed his friend with new suspicion. "Why?"

"Well, when I say he'll be coming back, it'll probably only be overnight, because we'll be heading for Harwich to pick up a ferry," said Robbie. The words came tripping out a little too quickly.

"Whatever for?"

"To go to Denmark," said Robbie, settling himself in his chair and lighting his pipe.

"Is this another holiday, then?"

"No, nothing like that. It's more of a fact-finding mission."

"In Denmark? What's in Denmark?"

"Nothing, apart from the port from where we'll sail to Norway."

He'd said it at last, what Bernard feared was coming. "You mean, you and this Carl chap are going to Norway?" *Without me?* he nearly added but stopped himself just in time.

Robbie sucked on his pipe and sighed. "You know full well, Bernie. To find these poor children's ghosts."

"Oh, so the hotel man was lying about that newspaper headline, then?"

"Yes, old boy, I'm afraid he was. My friend, the professor, gave me the real translation." Robbie took out a piece of paper from his top pocket and unfolded it. "Here," he said, "read it for yourself."

Bernard took the sheet of paper tentatively from his friend and began to read:

Following the discovery of the body of Mrs Marianne Dahl, 34, of Dyrdal Farm, Bergen Police are searching for the dead woman's missing children, Halle, 10, and Birgitta, 6. Mrs Dahl's body was found by a homeless young man when he entered what he thought was a deserted farmhouse to find shelter for the night. It is understood that her body had been there for nearly two months, according to pathologists. The gun which killed Mrs Dahl has so far not been discovered. Mrs Dahl was a widow whose husband was killed by the Nazis in 1944.

Her death is being treated as murder, and there are fears for the safety of her two children. It is understood that a man who sometimes worked on the farm has yet to be identified, and police are anxious to talk to him as soon as possible. Anyone having any knowledge of this man or his whereabouts, or of the two missing Dahl children, please contact the Bergen Police immediately.

Bernard looked up from the paper and stared at his friend. "Oh, Robbie, how awful. I'm sorry I doubted you."

"It's all right, old boy. I would probably have taken some convincing myself if you'd seen them and not me. Anyway, now that we know, I have to go back and try to contact those children. If I can get them to speak to me, I'll need Carl with me to help translate."

"Hang on a minute," said Bernard. "How can he help? I mean, he's not any more likely to see or hear them than I am."

"That's the difficulty, of course. My friend may be psychic, but it's not likely, I suppose. If the children try to communicate by speaking to me, I'll just have to speak the words and relay them to Carl as best I can."

"I see," said Bernard, doubtfully.

"Look, Bernie, those poor children have been murdered, and we need to find out by whom and where the bodies are buried. It looks like I'm the only one who can help the police with this."

"So it would seem," said Bernard. "But surely the Bergen police are doing what they can to find these children? And this man they mention?"

"Well, I don't know. I mean, the body of this poor woman had been undiscovered for two months, so the trail will have gone cold."

"Don't you think you'd better check if the case has been solved before you go off on a wild goose chase?"

"I already have. Well, Carl has. He called the Bergen police. They haven't found the children or the man. Carl said they didn't seem particularly interested. Said the murder had happened too long ago."

"God, how callous! But surely they tried to find the children?"

"Carl said they'd searched the surrounding woodland, but how thoroughly is anyone's guess."

"So, you're determined to go back, then?"

"I have to, Bernie. I've no choice. Those children appeared to me. I'm the only one who can help them. You do see that, don't you?"

"Yes, Robbie, I do see that," said Bernard, studying the translation again. "But what about your patients?"

"Old Winfield will step in as before."

"But you told me he keeps making mistakes," Bernard pointed out.

"It's no good trying to put me off," smiled Robbie. "You know I'm going."

Bernard looked at his friend thoughtfully. Yes, he knew. Robbie was a good man. He just hoped he would return safely. He was doubtful he would achieve anything useful by going back to Bergen, but he supposed he felt it his duty to do so. Bernard wanted the children found and laid to rest, just like his friend, but he was selfish enough to wish he wasn't going. He was going to miss him dreadfully.

London, August 1948

A fortnight later, Carl was back under Robbie's roof, much to the delight of Lucy Carter. She couldn't do enough for him, which began to make Robbie feel just a little bit jealous. Although he didn't have any particular intentions towards her, himself, he didn't quite like the idea of any other man muscling in on what he saw as his 'territory'. That was one thing he could say for good old Bernie: he was no threat where the womenfolk were concerned.

Robbie could see that his housekeeper had grown very fond of Carl. She was all of a dither every time she was in his company. He watched her primp her hair and check her lipstick when she knew Carl was going to put in appearance for his meals or whatever. Did he have any serious intentions towards her? he wondered.

The night before they were due to set off for Harwich, Robbie broached the subject with him. "Carl, dear boy," he said, "you're fond of Lucy, aren't you?"

"Sure," he replied. They were playing cards, and Robbie was winning. "What's not to like? Your turn to deal," he prompted. "Why d'you ask?"

"Oh no reason," said Robbie, shuffling the pack. "You seem very friendly with her, that's all."

"Well, she's a peach," observed Carl. "I'm surprised you haven't made a move on her yourself. I don't remember you holding back when you saw a pretty girl in the past."

"No, well. I'm her employer. It's not so easy," Robbie replied.

"Gee, I'm sorry. I'll back off if you're keen," said Carl, trumping Robbie's Queen.

"Oh no, I've no intentions towards her," Robbie told him, gathering up the cards and dealing them out again. "I just don't want her to get hurt, that's all. You forget, Carl, I know all about you. Love 'em and leave 'em: isn't that your motto?"

"Yeah, well I guess you're right," admitted Carl taking up his cards. "I don't want her to get hurt. She's too nice."

"Yes, she is," said Robbie sternly. "And she's already had her heart broken by a GI she met during the war."

"Oh, I didn't know."

"Yes, well, just you think about what you're doing, that's all."

Carl looked sad for a moment. Then sighed. "Anyway, I can't be serious with her, or with anyone else come to that."

Robbie put down his cards and looked into his friend's face. There was a look he hadn't seen there before. He couldn't quite describe it but, if anything, he thought he looked scared. Also, he noticed the dark lines round his blue eyes were more pronounced than when he had first seen them a few weeks ago. He looked worn out.

"What on earth do you mean by that?" he asked, concerned.

"Just that. You see, I'm not going to make old bones. So I *can't* ask anyone to marry me. *That* wouldn't be right."

"What makes you think you're going to die young?" Even though Carl looked tired, he hadn't suspected it was anything more than that.

Carl sighed and threw in his hand. "I'm out," he said. "Shall we have another game?"

"Not for the moment. Tell me what you mean by 'not making old bones'. I'm a doctor, remember? Perhaps I can help."

"No one can help, Robbie. I've had all the tests. You see, it's my heart. A faulty valve. Any form of exertion could be fatal I've been told."

"Oh, Carl, I'm so sorry. I'd no idea."

Carl smiled bleakly. "Of course you hadn't. I never told you. But that's why I can't be serious about my affairs with women. But I want to have fun with the time I've got left."

"It's so unfair," Robbie said. "How can someone like you, with such a brain, be doomed like that? We've got enough idiots in the world, why not get rid of some of *them* first? Anyway, who says you're going to die? I'll make it my life's work to keep you alive, you see if I don't."

Carl laughed. "Okay, man, whatever you say. But in the meantime, don't tell anyone, will you. Especially not Lucy."

"Why *not* tell her? She has every right to know, the way you've been buzzing around her. She probably thinks you're about to propose. You've got to put her straight, Carl."

"Okay, okay. I'll tell her, but not until after we get back from Norway, eh?"

Robbie reluctantly agreed. Then he had a thought. "I say, are you okay to travel all the way to Norway?"

"Oh sure. I've made it to Edinburgh and back, haven't I? Life has to go on, you know. Well, until it doesn't, I suppose."

"What medication are you on?" asked Robbie.

"Oh, tons of stuff. I'll get them for you, if you like."

"Yes, please do. And I'm going to give you a thorough examination before we go," he said with determination.

"Okay, you're the boss," smiled Carl as he left the room to retrieve his medicine.

In his absence, Robbie put a call through to Bernard and told him about Carl's poor state of health. Bernard was shocked.

"The thing is, I'd like it if you'd come with us tomorrow," said Robbie. "Just for moral support. If anything happens to Carl, I'd rather I wasn't alone with him."

"But I haven't got a ticket or anything," protested Bernard. "Anyway, I can't leave my parish again so soon. How long will you be away?"

"Only a couple of days, hopefully. There and back."

"Look, I really can't come now. I'm sorry. But I'll see you both off from the station, if you like?"

Robbie sighed. "Okay, that'll help. Do you mind?"

"No, not at all. I was planning to come and see you off anyway. What time do we leave?"

"We need to get to Liverpool Street to catch the ten-five to Harwich, so we need to get a bus to the underground for nine o'clock, to make sure we have enough time."

"Okay, I'll be ready."

"Thanks, Bernie," said Robbie gratefully. "I appreciate it."

As he replaced the receiver, Carl re-entered the room carrying several pill boxes and a bottle of a luminous-looking green concoction. Robbie studied the labels and nodded sagely. "Well, all I can say is most of these are doing you no good whatsoever, especially not this green stuff. Get your shirt off and let's examine you now – properly."

Bernard was as good as his word and accompanied Robbie and Carl to Liverpool Street to see them off. He waved goodbye, watching their two heads and arms protruding from the carriage as the ten-five to Harwich pulled out of the station.

The platform was nearly empty now, and the unseasonal chilly summer had suddenly bucked its ideas up. It was already very hot at that time in the morning and promised temperatures in the nineties by midday. Bernard felt the heat as he tried to loosen the pressure of his dog collar on his sweaty neck. He was concerned for the safety of his friend. Who knew what dangerous waters he and Carl were heading into? Apparently, there was a maniac on the loose who'd murdered at least one woman, and probably her children too. He should have stopped them going, somehow. He began to feel faint as he headed for the buffet for a refreshing cold drink before starting back home.

As he approached the buffet door, he suddenly felt a presence at his side. He looked around quickly and there was that weird little man who called himself Diabol standing there. He sported a different jacket this time, a bright red one, but his sparse hair patches and strange, changing coloured eyes were the same. He still had that funny little jerk of the elbows too.

"Not you again!" Bernard gasped. "Have you come for me *this* time?"

"Actually, no," said the little man, as his eyes flashed as red as his jacket.

"Did you find the correct Paltoquet by the way?" Although Bernard was horrified at seeing this strange apparition again, he was also very curious.

"No. He escaped me. But I'll get him soon, have no fear."

"So, what do you want with me now?" Bernard thought he really was going to faint if the man didn't go away soon.

"I'm looking for an acquaintance of yours who I was given to understand would be with you this morning." The man jerked his elbows and scratched his meagre crop of hair while anxiously looking around him.

"Do you mean Robbie MacTavish?"

"No. It's another funny name. I get all the funny names, me. Still, I'm sure I'll earn my horns one day." The man gave Bernard a leering grin, which made him feel almost physically sick.

"Well, I'm all alone, as you can see," said Bernard, "so I suggest you go and look elsewhere." Please go, he prayed under his breath. He just hoped God was looking after him this morning.

"Oppenheimer – that's the name – Carl Oppenheimer. You know him, I'm led to believe."

"Well, slightly, yes." Oh, dear, he thought. Was Robbie's friend ill enough to be carried off while he was still so young?

"So, where is he?" asked the little man impatiently. "I haven't got all day. I've got to escort a Mrs Fanackerpan and a Mr Moses Ofarim before twelve o'clock."

"I see what you mean about funny names," observed Bernard, amused, despite the weird situation, which was growing weirder by the second. "But I'm afraid you've just missed him. He was on the train that just pulled out. He's on his way to Harwich."

"Damn! Sorry, I mean Heavens!" exclaimed the man. "Foiled again!"

"Does that mean Carl won't be leaving us now?" asked Bernard, hopefully.

"Yes, at least not for a while. He's a marginal, in any case. Now he's got a reprieve, he may end up upstairs. He's been a bit of a bad boy with the ladies, but he's got a heart condition so that could account for his behaviour."

"How do you mean?"

"Well, sometimes, when people don't think they've got long to live, they try and cram as much living in as possible. I presume that's what your Carl has been doing, so he may get away with it. Mind you, he'd have more fun downstairs, if you get my meaning." And the little man gave Bernard another of his leering grins.

Bernard wondered if he was going insane, talking to somebody who wasn't really there. As he thought this, the sounds of the station crashed in on him and he heard the puffing of a great iron monster as it roared along the platform. The steam from the train engulfed him, and suddenly there were people everywhere, but no sign of Diabol. Bernard ran for the buffet and cursed that it was too early for an alcoholic drink.

When he reached the vicarage later that morning, he was still feeling faint and light-headed. Mrs Harper noticed his pallor at once and poured him a sweet sherry.

She sat him down in his chair in the study and threw open the windows. "Here," she said, "get this down you."

Bernard gulped the sweet sherry with relief. He smiled wanly and thanked her for her concern.

"I'll fetch you some strong hot tea right away," she said. "Dinner will be in about half an hour."

Bernard settled back in his chair and mulled over his second meeting with Diabol. He wasn't all that scary, he had to admit; he was too comical looking for that. But he couldn't understand why he had singled him out in this way. He knew, beyond any doubt, that these experiences had been psychic, and he silently apologised to Robbie for ever doubting him. Both men, in different ways, had some kind of psychic gift, which they would have to use carefully.

He wondered whether he should tell Robbie about his friend's narrow escape, but he thought better of it. It wouldn't serve any purpose; it would just make him worry. His friend's time would come when it would, and there was nothing either he or Robbie could do about it.

Gradually, he felt calmer and less faint, as he listened to Mrs Harper clattering up the stairs with the tea tray.

"There you go," she said, settling the tray on the little table next to him.

"Thank you, Mrs Harper."

Bernard decided to spend the time before his next meal (on the table at one o'clock, precisely) reading his

Bible. He had been neglecting the good book lately and was beginning to feel guilty about it. He needed to constantly improve his mind, as well as his knowledge of the Word of God, in order to be a good priest. He hoped he was one already, but sometimes he didn't feel too sure about that.

After his substantial dinner of shepherd's pie and rhubarb tart, he decided to take a stroll over the common, his Bible tucked under his arm. He didn't want to admit to himself that the meetings with Diabol had shaken him up but they had, and he decided to take them as a timely warning to keep him on the straight and narrow.

The afternoon, as presaged, was unbearably hot, almost oppressive. He wouldn't be surprised if there wasn't a thunderstorm soon, which he hoped would bring some much-needed rain. His head ached as he walked across the common, stepping between the bodies lying there, basking in the sun. How could they? he wondered. They would get burned. But, if they were under-dressed, Bernard was overdressed, still in his dog collar and tweed jacket. Sweat was pouring off him as he found a secluded and, thankfully, shady bench.

Mopping his brow, he took out his Bible and opened it at St Mark, chapter 9, verse 24, the bit about 'helping thou mine unbelief'. Bernard thought this was very apt. He read on, absorbing the words of wisdom that never failed to give him comfort in times of stress.

"Where did you say this Carl Oppenheimer had gone?" came a voice next to him.

Bernard nearly jumped out of his skin as he turned to see Diabol sitting on the bench beside him.

≈

The hot weather had broken at last. Rain drenched the drab South London streets from Inkerman Terrace, down Bockhampton Road, and round the corner to the vicarage itself in Canonbie Street. Bernard was completely out of sorts. Even Mrs Harper's sumptuous afternoon tea did not cheer him.

"You all right, love?" she asked him, as she placed the tray on the small table by his chair. "You look miles away."

"Oh, I'm fine," he replied, making an effort. It was all very well what the Bible told him: to be a Christian and do Christian things, but it wasn't always so easy. He seemed to feel nothing for the people in need of his ministrations; all he could feel was sorry for himself. "It's the weather. Looks like the summer is over."

"Yes, I suppose so," agreed Mrs Harper, casting a solicitous eye over her young vicar. "It's cats and dogs out there. Is that all that's bothering you?"

"I've been thinking," he said with even more of an effort, "we ought to do something for the poor of the parish."

"That'd be nice," she replied. "What did you 'ave in mind, like?"

"Maybe a dinner and dance? Or buffet, rather than dinner. We could sell tickets and raffle prizes, and the takings could go towards a slap-up Christmas dinner for the old age pensioners and anyone else who can't afford it or are alone at that time of the year. What do you think?"

"A good idea. And I'll provide the buffet," she said proudly.

"Are you sure, Mrs Aitch? It'll be a lot of work."

"Pish pash! Not for me. I can get some 'elp, if I need it. Better than paying fancy prices to the bloomin' caterers."

"Well, thank you, dear," said Bernard. "If you're sure?"

"'Course. You leave it to me," she said, as she left the study. "I'll start making a list right away."

He sank back in his chair and smiled. He was always changing his opinion of his housekeeper. One minute she was a scold, the next a nuisance, the next a saint. But, he supposed, taking her all in all, she was a bit of a treasure.

He felt cheered to be doing something for someone else. It was true that it was better to give than receive. He felt very pious, now that he was doing the charitable thing. He hadn't been doing enough of that lately. He just had to pray to God to make him a better person.

Then his thoughts turned to his further encounter with Diabol the previous afternoon. Even though he'd had his Bible for protection, it hadn't been proof enough against that horrid little man. He'd come back to ask him where Carl was once more. Bernard had known what that meant, of course; his time was up after all. There had been no reprieve for the Professor.

He had tried to put Diabol off by saying he had no idea, which was practically true, anyway. But the little man had persisted. He only wanted his confirmation, he'd said, as to where the young professor was going. Bernard had again told him he didn't know, which was a lie, of course. But it was in a good cause. Diabol had only grinned, though. He knew, anyway. So why had he bothered him? Bernard had then asked. But the man had already disappeared.

It seemed such a strange way to get premonitions, Bernard had thought, because surely these meetings with Diabol amounted to just that. Had Carl Oppenheimer already died? If so, Robbie would be beside himself. He wished he could call him to find out but, even if it were possible, what good would it have done? And what could he have said? 'Has Carl died yet?' No, of course he couldn't.

Now, all he wanted was to see Robbie again, to comfort him, if necessary. The problem of the ghostly children would have to be forgotten, too. If Carl was gone, there would be nobody to translate what they had to say, anyway. It would be a double disaster for his friend, of course.

But it would be a blessing, really. Robbie hadn't considered the possible danger he was getting himself into. If Carl was dead, Robbie would come home as quickly as possible, wouldn't he? There was nothing else he could do.

Mrs Harper returned with the afternoon post as he came to this conclusion. "Where's your doctor friend today?" she asked, handing it to him.

"Oh, he's gone on another trip abroad," Bernard told her gloomily, glancing at the letters, but seeing no airmail envelope which would have suggested a letter from Robbie. "He'll be back soon though, I expect."

"You miss 'im when 'e's away, don't you?" she observed, almost kindly.

"Yes, I have to say, I do," he admitted, flinging the post aside.

"Vicar?" she said, picking up his empty tea tray.

"Yes, Mrs Harper?"

"Tell me to mind my own business, if you like, but 'ave you got a girlfriend?"

Bernard was taken aback by the bluntness of her question. She was quite right. It really wasn't any of her concern. "Er, no, Mrs Harper, I haven't."

"It's just that you're on your own such a lot. It would be nice for you if you 'ad a girlfriend," she said.

"Maybe it would," said Bernard quietly, thinking about his long-lost Sophie. "But I've been too busy to think about it. Time enough, Mrs Aitch, time enough."

"You need to get out more," she observed. "I know some nice young women who'd suit you down to the ground."

"Please, Mrs Harper – no matchmaking," he protested. "I'll find someone when I'm good and ready."

"Well, mind you do," she said, opening the study door. "It'd do you a power of good."

Bernard smiled grimly as the door closed on his well-meaning housekeeper. The last thing he needed was a succession of 'suitable young women' paraded before him by Mrs Harper. He was content with his life as it was, thank you very much.

Except was he – really?

☙

Two days later, Mrs Harper opened the door to a very wet Robbie MacTavish. The rain hadn't stopped for over three days.

She sniffed. "So, it's you, is it?" she greeted him, as if there was a possibility that he could be someone else. "I suppose you'd better come in," she added grudgingly.

"Thank you, Mrs Harper," he said, stepping into the hall.

"Wipe your feet," she instructed, noticing he wasn't his usual ebullient self. "Is anything wrong, Doc?"

"Oh, not to worry," he said dismissively, removing his sodden jacket and giving it to Mrs Harper to deal with. "Is the lad in his study?"

"Yes, go on up," she said, hanging his coat on the hallstand.

"Thank you," he said, as he climbed slowly up the stairs.

It may have been a coincidence but, as Robbie entered the room, the sun peeked from behind a cloud, letting in a thin, watery stream of light that played gently on his sandy hair.

"Welcome home, Robbie," Bernard greeted him, clapping him on the shoulder and shaking him vigorously by the hand.

"Thanks, old boy," Robbie replied. "Nice to be back." He didn't look it, though.

Bernard was shocked by his haggard and drawn features. "What's up?" he asked, fearing he already knew the answer.

"Prepare yourself for a shock, Bernie," Robbie replied, seating himself opposite his friend. "Carl's dead."

"Oh, I'm so sorry," Bernard said, unsure whether to give the big bluff man a comforting hug. Their friendship had never been demonstrative in that way, and he didn't know how to start. He settled for a sympathetic tap on the shoulder. "What happened?"

"He had a heart attack on the train to Bergen," Robbie told him. "I tried to resuscitate him, but it was no good. He was gone. I can't say I was surprised, although I hadn't expected him to keel over quite so soon. I would never have let him travel if I'd thought that."

"I'm so sorry, Robbie. What did you do?"

"I called his parents in the States. I found his home address among his effects. They were really upset and shocked, because they knew nothing about his illness."

"So, are they arranging everything. All the formalities?"

"Yes, well, they want him to be buried in the family plot. In Manhattan, I think. Somewhere there. Long Island."

"I see." Bernard didn't know what else to say. There didn't seem anything he could usefully add.

"He hated his home town, he told me once," said Robbie with an ironic smile. "I hope he won't mind."

"I don't suppose so," said Bernard encouragingly. "It's better for him to be among his own family, don't you think?"

"Probably," said Robbie, not looking all that sure.

"It's such a shame," said Bernard. "Oh, here's Mrs Harper with the tea. That's most welcome."

She placed the tea tray on the table beside Bernard and left without speaking. She had heard the sad news through the study door and, for once, had nothing to say.

The two friends drank their tea in silence, listening to the comforting sound of the rain spatter against the window pane. Then Bernard spoke. "So, I suppose, what with all that happening, you didn't manage to find the children again?"

"What do *you* think?" Robbie said drily. "When would I have had a chance? Carl died on the train just before we arrived at Bergen. I spent the rest of the time talking to his parents and the Bergen authorities."

"It was a silly question. I suppose you'll drop the whole thing now, will you?"

"Not on your life!" exclaimed Robbie, searching his pockets for his trusty pipe. "Have you got any matches?"

Bernard retrieved a box from the mantelpiece. "Here. But how are you going to translate what they say?"

"Oh, I'll find someone, don't you fret," Robbie replied. "But I need to find the spot again. It was under a particularly fine spruce, if I remember rightly. I think I'll be able to find it, but I must go back soon, or I'm sure to forget. You must come with me this time, man. It's nearly the end of August, so you must be due for a few days' leave now."

Bernard looked at his friend in bewilderment. "I'll come with you, by all means, as soon as I can arrange it. But what use will I be? *I* can't speak Norwegian."

"No matter. You know the spot where I saw them. At least you can help me find that."

"Certainly, Bernard. But I don't know what'll happen then. If you see the children again, how will you communicate with them?"

"We'll have to see, won't we? First things first. Let me find them again. I simply must find them again."

Bergen, September 1948

A week later, Bernard and Robbie were back in Bergen. It was the beginning of September and Bernard had promised the Archdeacon to be back in London for Harvest Festival at the end of the following week. It was a matter of life and death, he had told his superior, which was true. The Archdeacon, like Pontius Pilate, washed his hands of the matter. If Bernard could arrange for his congregation to be looked after, he supposed he could see no problem.

The two friends booked into the hotel they had stayed in last time, but there was a different man behind the reception desk. On enquiry, they learned that the manager was himself on holiday – in London, of all places.

Their first morning dawned sunny and quite warm, and they set out with the hotel's standard packed lunch of spam and cheese sandwiches, plus a tomato. This was an addition to last time and seemed to indicate that things were looking up. The fruit was still as strange, though.

The pair set off but were astounded at what they saw when they reached the edge of the forest. What was once a densely tree-populated area, was now a sparse wilderness. They looked all around them, and then stared at each other in bewilderment. There was no doubt about it, the trees had been decimated. There was no way of knowing where that special tree was now. In fact, it didn't seem to be there at all. It had, along with

117

many others, been chopped down for the Christmas market.

Robbie rushed round and round in panic. "The trees have all gone!" he cried, stating the obvious.

He slumped down beneath one of the few remaining trees by the lake, and Bernard sat down beside him. "It's a blow," said Bernard, "but we should have thought about it, you know."

Robbie sighed. "What d'you mean?"

"It's the time of year when Norway exports its trees. It's probably one of their most lucrative trades."

"Oh, my God," exclaimed Robbie. "I think you're right! So our tree's probably on its way to somewhere to be sold as a *Christmas* tree?"

"That's what I would guess," said Bernard, opening up his sandwiches.

"What can we do now?" said Robbie hopelessly. "It's a bit of a facer, isn't it?"

"Yes, I'm afraid so." Bernard couldn't think of any words of comfort. Poor Robbie. He had lost a close friend and now he'd been foiled in his attempt to find out what had happened to those poor children. He must be feeling pretty sick, he thought. The two made their way back to the hotel disconsolately. The young man behind the desk smiled at them as they came in.

"Will you be dining here tonight, gentlemen?" he asked them brightly.

"Yes, please," said Bernard. "We'll be checking out tomorrow morning, so can you please have our bills ready?"

"Of course, sir," said the young man. "But I thought you were staying till the end of the week?"

"Yes, we were, but our plans have altered. Or rather they've been altered for us."

"Indeed?" The young man cocked an enquiring eyebrow. "May I ask what's happened, sir? Maybe I can help?"

"Your English is very good," observed Robbie.

"That's because I *am* English," said the man.

"Ah, that would explain it. Well, maybe I can ask you..." Robbie glanced sideways at Bernard, who gave him a warning look. He decided to ignore it.

"Do you know anything about the murder that took place here back at the end of March?" he asked.

"You mean that young widow on the farm?"

"That's right. Do you know if anyone was convicted of her murder?"

"No. Not so far as I know. It's a complete mystery. There was this man the police were trying to track down, but they have drawn a complete blank. He just seems to have vanished. It was some workman or other that occasionally helped out on the Dahl farm."

"Do you know if they ever found the children?" Robbie then asked him.

"No. They never have. It's very sad, especially for the murdered woman's parents. They've offered a substantial reward for any information concerning them or the mysterious man."

"Really? Do you know their names?"

"Er – who? The parents?"

"Yes."

"I think they're called Heglund. The police will be able to tell you. But what interest do you have in the case? Are you private detectives? I thought your friend here was a priest?" Bernard's dog collar was, as usual, very much in evidence.

"Er, no, we're private eyes," winked Robbie. "My friend's in disguise."

Bernard gave him a black look but didn't say anything.

"Really? How exciting! Have you got any leads?"

"Young man, you know better than to ask that."

"Oh, of course not. Sorry. Anyway, are you still checking out tomorrow morning?"

"No. We'll be staying another night, thank you," said Robbie, before Bernard could speak.

Later, after dinner, Bernard grumbled darkly. "What are you playing at, Robbie? Making out we're private detectives, of all things. Are you completely barmy?"

"Probably. But we *are* private eyes in a way. Me, especially. I'm acting for those poor little children. They've got no one else."

"What about the police?"

"Well, yes, them..." Robbie said slowly. "But they don't know what we know..."

"Oh, you mean about them being dead?"

"Precisely."

"But we don't *really* know that for sure, do we?"

"Now, Bernie," said Robbie warningly. "I thought you believed I'd seen their ghosts?"

Bernard laughed. "Okay, okay. Point taken. But why stay another day? We can't usefully achieve anything now that the tree's gone."

"I want to talk to the Heglunds before we go back. Maybe we can get some clue from them."

"But what if they don't speak English?" asked Bernard reasonably.

"Hmm, I hadn't thought of that. Never mind, we won't know until we meet them, will we?"

"But what good will it be to meet them? They don't know anything more than we do," Bernard pointed out. "And, anyway, should we be intruding on their grief?"

"Not in the normal way, no. But I'd still like to meet them."

Bernard gave up. He decided to go along with whatever his friend wanted. Maybe he would solve the case in the end. He certainly deserved to.

The next morning the two friends made their way to Bergen police station in their quest to find the Heglunds. Robbie had wondered whether he should tell the police about his sighting of the ghostly children, but Bernard had been doubtful.

"What would be the point?" said Bernard, over breakfast. "The police will just think you're mad and probably ban you from bothering the Heglunds altogether. If they don't lock you up for wasting police time or being a lunatic, or whatever."

Robbie had to concede and agreed not to mention any psychic manifestations to the Politimester.

They entered the police station with some trepidation. It was an austere building, almost forbidding in its grey stone aspect, and they felt like they were entering some kind of mausoleum. Very unlike a typical English police station, this was more like a library or museum, with its high ceilings and rarefied atmosphere. Nobody was speaking above a whisper.

Robbie approached the desk sergeant, who was standing stiffly behind the glass-fronted counter. He could hear his footsteps echo hollowly on the polished tiled floor and began to feel intimidated the closer he got to the officer. The man looked very spruce in his smart uniform, but he had a forbidding air of gloom and despondency that seemed to brook no nonsense.

"Do you speak English?" Robbie asked.

The policeman gave him a look of utter disdain. "A little," he said. "What is it?"

"Ah, well, my name is Doctor Robert MacTavish, and my friend here is Reverend Bernard Paltoquet. We are from London – England."

"I know where London is. State your business." The man wasn't exactly rude but bordering on it.

"Er, we, er, wondered if we could have the address of the Heglunds – the parents of Marianne Dahl who was murdered in March this year."

"And why do think I should give it to you?"

"We think we may be able to help them get over their loss."

"In what way?"

"That is personal. Between ourselves. It is a matter of extreme delicacy, you understand?"

"No." The answer was blunt, leaving no possibility of misinterpretation.

Bernard nudged his friend. "Come on, Robbie, let's go. We're not getting through to him at all."

But Robbie was having none of it. "No, Bernie, I need to do this." He turned back to the policeman who was now writing something in a thick, leather-bound ledger.

"I'm sorry to be insistent," said Robbie.

The man looked up from his ledger, seemingly surprised to see him still standing there. "What now?"

"I genuinely think we can help this couple in their hour of sorrow. I can't explain, but, believe me, we wouldn't have come all this way from England if we didn't think it would serve any purpose."

The man sighed. "Your travel arrangements are no concern of mine. If you visit Norway, that is for you. My concern is to stop interfering – er, how do you term it in your country? – 'busybodies' from bothering the bereaved family. We are working on solving this case, and it is people like you who are stopping us from doing our job. Are you in any way related to this family?"

"No. We've never met any of them. Well, I say that, but in a way, I have. But I don't think it will make sense to you." And looking at the man's stolid expression, he could see that was obvious. Robbie was sensible enough to realise that any mention of ghosts would have him thrown out in seconds.

"Is it possible to see whoever is in charge of this case, do you think?" Robbie decided to try another tack.

"No. Not unless you have any evidence to give him." The man was still bordering on rudeness without quite overstepping it. "Otherwise, would you and your friend please leave? We are too busy to listen to you anymore."

Bernard decided to intervene at this point.

"I wonder if someone who is not involved directly may not be of comfort to the family? I'm a man of God, you see, and my friend here is a doctor. We *do* have some connection with the case, I can assure you and, as Dr MacTavish just said, we would hardly come all the way from England just on a whim."

"On a whim?" The man obviously didn't understand. "Is that some kind of aeroplane?"

"No, no," grinned Bernard. "Look, we have something serious to tell the family. Please help us to help them. Just give us the address, that's all we ask."

Just then, a younger officer appeared behind the counter. "What's going on, Karl? Who are these gentlemen?"

Robbie jumped in. "We are concerned with the Dahl murder," he said, "and we need the Heglunds' address."

The second policeman seemed much more approachable than the first one, who had retired into a side office.

"In what way are you concerned?"

"We are English and have come all the way from London," he told him. "We think we can bring some comfort to the parents of Mrs Dahl."

"How?"

Bernard spoke now. "Christian comfort," he said, smiling beatifically.

"You're not reporters, are you?" The young officer looked at them suspiciously.

"Of course not," said Bernard.

A few minutes later, Bernard and Robbie were outside the police station, looking pleased with themselves.

"Well done, Bernie!" exclaimed Robbie. "You little charmer, you."

"It's the collar," pointed out Bernard meekly, handing the piece of paper with the Heglunds' address to his friend. "No one can distrust a vicar – well, unless they're just pretending to be one. Although I think he gave us the address in the end just to get rid of us."

"You're probably right," laughed Robbie.

The Heglunds lived in Oslo, not Bergen, which was a bit of a blow to the pair. But, nothing daunted, they bought train tickets and set off right away.

Bernard looked at his friend as they sat facing each other in the rather rickety steam train heading for the Norwegian capital. He pondered whether to tell Robbie about his further encounters with Diabol, and how he had known that Carl was going to die. It wouldn't make any difference, of course, whether he knew or not, but he felt he had a right to know anyway.

"Nice scenery," observed Robbie, as he settled back in his seat and lit his pipe.

"Yes, indeed, most pleasant," concurred Bernard. They rode in silence for several minutes. Then Bernard cleared his throat. "Robbie?"

"Yes, old chap?"

"I've got something to tell you, and I don't know how you'll take it."

"Well, you won't know till you tell me," said Robbie, reasonably.

"No, of course."

Clearing his throat again, Bernard proceeded to tell him about his further encounters with Diabol, and what had passed between them.

Robbie was horror-struck. "Dear God, are you telling me you knew all the time that Carl was going to die?"

Bernard looked out of the train window as he replied. "Yes, I suppose I did. But it's not my fault,

Robbie. I didn't ask that horrid creature to confide in me."

"Of course you didn't, old boy," said Robbie, looking thoughtful. "I'm just surprised Carl was supposedly taken down below. He didn't deserve that. He was a bit of a one for the ladies, but he'd never done anything really bad, I'm sure. It must have been some sort of a mistake. A mix-up of names, maybe."

"You know, you could be right. Diabol got *my* name mixed up before, remember?"

"Yes, that's right, he did. So, do you think this Diabol could have got the wrong Carl Oppenheimer?"

"Well, it's possible, I suppose. But there's obviously nothing to be done about it now."

Robbie hunched his shoulders and stared gloomily at his friend. "Apparently not," he said sadly. "Poor Carl."

They continued their train journey in companionable silence, both lost in their own thoughts.

They reached their destination quite late that afternoon, and it was growing dusk as they approached the apartment where the Heglunds lived. It was a tall block situated not far from Oslo Central station. The imposing building, in some ways, looked more like a prison than residential apartments. But inside, it was much more pleasant. The main hall was well-lit and carpeted, and the walls were painted in a soothing pale green. There were a few pot plants in evidence, which added a homely touch to the place.

The Heglunds' flat was located on the third floor, which was reached by a rather unwieldy lift that carried them creakingly and slowly upwards. As it hit the third floor, they were practically thrown off their feet as it jerked to a halt.

They stepped out into a long corridor, with warm, russet carpeting along its length, soft lighting and a pleasant aroma of lavender polish. The Heglunds' flat was the last one on the right side. As they stood outside the door, they almost wondered why they had come. They just hoped the couple would be pleased to hear what they had to say.

Robbie pressed the bell with determination. The door was opened almost immediately by an ancient-looking, bent-up little woman. This couldn't be the grandmother, surely? She must be the great grandmother.

"Hello," said Robbie. "We are here to see Mr and Mrs Heglund, the parents of Marianne Dahl. Are they in?"

"Yes, we are," she replied. So, she *was* the grandmother. At least she understood English, which was a blessing. A man, looking a good twenty years younger, came to the door and shook Robbie and Bernard by the hand. "Come in, please. We have been expecting you."

"Er, thank you," replied Robbie, following them into the flat, with Bernard trailing behind. "You were expecting us?"

"Yes," said Torrad Heglund. "The police called us. They told us you were coming to see us. They said they hoped you were not going to cause trouble and to call them if you did. But I can see you are not trouble." And he smiled at them.

"I hope you won't think so, after you've heard what we have to tell you," said Robbie, averting his eyes from the open face of Mr Heglund.

"What news do you have, young man?" asked Mrs Heglund, addressing Robbie, as she ushered them both into the living room and invited them to sit down.

Torrad said something to his wife in Norwegian. "Would you like some tea?" she asked.

"No, thank you," said Robbie at once. "Listen to what I have to say first. You might just want to kick us out afterwards."

The Heglunds looked bewildered. "I don't understand," said Torrad. "Do you have news that will upset us?"

"I fear so," said Robbie. "You see, I've seen your grandchildren." Bernard gave him a startled look. He didn't think he was going to break it to them quite so bluntly.

Edda Heglund clapped her hands in joy. "You have? Where?" she cried.

"I'm sorry. I didn't mean to raise your hopes," said Robbie. "I saw them, but they were in the spirit world. They were ghosts. Do you know what that means?"

Torrad's face took on a horrified expression. Mrs Heglund just looked puzzled. She turned to her husband, who again spoke to her in her native language. Then it was her turn to look horrified.

"You mean they are *dead*?" she screamed at Robbie.

He cast his eyes down to his shoes. "It looks that way, I'm afraid," he murmured.

Edda Heglund let out a yell and collapsed into her husband's arms. A yell, being the same in any language, Robbie and Bernard knew that she had taken this news as badly as they feared.

"I'm so sorry," said Robbie, "but I had to tell you the worst because something positive could come out of this, if you stop and think for a minute."

Torrad glared at him. "I think you've done enough damage, Mr – er, Dr MacTavish," he said sternly. "You come here with some story about seeing the *ghosts* of our grandchildren – how do you think that makes us feel? You cannot possibly state that they are dead, can you? You saw some sort of a vision. That's no proof. How dare you upset my wife like this? Please go – now!"

Robbie and Bernard rose to leave. They had done what they had set out to do, but they hadn't succeeded in convincing the couple of their story. Perhaps it was inevitable.

Edda Heglund stopped them as they were about to go out of the door. "Wait," she called in a small, thin voice, completely calm now. "You tell us that you have seen our grandchildren? They could have been real, couldn't they? I mean *alive*. Not – ghosts at all?"

Robbie saw a way now to help soften the blow. "I don't know for sure, Mrs Heglund. All I can tell you is that I saw them under a tree in the forest near their home. Pretty blond children, the little girl had her hair in a plait, and they were both dressed in blue. They could have been playing or just waiting for some help. They tried to talk to me, but I couldn't understand what they said. I was on holiday then with my friend here. I couldn't rest when I got back to England, and I made it my business to find out what had happened to them. I came back to Bergen to find them again, but the tree where I saw them has been cut down."

"It would," said Mr Heglund. "It's the Christmas market. So they *are* alive?"

"I didn't say that, Mr Heglund. My friend here, Bernard, was with me, but he didn't see them. That's why I fear they may have been ghosts. Do you understand?"

"But your friend could have been looking elsewhere and missed them, couldn't he?" Edda Heglund asked, hopefully.

"Yes, Mrs Heglund," Robbie sighed. "It's possible." He didn't have the heart to contradict her further.

Bernard touched her arm gently. "Mrs Heglund, if your grandchildren have passed over, they may be trying to get in touch with someone to tell them about what happened to them and, I'm sorry to have to say this, also to tell them where their bodies are. Also, they will probably know who their murderer is. Do you see?"

As before, Bernard was able to pour a little oil on troubled waters. Mr Heglund still looked very cross, but his wife was calm, almost serene. She seemed to understand. He told them that he and Robbie would make every effort to find out what happened to their daughter and grandchildren.

"Phew! That wasn't easy," observed Bernard, once they were out in the dark street once more.

"But they needed to know," said Robbie grimly. "We must come back and see them tomorrow, Bernie, once they've had a chance to assimilate what we've told them. Maybe, by then, they'll be able to tell us something about this man that helped out on their daughter's farm."

"Do you think that's a good idea? Don't you think we've upset them enough already? And don't you think they would have told the police all about this man? They're not likely to tell us anything new, are they?"

Robbie shrugged. "I only know I need to do this, Bernie. I must talk to them when they've calmed down. You never know, the police could have missed something."

"Do you think that's likely?"

"I don't know, Bernie, I only know we've got to try. Anyway, we'd better book into a hotel for the night. Come on."

Bernard thought his friend was taking too much on himself. If the tree had still been there, all well and good. If he had seen the children again, all well and good. And if Carl had still been alive to translate what they said, all well and good. But with all these things no longer possible, what other options did Robbie have?

∿

"Oh, it's you," said Torrad Heglund, as he opened the door to Robbie and Bernard the following morning. His welcome was nowhere near as friendly as it had been the evening before. "My wife has been upset enough without you two coming along to stir it all up again. Can't you leave us in peace?"

"Believe me, Mr Heglund, there's nothing I'd like better than to do just that," said Robbie, "but those children are crying out for help, and I'm not going to turn my back on them. Now, I just need to ask you a few questions, that's all. That can't hurt, can it?"

Mr Heglund stared at him, then looked at Bernard. His expression softened after a moment and he sighed. "All right, you had better come in," he said.

His wife was standing in the living room as they entered. She looked friendlier than her husband, but she had obviously been crying. Robbie apologised for disturbing them again and sat down in the chair indicated by the old woman. Bernard sat in the chair opposite. The bereaved couple held hands and seated themselves on the sofa in the middle of them.

Edda smiled thinly. "Well, what would you like to know, gentlemen?" she asked.

"This man the police are looking for, the one your daughter apparently hired to help out on the farm, have you any idea who he is?" Robbie asked.

Edda looked at her husband, who shrugged dismissively. "You must understand, Dr MacTavish ..."

"Robbie, please," interrupted that gentleman.

"Yes – thank you," replied Mr Heglund. "You must understand, er – Robbie, that we didn't see so much of our daughter since this man came along. We did not approve of him, you see."

"Why was that?" asked Robbie.

"We did not like that he was – well, to be blunt, he was sleeping with Marianne. She told us he was some odd job man, not one of our class. A mere peasant."

Robbie nodded, as if in sympathy. "But how do you know he was sleeping with her? Did she tell you?"

"No, it was things the grandchildren said." Torrad Heglund looked almost shamefaced. "I know what you think, that we are snobs."

"I wasn't thinking that," said Robbie, untruthfully.

Bernard came forward now and leaned towards the distraught man. "We understand, of course," he said, also untruthfully. "We just wondered if you knew anything about this man at all. Something you didn't tell the police, but have since remembered?"

"No, we know nothing about him, only that he is of lower class and took advantage of our daughter," said Edda Heglund, looking ready to cry again.

"I see," said Robbie. "Never mind, it was worth a try."

"Wait a minute," said Edda suddenly. "Now you say it, I *do* remember something Marianne told me the last time she visited."

"When was that?" Robbie leaned forward eagerly.

"It was last Christmas. She came with the children to spend Christmas with us here in this apartment."

"Right," said Robbie. "What did she say?"

"Just that she was employing this man to help out at the farm. We were pleased then. It was only later when we realised he had moved in. That he wasn't just working there…"

"Did she know who he was – I mean, when he turned up looking for work? Had she ever seen him before?"

"Well, that's the thing. She *thought* she knew him from somewhere, but wasn't sure," said Edda, dabbing her eyes with her handkerchief.

"This is interesting, Mrs Heglund," he said eagerly. "So she may have known him? He may have lived nearby? In Bergen itself? He may even be living there now."

"Well, yes, it is possible, I suppose," said Edda. "But the police questioned so many people about this man, and no one seemed to know him. I think the police assumed he was a stranger and had left Bergen altogether. They said he could be anywhere by now."

"But there's just a chance that he's still living there," Robbie persisted. "Did your daughter describe him to you at all?"

Edda Heglund screwed up her already very creased-up face in concentration. "I told the police all I knew about him at the time. Marianne did say he wasn't very good looking. She said he was – how did she put it? – a 'big brute of a man'. But it is hardly enough for the police to find him, is it?"

Robbie had to agree. "So you told the police this?" he asked.

"Yes," replied Edda.

"Hmm. I don't suppose she mentioned his name to you?" Robbie wasn't hopeful.

Torrad Heglund interrupted at this point. "Do you know, I believe she did," he said.

"Can you remember what it was, Mr Heglund?" Robbie gave Bernard a quick look. It was as if he was saying 'this could be the break we have been looking for, Watson'.

"Wait – let me think," said Torrad, slowly. "Not his full name – just his first name. It began with an 'H' I think. Or was it a 'B'?"

"Right – go on, try to think, Mr Heglund, please."

"I *am* trying," he said with irritation. "Give me a chance. No, it's gone. It could have been Baldric, possibly, but I don't think that is quite right." He sighed. "Sorry, I wish I could remember." He looked at his wife. "Can you remember, dear?"

"No," she replied. "I only wish I could. I'm sure it wasn't Baldric, though."

"Never mind," said Robbie, "At least we've got some sort of a description of him."

He got up, pulling Bernard up with him. "Come on, man, let's go," he said. "Don't you worry, Mr and Mrs Heglund, we'll find your daughter's killer and find out what happened to your grandchildren. Never fear!"

Edda smiled at them. "Thank you for taking such trouble," she said, accompanying them to the door. "I don't know why you should – after all, you don't owe us anything. You don't even know us."

Robbie took the old lady's hand and cupped it gently in his own. "I have an obligation in this matter, Mrs Heglund. That is all."

Shortly after their second visit to the Heglunds, the pair of amateur detectives checked out of their hotel and made for Oslo Central station. On the rickety steam train heading back to Bergen, Bernard asked Robbie what he hoped to achieve with the meagre information he had gleaned from the bereaved couple.

"After all, it's not much, is it?" he pointed out.

"Not in itself, no," agreed Robbie. "But we know the man's quite big and unprepossessing, and that his name is something like Baldric. He's probably a native of Bergen, too, so people might know him when we circulate his description."

"Circulate? What do you mean? Are we going to print a 'wanted' poster or something?" Bernard was at a loss.

"No, of course not. We'll just ask around. In the bars and shops, maybe," he replied. "And we must go back to that wood again. If we go back to the lake, I think I can more or less remember where that tree was in relation to it. I think I need to then sit there for a while and see if the children reappear to me."

"But that could take ages," grumbled Bernard. "And I need to get back for Harvest Festival. Remember?"

"We've still got a few days, Bernie, don't be difficult. Don't you want to help solve this crime?"

Bernard looked at his companion with something like exasperation. "Not really, no. I think it's a matter for the Bergen police. Why should we get involved? It doesn't really make much sense to me."

"Bernie, Bernie! You know why."

"All right," said Bernard grudgingly. "But without that tree, I don't see what you can do. Don't you think you should get back to your patients? You've been neglecting them lately." He fumbled in his pocket for his pipe and matches.

"I know, old boy. Don't think I haven't thought of that. But there's something driving me on with this. I can't stop now. You can go back to London, if you like. But I must stay at least another couple of days."

Bernard lit his pipe and began to draw on it. "No, I'll stay with you, Robbie. I admire you for what you're trying to do. I just wish I was more hopeful that something would come of it."

"Don't be defeatist! We'll get there, I'm convinced of it. Now, how about a slap-up dinner when we get back to Bergen?"

❧

The next day dawned bright but cold. Autumn mists were beginning to appear but had dispersed by mid-morning. Bernard and Robbie got their inevitable, unappetising packed lunch from the hotel's catering staff and headed off to the forest once more.

They came to the lake shortly before midday, and the sun was now pleasantly warm. Bernard was all for eating his lunch straightaway, but Robbie suggested they save it for at least another hour. It could be a long day. Bernard sighed and folded up his cheese sandwiches again.

They made their way to the spot where Robbie thought he had seen the children. But it was difficult to be sure they were in the right area now that the trees had gone. The forest paid dearly for people to enjoy their Christmases. However, Robbie was determined to sit it out. If the children were still haunting the place, sooner or later they would find him again, he was sure of it.

By ten minutes to two, Bernard couldn't wait any longer. Sitting beside Robbie, he opened his cheese sandwiches, which were now even less appetising and very sweaty. But he was starving, and they were soon safely inside his stomach. He swigged down the lukewarm tea and rummaged around for the apple and banana he had also been given by the hotel. Robbie, unlike his friend, didn't feel in the least tempted to eat his lunch. Bernard willingly helped him out.

The afternoon wore on and Robbie stood up to stretch his legs.

"How much longer are we going to stay here?" Bernard asked, looking up at his friend, shielding his eyes from the sun as he did so.

"I don't know, Bernie," he replied. "I just need to stay a bit longer, although I fear the children aren't here now."

"If they ever were," Bernard muttered under his breath.

"You were saying?"

Bernard coughed. "Sorry, Robbie, but don't you think you may have been mistaken?"

"How do you think I could have been mistaken? Maybe I mistook them for a passing deer or a badger?"

"No, no," said Bernard, standing up and brushing off the grass that was clinging obstinately to the seat of his trousers. "I don't mean that. But it's a long time since you saw them, it could have been a one-off. Maybe you were particularly susceptible that day, or something."

Robbie sighed. "I suppose you could be right," he said sadly. "But I did so want to help them."

"Well, maybe you still can," Bernard said, putting the empty food and drink containers back in his rucksack. "We can still ask around about this man. Maybe someone will know who he is."

"Yes, we can do that, at least," agreed Robbie, getting ready to leave too. As he got to his feet, he suddenly tripped over and fell with a crunch to the ground.

"Ouch!" he yelled. "I think I've sprained my ankle."

"Oh dear," cried Bernard, kneeling down beside him. "What happened?"

"I must have tripped over that tree stump," said Robbie, rubbing his ankle, which was swelling fast.

"Oh dear," said Bernard. "What a nuisance! Will you be able to walk?"

"Not very well," grumbled Robbie. "I'll have to hop, or lean on your shoulder, old boy."

"Feel free," said Bernard, his heart sinking. The man was at least five or six inches taller than he was, as well as a whole lot wider and stockier. He'd have him over in no time.

Just then, Robbie noticed that the ground around the tree stump had been disturbed. There was a mound of earth that looked like it had been piled up neatly by a human hand.

"Look at that, Bernie," said Robbie. "Do you see what I see?"

Bernard couldn't; he was too busy wondering how he was going to support his friend back to the hotel. "Where?" he asked, absent-mindedly.

"That pile of earth. It looks like there's something buried under it."

"How do you mean? It's just a pile of earth."

Robbie was scrabbling at it, however. Bernard was about to pull him away when he saw with horror what he had in his hand.

"What's that?" he cried.

"What does it look like? It's a gun," said Robbie grimly.

"But what's it doing here?"

"It was buried by that tree stump I fell over. Don't you see, Bernie, it's another sign? I was meant to fall over and find it. It's the murder weapon!"

"Murder weapon?"

"The weapon that killed Marianne Dahl. Keep up, Bernie, please!"

"Oh! Are you sure?"

"What else can it be? Don't you see what this means? Those children were killed near this spot and the killer buried the weapon here too."

"So, do you think the children are buried here as well?"

"Could be," said Robbie. "Could well be."

"Don't tell me you're going to start digging?"

"No – not me. The police. We have to tell the police. With this gun as evidence, they'll have something to go on. They can begin a search of the whole area for the bodies."

Bernard was relieved that Robbie wasn't suggesting they go and get some spades themselves. But then he wasn't up to digging now, of course, with his gammy ankle, thank goodness.

London, September 1948

Harvest Festival had come and gone, and Bernard was back in his ecclesiastical routine. Robbie was tending his patients once more, his ankle still strapped up. But he was hobbling around nicely now.

The Norwegian police had taken possession of the gun, although they had been sceptical that it was the murder weapon. It could be any old gun, they said. But, Robbie had insisted it was the gun that killed Marianne Dahl, otherwise why had it been buried? That reasonable question had been met merely with a shrug. However, they were less slothful in nearly arresting Robbie, and it had taken Bernard some convincing that his friend had only *found* the gun, not used it.

Both men had then insisted the police searched for the bodies of the children in the same area where the gun had been found, but the police pointed out that two mere 'foreigners' were in no position to tell them what to do. It was frustrating, to say the least.

Undeterred, however, Robbie had spent the time remaining in Bergen hobbling around, supported by Bernard, asking anyone and everyone if they knew of someone with a name like Baldric answering to the sketchy description they had gleaned from the Heglunds. Needless to say, he had got nowhere. Most people he asked, asked him a question in return: what was an Englishman doing asking questions about a Norwegian crime? Apart from the insult of calling him

'English', the Scotsman in Robbie had continued on his quest more or less until their boat sailed homewards.

Bernard contributed what he could, which consisted mainly of prayers for the lost children, but short of that, what else could he do? What could either of them do? He had to concentrate on his parish duties and Robbie had to understand that. They had come to the end of the road.

London, November 1948

Robbie MacTavish was sitting in his surgery after the last patient had gone. Lucy Carter had looked in on him as she left for the evening, telling him his supper was in the oven. "Don't let it burn to a crisp," she had instructed. Robbie sighed, going to the window and watching the shapely figure of his housekeeper try to hold up her umbrella as the wind and rain did their best to turn it inside out.

He was on his own again. The whole place was getting on his nerves. Rattling around in his large flat above the surgery every night gave him too much time to think. Too much time to wonder what else he could do to help those poor children. Then he did what he did on most evenings when he was at a loose end.

He picked up the phone and asked the operator to put him through to the vicarage. "Hello, vicarage. Mrs 'Arper speaking. Who's that?"

"Hello, Mrs Harper," said Robbie cheerfully. "Is the rev at home?"

He could hear her sniff even on the indistinct line. "If you mean 'is vicarship, 'e is, but 'e's busy."

"Can he come to the phone for a moment, do you think?"

"I suppose I could go and ask 'im, if it's that important," came the grudging reply.

"Yes, please do," said Robbie a little impatiently. Bernard was probably doing a crossword at that time in the evening, he thought. "I think he'll be pleased to hear from me."

"Wait there, then. Don't go away," said Mrs Harper, and he heard the clatter of the receiver as she clumsily put it back on the rest. Bother! thought Robbie, will the woman never get the hang of using the phone? He asked the operator to put him through again.

"Why can't you wait?" came Mrs Harper's angry tones. "I only got 'alfway up the stairs."

"You cut me off, Mrs Harper," explained Robbie. "Don't put the receiver back on the hook this time. Just lay it down beside the phone – gently." He said this last word too late, as the loud clatter of the receiver being put down threatened to burst his eardrums. But at least this time she hadn't cut him off.

He drummed his fingers on the desk, looking gloomily out of the window at the November night. There was a spattering of raindrops on the glass, and every now and then the whistle of the wind could be heard as it made its way around the eaves. Finally, he heard his friend's cheerful voice.

"Hi Robbie, why the call? Why not just come over like you usually do?"

"Mrs Harper told me you were busy."

"She did, did she?" said Bernard. "I wasn't doing anything in particular. Come over."

"Okay," said Robbie, studying the rain. Should he get the car out? he wondered. It seemed ridiculous for so short a journey, but the weather was atrocious. "Give me five minutes."

As Bernard put the phone down, he heard his housekeeper sniff behind him. "You shouldn't encourage that Doctor MacTavish," she admonished him. "'E's a bad influence on you. So far, 'e's taken you on two trips abroad, leaving your parishioners in the lurch. And 'eaven knows what 'is patients think. It's a good job I ain't 'ad a bout of my lumbago lately, that's all I can say."

"It was only a few days the last time," Bernard pointed out. "We have every right to some free time, Mrs Harper."

She stood her ground. "I'm only thinking of you, Vicar. You take on too much as it is."

"Thank you, Mrs Harper, but I think I know better than you what I can and can't do."

She gave a sniff and stalked off into the kitchen, while Bernard made his way back up to his study. He banked up the fire and got out the bottle of Glenfiddich, which he kept well hidden from the prying, disapproving eyes of his housekeeper at the back of his desk drawer, under lock and key.

When Robbie arrived, the fire was burning cheerfully, and the whisky had been poured. Bernard had his sweet sherry as usual. The lamps were lit, casting a warm glow around the room, cancelling out the bitter November night outside. Robbie had decided to walk from his surgery in the end and was glad to toast his outer self dry by the fire and his inner self with the whisky.

"I've been thinking about those poor children, Bernie. I can't get them out of my mind," he said.

Bernard sighed. "Here we go again. Look, Robbie, I know it's hard, but there's really nothing we can do now."

Robbie smiled bleakly. "I know, I know. But I can't seem to let it go, somehow," he said, swigging his whisky. "It's unfinished business, as far as I'm concerned."

"It's a shame," said Bernard. "But never mind, you did your best."

Robbie sighed again. He knew he had the gift, and he knew he was meant to use it, but events had stopped him at every turn. "Maybe. Anyway, let's have a game of chess to take our minds off it," he said. "I'll be black this time?"

"Mrs Harper, you're a treasure!"

It was the following morning. The rain had stopped, but the wind could still be heard whistling down the vicarage chimneys. Mrs Harper had told him that she had managed to sell all the tickets for the dance and buffet to be held in the church hall the second Saturday in December.

"And they all paid up, too. On the spot," she said proudly. "When I said it was in a good cause, for the old folk with nowhere to go at Christmas, they didn't 'esitate."

It was at times like these, Bernard thought, that restored his faith in human nature.

"And I've managed to rope in lots of 'elp with the catering, like. Ada's cooking ain't as good as mine, but she can't do much 'arm with the jam tarts."

"I've said it before and I'll say it again: you're a treasure, Mrs Aitch."

"I was thinking, Vicar," she said, as she turned to leave the study, "shouldn't we be thinking about getting the Christmas tree for the 'all?"

"Good idea, Mrs Aitch," Bernard said happily. "Shall you and I go and buy one later?"

"They've got some lovely big ones at the greengrocers," she said. "One of those'd look lovely in the 'all."

"Good!" said Bernard happily. "But not too expensive, I hope?"

"Oh, don't worry about that. Morrie's a mate of mine – at least 'is wife is."

"Morrie? Who's he?"

"The greengrocer. He always lets me 'ave a bit over the odds. Potatoes, greens, cabbages, what 'ave you. I don't see why the same can't go for Christmas trees."

Bernard smiled. "You seem to know all the right people, Mrs Aitch."

"'Course I do. You can't get by without 'aving the people who matter on your side. Where do you think the lovely tender meat in your steak and kidney pies comes from, eh?"

"Quite," said Bernard, giving a nervous cough. He had tried not to think about it too much.

"What you don't know can't 'urt you, that's my motto," she said. "Things keep falling off the backs of lorries all the time. Must be the pits in the roads left over from the German bombing."

"Mrs Harper!" Bernard was shocked.

"Come on, Vicar. In times of 'ardship, it's every man 'isself."

So, later that morning, the ill-assorted couple set off for Morrie's in the High Street.

∾

While Bernard and Mrs Harper were haggling over the price of Christmas trees with Morrie, Dr Robbie MacTavish was examining a young woman who had come to him complaining of fatigue and headaches.

"Well, Mrs Plunkett," he said, writing something on his prescription pad. "It looks to me like you've been overdoing it lately. You seem well enough in yourself, but the fatigue and headaches are symptomatic of overwork, nothing more serious than that. I can prescribe some pills for the headaches, but what you need more than anything, is complete rest."

"Well, thank you, doctor. It's *Miss*, by the way."

"Oh, sorry – yes, Miss Dorothy Plunkett. I haven't seen you before, have I?"

"No. I've only just moved here from Exeter."

"Oh, right. Do you have any work at the moment that's making you particularly tired?" he asked.

He gave his new patient an appraising look, not in an entirely detached, medical way. She was certainly an attractive woman, if a little on the plump side. Her skin was good, her eyes a clear blue, and her hair an abundant brunette. Rather nice, in fact.

"Well, you might not think it *work* as such, doctor," she said meekly.

"Try me." He smiled encouragingly at her.

"Well," she began, "I'm a – I'm a medium." She smiled apologetically at him. "I don't know if you know what that is?"

Robbie knew exactly what it was, and his heart leapt. "You mean you give séances and that sort of thing?"

"Yes, that's right. It doesn't bring in much of an income, but I have a small annuity of my own and that helps keep body and soul together."

"So, have you been doing lots of medium work lately? Giving lots of séances? I mean, to account for your tiredness and headaches?"

"No more than usual, doctor. More's the pity. But, having just moved into the area, I haven't built up any sort of clientele as yet. I've advertised in the local paper and put ads in the newsagents' windows, of course. But it takes time to build up a reputation. I'm getting *some* work, though. Mostly war widows. They come to me to help them get in touch with their husbands killed in action. It's all very sad."

Robbie nodded sympathetically. "You must see a lot of tragedy in your line of work. It must be hard."

"Well, you say that. But in fact, I feel I'm helping these poor women. If I get in touch with their husbands and they say they're happy and just want their wives to be happy, that makes a lot of difference to them. Some women just want their dead husbands to give them the okay to marry again. That's another positive thing."

"And are you able to get in touch with dead people all the time? Is it easy for you?" Robbie was very interested, not only in the woman herself, but in the gift she seemed to have. A gift he thought he shared to some degree.

"I'm quite successful, yes. Not all the time, of course. Sometimes I make no contact at all and they go away very unhappy, calling me a charlatan and a quack. Understandable, of course, although I do tell them at the beginning that I can't always guarantee success. And there have been occasions when I can't get in touch because the person I'm trying to contact hasn't actually died. That's when it's hard."

"How do you mean?"

"Well, say a young widow comes to me, telling me her husband was killed in the war and, say I can't get in touch with him. It could be that he hasn't returned home because he's met someone else."

"Goodness, how dreadful. Does that happen a lot?"

"Thankfully, no," she smiled.

"That's a blessing, anyway. But getting back to you, Miss Plunkett," he said, tearing off her prescription from the pad. "What do you think can account for your malaise if it's not due to overwork?"

"I really don't know. I was fine before I moved here. I moved into a nice little house in Park Grove Avenue, just round the corner from here, two weeks ago, and I was perfectly well then."

"So, it's since you've been here in Wandsworth you've not been feeling well?"

"That's right. The first time I felt strange was when I was out doing a bit of shopping last week. I remember coming out of the Home and Colonial feeling perfectly fine and going into the greengrocers. I bought a cabbage and a pound of potatoes. When I came out I had a splitting headache and felt very lethargic. I got back home and lay down for a while. I felt better shortly afterwards, so I thought no more about it."

"Right," said Robbie, writing in her file. "So, when did you next feel bad?"

"A couple of days later. The coincidence was I got the headache as soon as I came out of the greengrocers again."

"Hmm," he said thoughtfully, writing again. "So it seems to be shopping that takes it out of you. Would you say that?"

"Yes, I would. Although it only seems to be when I visit the greengrocers. Perhaps there's something in there that I'm allergic to?"

"That's very possible. A type of vegetable or fruit, perhaps? I've never heard of anything like that, though."

"Trust me to get some rare allergy," she laughed.

"Anyway, these pills will help the headache," he said, handing the prescription to her. "And if you don't feel any better in a week come back and see me again."

"Thank you, doctor," she said, putting the prescription in her handbag and standing up to go. "It was nice to meet you."

They shook hands. "Er, I hope you don't mind me asking this but, as you're new to the area, would you like to go for a drink sometime?" He coughed nervously. Asking a patient out was strictly against the rules. But he didn't think there'd be any harm in taking her for a drink. He would have to transfer her to another doctor, if things progressed, of course.

Dorothy Plunkett smiled again, and studied his kind, handsome face with interest. "That would be very nice," she said. "As soon as I feel better, I would love to. You have my address and phone number on my file. Give me a call."

"I'll do that. By the way, are you going to the Christmas do at the church hall? I'm sure it'll be a great evening and you'd get to know your neighbours as well."

"Oh, yes. I saw the advert in the newsagents," she said. "I was thinking about it but was waiting till I felt better."

"All the tickets are sold now," he told her. "But I've got a spare one, so why don't you come with me?" Was he moving too fast? he asked himself. He wasn't an impetuous man as a rule, but there was something so pleasing about this woman, he couldn't help himself.

"Well, I – " She hesitated for a moment. "All right. I'd love to," she said.

"It's a date, then. My name's Robert, by the way – Robbie to my friends, which I hope you will be."

He felt a lot more cheerful after she had gone than before her visit. What a godsend she was. Not only was she pretty, she was single and available. And, a big plus, she was a psychic medium. He would be able to confide in her about his vision of the two children. He was sure she would be interested and sympathise. He switched off the light and the electric fire and made his way upstairs to his living quarters. Lucy Carter was there to greet him with his lunchtime meal.

She placed the plate of sausages, mashed potato and onions in front of him with a smile. He munched his food, not really tasting it, thinking of Dorothy Plunkett. Up until he'd met her, he had been planning to take Lucy to the dance. He was glad, now, that he hadn't mentioned it to her.

There were several large fir trees lying in front of Morrie's greengrocery emporium that wintry morning. They looked and smelt wonderful, and Bernard was as excited as a child, trying to decide which one to choose. Mrs Harper just stood by and watched him in amusement. There were several other people examining the trees too.

"Hurry up and pick one, Vicar," she prompted. "There'll all be gone if you don't make up your mind soon."

"Which one do *you* like best, Mrs Harper?" he asked her, dithering between two likely candidates.

"They all look the same to me," she said, unhelpfully. She gave them a cursory glance. "That one." She pointed to the tallest tree propped up against the window. "I think that'll look fine in the 'all. Once we've got the lights on it and everything."

Bernard wasn't so sure. It looked a bit threadbare to him, compared to a couple of others he was considering. But it was definitely the tallest, and, as Mrs Harper said, once the lights and tinsel were on it, it wouldn't be noticed.

"Very well," he said. "I bow to your judgement. But look at the price. Five shillings. That's a bit steep."

"Don't worry," she said. "Leave it to me." So saying, she disappeared inside the shop, leaving Bernard to cool his heels outside. While he waited he changed his mind at least ten times about his choice. Finally, Mrs Harper reappeared. "That's done," she said with gratification. "It'll be delivered tomorrow morning."

"How much is it going to cost?" he asked anxiously.

"Nothing," she said in triumph.

"Nothing? What do you mean?"

"I just told 'im it was in a good cause – works every time."

"Just that? And he agreed to give it to you for nothing? I mean, I know it's for charity, but the man has to make a living."

"Well, when I say I got it for nothing …" she began.

"Well?"

"I said 'e and 'is wife could come to the dance for free."

"But isn't it already over-subscribed? They won't be able to move in the hall at this rate."

"Don't worry," she said dismissively. "There's always some who don't turn up. Anyway, 'e also promised to donate a basket of fruit for the raffle, so we can't pass that up, can we?"

"No, Mrs Harper. We can't. What would I do without you?"

Her only reply was a sniff. It spoke volumes.

"What's her name?"

"Dorothy – Dorothy Plunkett," said Robbie, supping his pint. Bernard and Robbie had met in the Bricklayer's Arms the next day. Unable to wait to tell him about the new woman in his life, Robbie had phoned his friend and asked to meet him in the pub after his morning surgery.

"A medium, did you say? What's that when it's at home?" Bernard asked, hunting for the bag of salt in his packet of crisps. "Do you know, I don't think there's any salt in here at all," he grumbled.

"Just as well," laughed Robbie. "Too much salt's not good for you," he said, with his doctor's hat on.

"Oh, but crisps are no good without salt," complained Bernard, eating them just the same. "Come on, tell me. What *is* a medium exactly?"

"Someone who contacts those who have passed over. They hold séances for the bereaved, that sort of thing."

"You don't believe in all that rubbish, do you?"

"I thought we'd had all this out before," said Robbie impatiently. "You said you believed me about seeing the children."

"Yes, I do. But there are a lot of charlatans about. Is she pretty?"

Robbie felt his cheeks redden. "Well, she's quite nice-looking, yes," he admitted. "But that's not the reason I believe her. If you met her, you'd believe her too."

"Okay, Robbie, whatever you say. So, you're bringing her with you to the buffet dance, then? That's pretty quick work. I thought doctors weren't supposed to date their patients."

"Not in the ordinary way, no. But she's only consulted me once, and it was only because of headaches and tiredness. I'll have to transfer her to another doctor if we continue to go out together, which I hope we will."

He finished his pint and opened his own packet of crisps. There were two blue salt bags in it and he handed one to Bernard.

"Well, I shall look forward to meeting her," he said, emptying the salt on what remained of his crisps. "The Christmas tree was delivered this morning, by the way. It's really tall, but a bit straggly in places. Still, it'll look great in the church hall once all the decorations are on it."

Robbie smiled. He couldn't wait to show off Dorothy to Bernard, as well as to all the people at the Christmas do. Wouldn't they be jealous!

London, December 1948

"Hello, Robbie. It's Dorothy Plunkett here."

Robbie hoped she wasn't going to tell him she couldn't come to the dance with him.

"Hello, Dorothy, how are you? This line isn't very good."

"Can you hear me all right?"

"Yes, just about."

"I just rang to say I'm feeling much better."

"You do? That's good news," he said, relieved.

"Actually, I felt better the very next day after seeing you," she said. "It was as if a weight had been lifted from my shoulders. I was out shopping and began to dread going into the greengrocers. But I needed some parsnips to make soup, so I had no choice. When I came out, I fully expected to feel rotten again but nothing happened this time. I felt absolutely fine."

"So, whatever it was that was making you feel ill wasn't there any longer?"

"Presumably. But I'm just so glad to be free of those headaches. I can now look forward to the dance without worrying I'll be too ill to enjoy it."

"Indeed, you can," smiled Robbie into the phone. "Shall I call for you at eight?"

"Yes, please. We'll have an aperitif before we go."

"Lovely. Take care, young lady."

"Bye for now, Robbie. And thank you."

Robbie felt very happy as he replaced the receiver. It was going to be a grand night. The only fly in the ointment was his housekeeper. He knew that Lucy had seen the tickets on the sideboard and had been expecting him to ask her to go with him to the dance. When he told her he was taking Dorothy, he could see she was disappointed and he felt like a cad. But he hadn't promised he'd take her, so there was no help for it. Never mind, Bernie would look after her, he thought.

⁂

As the evening of the Christmas dance and buffet approached, Bernard could hardly contain his excitement. It was going to cement his standing in the parish, he felt sure and, added to this, Mrs Harper was making not one, but two, superb Christmas cakes! One for himself, and one for the raffle. He crept into the kitchen when she had gone shopping and began licking the icing from the bowl, only to be caught in the act when she returned unexpectedly.

"Vicar!" she protested. "I 'ope your fingers are clean."

"Sorry, Mrs Aitch," he said meekly. "I just couldn't resist! I can't wait to taste the cake when it's ready."

"Well, you're just going to 'ave to," she told him, pushing him gently aside and removing the icing bowl out of temptation's way into the sink. "It'll need to mature for a while yet to get the full flavour out. You're not allowed to touch it until I say it's ready. Actually, I should 'ave made them earlier, but I've been that busy, organising the buffet."

"And you've done a wonderful job!" Bernard told her. "The hall looks lovely with all the decorations and the tree with all its baubles and tinsel on it. I love the fairy on the top. Where did you get it?"

"It's been in my family for generations. I want it back, mind, when the tree's taken down."

"Of course, Mrs Aitch."

Bernard's only slight worry about the evening was the promised advent of Dorothy Plunkett, whom Robbie was treating like the Second Coming.

"Mrs Aitch?" he began tentatively, nibbling at some freshly baked biscuits that were airing on a tray.

"Yes, Vicar?"

"Have you heard of a woman called Dorothy Plunkett? She's just moved here apparently, and she's some kind of psychic medium."

"Oh 'er," she sniffed, wiping her hands and removing the tray of fast disappearing biscuits from under Bernard's itchy fingers.

"You've heard about her?" he asked.

"Oh yes, she's made 'er presence felt all over the place. 'Aven't you seen 'er ads in the newsagents' windows?"

"No, I can't say I have. Have you actually met her, though?"

"No. Not to speak to. I saw 'er in the greengrocer's the other day. She was buying some parsnips. Morrie was all over 'er."

"How do you know it was her?" he asked, reasonably.

"Because Morrie called 'er by 'er name," she replied, also quite reasonably.

"Oh, I see, of course. What was she like?"

"Why all the interest? Are you thinking of asking 'er out?" She gave him a knowing look. "She ain't bad looking, and she'd be about your age. You could do worse."

Bernard flushed to the roots of his hair. "Don't be silly. I don't even know the woman."

"Well, why are you so interested in 'er then?"

"Because Robbie is bringing her to the dance."

"Oh, I see," she said. "You've been pipped at the post, then."

Bernard decided to ignore this remark. "He seems very taken with her."

Mrs Harper sniffed. "'E should be bringing Lucy to the dance. I bet she ain't best pleased."

"No, I don't suppose she is," said Bernard, thoughtfully.

"So, Vicar, if there ain't nothing else, can you run along out of my kitchen? I need to get on. Dinner is in 'alf an hour. One o'clock sharp."

"Thanks, Mrs Harper. I'll be in my study. I'm writing a thank you speech to give at the end of the dance."

"We'll look forward to it as long as it ain't as long as your sermons usually are. Now off with you."

With that, Bernard considered himself dismissed. As he sat at his study desk trying to concentrate on his speech, his mind kept wandering to Dorothy Plunkett.

Why should he mind about her? he asked himself. If Robbie was interested in her, he should be pleased for him, not jealous. But he *was* jealous, all the same. Not of Robbie for dating a pretty woman, but of Dorothy, for diverting his friend's attention from himself. He just wanted Robbie's undivided attention, that was at the bottom of it. He didn't want the nature of their friendship to change, as it assuredly would if this Dorothy Plunkett became a permanent fixture in Robbie's life.

Bergen, December 1948

Ever since the discovery of the gun, Baldur Hanssen had been nervous, even though he thought it unlikely the murder weapon could be traced back to him. Especially not by the incompetent Bergen police, anyway. And, as the days and weeks went by, he became more and more relaxed.

When he was sure he was in the clear, he decided it was time for a change and left his fitting and welding job to become a lumberjack. He preferred the outdoor life, and the work suited him much better. Also, he was working in the forest where the children were buried and was thus able to keep an eye out for any likelihood of their discovery.

So, with his new job, he felt more at ease, and his confidence had grown to such as extent he had managed to get himself a girlfriend. Gunda, a woman somewhere in her forties, was a war widow who had been making ends meet by doing various cleaning jobs. He'd met her in the local inn one evening and they had got to talking. She wasn't what he'd call pretty and looked a little the worse for wear, but she had kind eyes and a nice smile. He had seen her home that first evening and, when she invited him in, he realised she was just as lonely as he was.

All in all, Baldur Hanssen was happy with his lot. The money earned chopping down trees was good and he was looking forward to a quiet, but pleasant, Christmas with his new love. If he thought he didn't deserve such luck, he didn't dare admit it. Not even to himself.

London, December 1948

Robbie stood on Dorothy Plunkett's doorstep the evening of the dance, carrying a large bouquet and a box of Black Magic chocolates. He felt very nervous, done up as he was in his dinner suit which smelt unpleasantly of moth balls. Lucy had hung it out of the window all day to try and shift the smell, but every now and then he caught a whiff of it and it turned his stomach. He only hoped that other people didn't notice it, especially not Dorothy.

She opened the door to him almost immediately. She looked lovely in a rose-coloured evening gown and long white gloves. Her dark hair was freshly washed and shining, pinned up in a pile on top of her head. He swallowed hard as she led him through to the living room where bottles and glasses were arranged in readiness on the sideboard.

"What would you like?" she asked.

He tried to speak but his mouth had gone dry. Her beauty had taken his breath away. He coughed to release the frog trapped somewhere down his throat. "Er – whisky for me, please," he managed.

"Dear me!" she said, "Have you got a cold?"

"No, I don't think so. You look lovely."

She blushed at the compliment and reciprocated. "You look very dashing in your evening suit," she said, handing him the whisky. She poured herself a gin and Italian and they clinked glasses. "Here's to a pleasant evening," she said.

"Cheers," he said, swigging the whisky a little too eagerly, almost choking as he did so.

"Thanks so much for the flowers and chocolates," she said.

"Charmed, charmed," he replied, smiling at her as the whisky worked its magic on him. He'd be the envy of everyone at the dance. There wasn't a woman in the whole parish that could compare to her, he felt sure.

He coughed again, as Dorothy refilled his glass. "I hope you don't mind," he said, sipping this second drink more slowly.

"Mind what, Robbie?" she asked, smiling.

"I've told my housekeeper that I'd go back and fetch her to the dance – after I've dropped you off, that is. You see, she hasn't got anyone to go with."

"Of course, I don't mind. How kind you are," she said.

"You see, I think she had the idea that I would be taking her. Don't get me wrong – I hadn't said anything, I think she must have just assumed. I probably would have taken her if you hadn't come along, you see."

"I suppose she doesn't like me very much," observed Dorothy, sitting on the sofa and inviting Robbie to join her.

"Don't be silly, she doesn't even know you," said Robbie, careful not to sit too close to her. "It's just that she's on her own now. Her fiancé was killed in the war."

"Oh, how sad. So many women lost their men that way. It's good business for me, but hard on them."

"Yes, it must be. You must see some very sad people in your line of work," he said. He finished his drink and stood up. "Now, perhaps we'd better get going?"

Dorothy went to fetch her wrap. "Do you have a car or are we walking?" she asked.

"Walking, as it's not far. It's a nice night for a stroll, but I think you'll need more than just that flimsy thing," he said.

"Yes, you're probably right. I'll fetch my coat."

Moments later, they were walking along the street towards the church hall which they could see was all lit up and looking very festive. As they made their way inside, Robbie could sense that people's eyes were all on his lovely companion, men and women alike. Admiring glances from the men, and envious ones from the ladies. He felt very proud as she took his arm, but he remembered he would have to leave her to go and fetch Lucy. She would soon get snapped up if he left her alone. He would make sure he left her with Bernard; that should stop the wolves from gathering, he thought.

Bernard was in his element. The evening was going to be a great success, thanks, mainly, to Mrs Harper. It would never have got off the ground if it hadn't been for her organising skills and knowledge of the locals.

The food alone was worth the price of admission. The buffet tables were creaking under the weight of all sorts of tempting goodies which she and her army of female friends had provided. It all looked delicious: the delicately cut corned beef and ham sandwiches, pork pies, various sweet and savoury flans, jellies, blancmanges, trifles, cakes and the centrepiece, Mrs Harper's triumphant Christmas cake which was to be raffled off later in the evening.

As the people arrived, he stood by the door and greeted each one, thanking them for coming and for supporting the good cause. He could see that everybody was determined to have a good time, and he was certainly going to see that they did.

Over on the stage, the four-piece band was tuning up. Mrs Harper had obtained the services of her friend, trumpet player Eddie Wells, and the other three musicians for free. Bernard hoped they would be all right, because they looked quite old. Eddie looked at least seventy, and the other three didn't look much younger. He wanted the evening to go with a swing and everybody up and dancing. He only hoped these old-timers knew some modern tunes. He, himself, particularly liked Cole Porter songs, like *I've Got You Under My Skin* and *Begin the Beguine*. The latter was a special favourite of his. He and Sophie had danced to its romantic rhythms many times in the good old days.

Just then, he saw Robbie approach with an enchanting female on his arm. So that's Dorothy Plunkett, he thought. No wonder he's besotted with her.

He went over to his friend and shook him warmly by the hand.

"And may I have the pleasure of an introduction to this lovely lady?" he said gallantly. He felt an instant attraction pass between them as he spoke.

"Bernie, this is Dorothy Plunkett. Dorothy, this is my dear friend, Bernie Paltoquet, vicar of St Stephen's church."

Bernard took her hand tentatively. She smiled warmly at him.

"Bernie old chap," said Robbie. "Would you mind taking care of Dorothy for me while I go and fetch Lucy? I said I'd escort her to the dance too."

"Ooh, you rogue," admonished Bernard light-heartedly. "You mustn't be greedy, you know. Isn't one lovely lady enough for you?"

Robbie coughed in embarrassment. "You know how it is, Bernie. Lucy's on her own. I can't let her miss out on this occasion."

"No, of course not," said Bernard.

"Anyhow, I shan't be long. Take care of her for me."

"Of course I will," Bernard assured him, watching his friend disappear through the throng of people still pouring into the hall. He turned to his fair companion and smiled.

"May I offer you some refreshment, Miss Plunkett?" he asked politely.

"Call me Dorothy, please," she insisted.

She took his arm as he led her to the buffet tables.

"Shall I get you a drink while you choose what you want to eat?" he asked, as she picked up a plate. "A glass of wine, perhaps?"

"No, nothing for me, thank you," she said. "Do you know, I think I'd better sit down, I've got rather a nasty headache coming on."

Bernard looked at her with concern. She had gone as white as a sheet. "Oh dear," he said solicitously. "Do you suffer from migraines?"

"No, not usually. But I've been getting these headaches a lot lately, although I thought they'd stopped. That's how I met Robbie, by the way, did you know that?"

"Yes, he did mention that you'd consulted him," said Bernard, leading her to a chair at the side of the hall. The band was just striking up and people had begun to gravitate onto the dance floor, ready to strut their stuff. Bernard prayed that the first tune, at least, would be a lively one. With relief, he recognised the strains of *Alexander's Ragtime Band.*

He sat next to Dorothy, who was holding her head in her hands. "It's never been as bad as this before," she muttered. "Have you got any aspirin?"

"In the vicarage," he said. "Maybe you should come over with me and rest there? This noise can't be doing your headache any good."

"Maybe I should," she agreed. "Thank you."

She rose unsteadily and took his arm. Bernard led her gently out of the hall into the cloakroom. "Which is your coat, Dorothy?" he asked, rummaging among the piles of outdoor wear that had been dumped anyhow on the pegs, a lot of which had since fallen to the floor and been trampled on by eager guests.

"Oh dear," she said. "What a mess. Why can't people be more careful?"

"Never mind," said Bernard. "Can you see your coat among this lot?"

"No, I can't," she said. "But I can hardly see anything at the moment. This headache is blinding me."

"Don't worry, we'll find your coat later. Here, put my jacket on." And, so saying, Bernard gallantly took off his jacket and draped it around her shoulders.

"Thank you, Bernard," she said gratefully, as he led her out of the hall towards the vicarage a few yards down the road.

When Robbie returned to the hall with Lucy Carter on his arm, he could see many eyes on him. He supposed it must have looked odd to see him with another pretty female in tow. That's no way for a doctor to carry on, those eyes seemed to be saying.

Lucy looked very charming in a kingfisher blue dress that twirled around her ankles. She smiled gratefully at Robbie as he took her coat and led her through the crowd to the buffet table. He fetched her a glass of wine and some food, then looked around for Dorothy. He was alarmed when he couldn't see her anywhere, nor, he realised, could he see Bernard. Where had they gone?

"Would you mind if I left you here for a moment, Lucy, dear?" he asked.

She smiled at him and sipped her wine. "Of course not," she said. "I can see a couple of people I know over there. I'll join them. You go and look after your *proper* date."

It was said with meaning, but Robbie was too worried about Dorothy to take much notice. He looked around him, searching the crowds. Was she on the dance floor? Had she been whisked away by some bloke? Maybe she was even dancing with Bernard. But no, he could see no sign of either of them.

As he continued to look around the hall, the music stopped for a break and the floor emptied. It was clear that neither Dorothy nor Bernard were there.

As he was thinking about checking the room at the far side of the hall which he could see contained quite a few people, he caught a flash of something out of the corner of his eye. He turned quickly and thought he saw a child dart through the people making their way to the buffet tables for refreshment. He rubbed his eyes. That's odd, he thought. There weren't supposed to be any children allowed. Still, maybe whoever's child it was had been let down by their babysitter at the last minute. Anyway, he was more concerned about finding Dorothy. And where on earth had Bernie got to?

❧

"Are you feeling a little better?"

Dorothy Plunkett was sitting by the fire in the vicarage study, having swallowed a couple of aspirins. She continued to sip the glass of water with which she had washed them down, and Bernard could see her hands were still shaking.

"A little, thank you," she said, although she was still very pale. Even the glow from the fire wasn't helping to dispel her pallor.

"Perhaps I should fetch Robbie to take a look at you?" said Bernard, sitting down opposite, regarding her with concern.

"No, please don't bother him. I'll be all right soon," she said, sinking back against the cushion with a sigh. "I'm so sorry to be such a nuisance."

"Don't be silly," protested Bernard. "You just sit there and relax."

Poor Robbie, he thought. He'd probably be wondering where they had both got to. He supposed he had better get back to the hall soon, but he didn't want to leave her on her own while she was feeling so unwell.

"Maybe I should fetch my housekeeper to look after you," he said, after a minute or two. "I'm afraid I'll have to get back to the hall."

"No, please don't bother her. I'll be all right here by myself. I'll probably have a little nap, if that's all right."

"Of course," said Bernard. "Go right ahead. I'll tell Robbie you're here. I'm sure he'll come and keep you company. I'll give him the key to let himself in."

"Thank you, Bernard, you're very kind. But, before you go, I think I need to tell you something." She made an effort to sit up straight.

"Not now, Dorothy. You're in no state to talk. Just rest."

"No, I can't. Not until you hear what I have to say."

She seemed determined, so Bernard sat down again. "What is it?" he asked gently.

"The reason I've got this headache is because – well, you know I'm a psychic medium, don't you? Robbie mentioned it?"

"He did tell me, yes." What on earth was she going to say?

"Well, I think I'm getting these headaches because of something very wrong in the hall. I felt it the minute I walked in there, and my headache started almost at once. I tried to ignore it, but it was no good. There's something not right and it's in the church hall somewhere."

"What do you mean? Not right?"

"I can't easily explain it," she said, stroking her forehead. "I just wanted to warn you, that's all. I don't want the evening to be ruined."

"I've no doubt of your good intentions, Dorothy," said Bernard, a little sternly. She may be lovely, he thought, but she needn't think I'm going to believe in any psychic rubbish. "But I'm sure everything is fine.

I'm sorry about your headache, but I don't see how anything in the church hall could have caused it."

"I can see you'll take some convincing," she said, giving him a wan smile. "I only know I first started getting these headaches when I visited the greengrocers in the High Street. Morrie's, I think it's called."

"Ah, yes. Morrie's," he said. "That's where the tree in the hall came from."

"Oh?"

"Yes. He donated it in exchange for free tickets to the dance."

"I think I'm beginning to see a connection," she said, her face becoming slightly more animated and a little flushed.

"A connection?" She wasn't making much sense to him. Maybe she was a little delirious?

"Don't you see? I got a headache every time I went to the greengrocers," she said. "And I remember there were Christmas trees propped up inside, as well as outside, the shop."

"Well, there would've been. It *is* near Christmas, after all," Bernard pointed out.

"Yes, yes. But don't you see? The last time I visited the greengrocers I didn't get a headache..."

"There you are then," he interrupted. "Can't be the Christmas trees."

"Yes, it can," she said impatiently, "because that time I noticed that his stock of trees had been depleted. There were only a few left. So the tree that caused my headache had probably been sold."

"How on earth can it have been a tree that gave you a headache?" Bernard was completely baffled.

"Because I know now what's been causing my headaches. I haven't usually suffered like this, but occasionally I've felt unwell when I'm close to some violent event which has taken place. Like murder, for instance."

"I think you need a drink," said Bernard, scratching his head nervously. "Would you like a whisky or a sherry?"

She ignored him. "I got a headache tonight because that Christmas tree in the hall was causing it."

Bernard sighed. "I think I'll have a sherry anyway." He got up to fetch it.

"Please, Bernard, listen to me. I'm not mad. Something horrible happened around that tree – I don't know when and I don't know where, but it did."

"Mrs Harper, have you seen Bernie or Miss Plunkett about anywhere?" asked a very worried Robbie. She paused in the act of dishing out the trifle and sniffed.

"No, Doc, I 'aven't. Not since they went out of the 'all."

"Oh? When was that?"

"About ten or fifteen minutes ago," she replied. "Wait your turn, Fred. There's enough for everybody," she turned to admonish a young man who was elbowing his way to the front of the queue.

"And you haven't seen either of them since?" Robbie was being jostled by the guests who were trying to get at the fast diminishing food on the buffet tables.

"No," she said huffily. "They must be about somewhere. Now, you can see I'm busy. If you don't want any trifle can you let them as do get a look in?"

Robbie turned away and headed out to the cloakroom. He began hunting for Dorothy's coat, but couldn't see it under the mêlée of outdoor wear that was festooned there. He had just started to pick up some of the coats that had fallen onto the floor when Bernard returned.

"Ah, there you are!" exclaimed Robbie. "I've been looking for you everywhere. Since I came back with Lucy I haven't been able to find you or Dorothy. What have you done with her?" He couldn't keep the accusatory note out of his voice.

"I've been looking after her at the vicarage," Bernard started to explain.

"You what?" yelled Robbie. "I wouldn't have put you down as a fast worker."

Bernard stared at him. "What on earth do you mean by that?"

"As soon as my back's turned, you whisk her away to your lair. What sort of man are you?" Robbie was red with anger. His complexion almost matched his hair.

"You idiot!" Bernard yelled back. "I don't even think I should reply to that insinuation. I'm no Lothario, for God's sake!"

Robbie's anger began to subside as he started to realise what a fool he was being. "Bernie, look, I'm sorry, I know you're not like that. I think it's just that I'm rather too keen on Dorothy for my own good. I'm not really the jealous type – normally."

"Well, I should think not," said Bernard, also somewhat placated. "I took Dorothy to the vicarage because she had a headache. I gave her a couple of aspirins. She's resting now. I said I'd send you to her. Here's the key." He handed it to him.

Robbie was suitably embarrassed by his outburst. "Thanks, Bernie. I should have known better, shouldn't I?"

"Yes, you should." Bernard was still a little upset by his friend's apparent mistrust of him. "Before you go, Robbie, could I have a private word? In here."

So saying, Bernard led Robbie into a little side room, which had also started filling up with people's outdoor apparel. Other than that, it contained a broom and a bucket, as well as various other cleaning materials. They inched in beside each other and Bernard closed the door.

"What's all this?" Robbie asked, puzzled. "It's a bit cloak and dagger, isn't it?"

"Look, I think I should tell you what Dorothy has just told me."

"What?" Robbie was starting to feel anxious again. Was she giving him the brush off via Bernard?

"Well, it's hard to explain, but it's about her headaches."

"Yes, I've been treating her for them, as you know, but she was much better – well, until tonight apparently," Robbie said.

"Well, that's just it. To cut a long story short, she said she had traced the cause of them to that Christmas tree in the hall."

Robbie stared at him. "The Christmas tree?"

Bernard explained to Robbie as best he could what Dorothy had told him. "She seems very worried that something bad could happen because of that tree," he concluded.

"But, come on, man, how can a bloody tree have such an effect?"

"She's supposed to be psychic, isn't she?" Bernard grabbed him by the shoulders. "You're not very quick on the uptake tonight. I thought you'd cotton on, like I did. Quicker than I did, actually."

Robbie didn't seem to be getting his drift. "Think back to Norway..." Bernard prompted.

A light dawned in Robbie's eyes at last. "You mean – you think that Christmas tree in the hall is the one where I saw those children?"

"Well, I don't know for sure. But it seems highly likely, don't you think?"

"But, surely, it's too much of a coincidence." Robbie wasn't convinced.

"It *is* a coincidence. But, then, coincidences do happen sometimes. That's why they're called 'coincidences'."

Robbie had to admit that it all fitted. Maybe the tree had been brought to the church hall by an outside agency. It wasn't only God who moved in a mysterious way, it seemed.

"My God, Bernie, do you know what this means?"

Bernard shrugged. "It's all too much for me," he said. "I wish we'd never gone to Norway in the first place."

"It's a second chance," he said, ignoring his friend's unenthusiastic response. "Maybe those children have come with the tree. Maybe I can still help them."

"Aren't you forgetting something?"

"What's that?"

"Even if you see the children again, you can't speak Norwegian."

"Minor detail. I'll write down what they say as phonetically as possible, then get it translated."

"But won't you need someone to question the children as well?"

"It would be best, but I'm the only one who can communicate with them, unless I'm lucky enough to find someone who speaks Norwegian and is psychic."

"A bit of tall order," grinned Bernard. "Anyway, I think we're jumping the gun, don't you? I mean, you haven't seen any sign of these children yet, have you?"

"No, not yet – hang on, actually, I think I have."

"You have? When?" Bernard looked excited.

"I didn't think anything of it at the time. I just thought someone had brought their child to the dance because they couldn't get a babysitter..."

"You saw a child? Oh God," said Bernard. "I'm sure there are no children at the dance. We specifically stated it was an adults only do. What did this child look like?"

"Well, I think it had blond hair, for a start. I only caught a glimpse, though, so I didn't even see if it was a boy or a girl."

"Where did you see this child?"

"Just pushing through the crowd that was around the buffet table. It was literally just for a second."

"Do you think that this child was one of the Norwegian children, then?"

Robbie looked straight into Bernard's eyes. "Yes, Bernie, I do, and I believe you do, too."

Dorothy sat on in the vicarage study, rubbing her temples. The throbbing in her head was beginning to ease now, and she felt more comfortable. She also started to feel sleepy. She snuggled down further into the big leather armchair and imagined the charming vicar seated there of an evening, sucking his pipe, and thinking up his sermons. There was something about the brown-eyed priest that she really liked. He seemed so gentle. She had recently seen *Bambi* and, apart from crying buckets like everyone else at the death of the baby deer's mother, the look in the pretty fawn's soulful eyes reminded her of the look in Bernard's. She smiled to herself as she realised that dear Robbie reminded her of Thumper in the same film. Just as she was wandering off on this train of thought, Robbie was at her side. She looked up at him, smiling, her headache completely gone.

"Ah," he smiled. "I can see you must be feeling better." He took her half-stifled laugh as a sign she was happy to see him and was beginning to recover.

"Yes, Robbie, thank you, I am. Thanks to your friend. He's a lamb."

"Did you get another one of your headaches, dear?" he asked, gently stroking her hot brow.

"Yes, it was very bad this time. I told Bernard I thought it was to do with that Christmas tree. No, don't look at me like that. I know you think I'm mad, both of you. But there's something wrong in the hall, I know there is."

"I do believe you, Dorothy," said Robbie, sitting in the chair opposite, and banking up the fire which was in danger of sputtering out. "I think I owe it to you to tell you what happened to me some time ago, in the spring, when Bernie and I were in Norway."

A while later, Robbie escorted Dorothy back to the hall, just in time for the raffle. They stood close to the door and as far away from the Christmas tree as possible to make sure her headache didn't return. Bernard had just won the Christmas cake, and was looking very pleased with himself.

"'Ere!" called out one of the guests, a stroppy looking individual with a florid complexion and egg on his dinner jacket.

Bernard looked up from his prize in astonishment. "Who said that?" he asked.

The man in question stood up. He was swaying slightly and was clearly the worse for drink. "It's me, Ernie Platt," he replied. "The local shoe mender. Your Mrs 'arper knows me." Mrs Harper was standing behind the now empty buffet tables, arms folded.

"Sit down, Ernie," she said firmly. "You're drunk."

"It's a fix!" persisted Ernie, undeterred by the thunderous look on Nancy Harper's face. "You made sure your *darling* vicar won the cake, didn't yer!"

There was a muttering among the crowd, some no doubt agreeing with this version of events. Bernard looked very embarrassed but continued to hold onto the precious cake.

"Don't be daft," said Mrs Harper, coming round the table to face him. "I can't 'elp it if 'e got the winning ticket."

Some of the onlookers began to laugh, as Bernard grew redder and redder. "Look, Mr Platt," he said, putting down the cake and going over to his table. "I won it, it's true. It was totally fair and above board, and I intend to donate it to the local children's home."

"I'd rather you give it to me and my family," said Ernie, sitting down with a crash, knocking over a couple of wine glasses on the table as he did so. "We've got eleven kids, never mind the bleedin' children's 'ome. We 'aven't even got a turkey for Christmas dinner. It'll be corned beef sandwiches as usual in our 'ouse."

His wife, sitting beside him, whispered urgently in his ear. "Sit down, Ernie. Don't make a spectacle of yourself! And don't tell everyone our business."

Ernie slurped the rest of the wine in his glass. "You stay out of this, Janet," he grumbled, but it was obvious he felt ashamed of his outburst now.

Mrs Harper was looking at the couple with something bordering on sympathy as Bernard returned to the buffet table and the controversial cake. A look passed between them. He picked up the cake again and walked over to Ernie's table, putting it down ceremoniously in front of him. "It's yours," he said. "I'm sorry, Ernie. I hope you and your family enjoy it."

Ernie muttered his thanks and Janet burst into tears. She jumped up and kissed Bernard on both cheeks. "Thank you, thank you!" she cried.

"There, there," he replied, stumbling back to the buffet table as the whole room erupted into applause.

"Three cheers for the vicar!" came a voice from the back of the hall. "Hip hip!"

"Hooray!" was the happy response.

Bernard's heart was full and, as he looked around the room, his eyes picked out Dorothy and Robbie still standing by the door. His friend was giving him a thumbs up sign, while Dorothy was looking at him with something more than just mere approval in her smile.

❧

Later that evening, after most people had left the hall, Bernard, Robbie, Dorothy and Mrs Harper surveyed the debris left behind. It looked daunting, but it was clear that everybody had enjoyed themselves thoroughly.

"Don't worry," said Mrs Harper. "Me and the girls'll clear it all up in the morning."

"Thank you, Mrs Harper," said Bernard. "You've done us proud. It all went off splendidly."

"I was 'oping there'd be a bit of food left over," she said, "to take to the kiddles in 'ospital, like."

"It's a shame, but your cooking's much too good. Even the mice will have to look elsewhere tonight."

"Pesky mice!" she grumbled. "Now, if you don't mind, I'm off to my bed, if there's nothing else you'll be wanting tonight?"

"No, thank you, Mrs Aitch," said Bernard. "You go to bed. I'll lock up."

After Mrs Harper had gone, Dorothy turned to Robbie. "Can you see me home, dear? My headache's coming back. I need to get out of here."

"Of course," said Robbie, taking her arm at once. "Did you see if Lucy had found someone to take her home?" he asked Bernard over his shoulder.

"No, I didn't see her go," said Bernard. "But I'm sure she must have found some young man or other to escort her. Don't worry. You see to Dorothy. Good night both of you. Hope you feel better," he added, addressing the lady, who again looked very ashen and unwell. The less time she spent near the Christmas tree, the better, he thought.

After they had left, Bernard strolled around the hall, picking up bits of litter here and there as he went. He surveyed the scene and smiled contentedly. His parishioners had had a great evening and he was glad. Maybe he should make it an annual event. Just as he was about to switch out the light he heard a nervous cough coming from the back of the stage.

"Who's that?" he called out, fully expecting to see a Norwegian child himself. But it was someone far earthlier. Lucy Carter, looking flushed and obviously very much the worse for drink, came forward and smiled at him.

"Hello, Vicar," she said sweetly. "I waited for them to go. I wanted to have a private word with you." She stumbled down the stage steps and sidled up to him, none too steadily. He noticed that the heel on one of her satin shoes had broken off, causing her to limp.

"Please, Mrs Carter, come and see me tomorrow morning. It's much too late now. I'm very tired."

She looked crestfallen as he said this. He sighed and wondered what on earth she wanted to talk to him about that couldn't wait a few more hours.

"Look, Mrs Carter, I'm sorry. If it's urgent, of course, I'll listen. But, if it can wait ..."

"No, it can't ... wait," she slurred. "I've drunk enough to get up the courage, you see."

"Yes, you do seem rather tipsy," he observed, slightly understating the situation, as she was practically falling into his arms. "Come and sit down," he said brusquely, "I'll see if Mrs Harper can make you some coffee before she goes to bed."

"No, don't bother her," she said, "I'm fine, really. Come and sit beside me for a minute."

Bernard sighed, seeing no way out. "Very well," he acquiesced. "But, just for a minute, mind."

He sat down beside her and looked at her blandly. He saw a rather plump, pretty woman of around his own age, not unlike Dorothy Plunkett in some ways, but there was a knowing look in her eyes which made him slightly nervous.

"I'm sorry to be a nuisance," she said, picking at a piece of fruit cake that had stuck to her dress. "But I wanted to say that I very much admired what you did earlier."

"What I did?"

"You know – giving the cake to that Ernie Platt," she explained.

"Oh, it was nothing," he said. "It was the least I could do."

"You're a lovely man," she continued, stroking his arm. He began to feel very ill at ease. Never the sharpest knife in the box, Bernard was beginning to wonder if she was making some sort of pass at him.

"Look, what is it you wanted to talk to me about, Mrs Carter?" he said with firmness. Where was Robbie when he needed him? He wished Mrs Harper hadn't gone to bed, she would have known what to do in this situation.

"Oh, just that, really. I think a lot of you, you know?" she said, in no way daunted by his frosty manner. "You need a good woman to look after you, you do."

"Thank you, Mrs Carter," he said, unsure whether she was offering her own services in that direction, but fearing she probably was. "It's very nice of you to say so, but I'm very happy as I am with Mrs Harper to look after me."

"But you need a *wife*," she whined, putting her hand on his. He swiftly removed it and abruptly stood up.

"One day, maybe, if the right woman comes along," making it as clear as he could that she wasn't that woman.

"How do you know the right woman hasn't come along already?" she wheedled, tottering to her feet and picking at the collar of his jacket.

"Please, Mrs Carter, you must go home now. It's very late."

"You don't want me, either, do you?" She started to cry.

That's all he needed now, he thought. "Come on, Mrs Carter. I'm sure there are lots of likely lads who would feel privileged to be going out with you. I bet you've got your pick of them."

"What? Just after a world war? You're joking, of course. What men there are, are either incapacitated or living on their nerves."

"Don't be silly, Mrs Carter. I know for a fact that the postman has a soft spot for you," he told her, fingers crossed behind his back. He knew nothing of the sort, but what he knew of Charlie, he had a soft spot for anything in a skirt that had a pulse.

"Oh, him! I wouldn't touch him with a ten-foot barge pole." She looked as indignant as it was possible to look in her drunken condition. "He's always chasing after the girls. Married or single, makes no difference to him."

"Well, I'm sure Charlie isn't the only possibility," Bernard tried. "You'll find someone soon, I'm sure." He ran out of steam. There was nothing more he could think of to say as, in his heart, he knew Lucy was right. There weren't many eligible males around.

At that moment, to his great relief, Robbie came back into the hall. "I've seen Dorothy home, but I can't find Lucy anywhere. I said I'd escort her ..." He stopped when he saw his housekeeper snuggling up to Bernard.

"Oh, sorry, have I interrupted something?" he asked, looking amused.

"No, not at all," said Bernard, extricating himself from Mrs Carter's clutches and giving him a stony stare. "Thank God you're here," he said through the corner of his mouth. "She seems to be – er – a little drunk."

Robbie grinned mischievously. "Don't worry, I'll take her off your hands. I bet she'll regret this in the morning – if she remembers it, that is."

So saying, Robbie took his housekeeper by the arm and led her limping out of the hall. He returned a few seconds later.

"What have you done with her?" asked Bernard, puzzled.

"I've propped her up in the cloakroom for a minute," he said. "Will you be here for a bit longer?"

"Not much. Why?"

"I wanted to come back and see if – you know – I could get in touch with those children again."

"What, tonight? Why not come back tomorrow?"

"All right. I will. Straight after morning surgery. Will there be anybody here then? I think it would be best if I was alone."

"Well, Mrs Harper and some of her friends will be here first thing to clear up, but I expect they'll be finished by the time you come. Do you want me to be here?"

Robbie thought for a moment. "No, Bernie. I think the children will be more likely to appear if I'm alone."

"Okay," said Bernard. "Come and collect the key tomorrow."

"Thanks. Great evening, by the way. See you later."

But, what if Robbie saw those children again? Bernard wondered as he took a last around the hall before switching off the light. What would it mean and where would it lead?

&

Robbie rushed through his morning surgery the next day. He saw the usual line-up of coughs, colds, sore throats, and other winter ailments. Luckily there was nothing more complicated with which he had to deal, apart from old Mrs Tozer, a patient who turned up on average at least three times a week with some imaginary illness or other. He knew she just wanted a chat and some sympathy. He felt sorry for the old girl who had recently lost her husband of fifty-five years and was feeling bereft and lonely. He made sure she was put on the list for the old folks' Christmas dinner and gave her a full fifteen minutes of his precious time.

Finally, the last patient having been despatched with a prescription for cherry linctus for a tickly cough, he called up to Mrs Carter that he wouldn't be requiring any dinner and rushed out immediately before she could complain that she had already put it in the oven, and what was she supposed to do with it?

Lucy had obviously been hung over when she turned up to cook his breakfast, but he didn't refer to it or to the events of the night before. Robbie had never been the most tactful of God's creatures, but even he could see she didn't need any snide comments this morning.

He had been surprised when he caught her making a pass at Bernard, but he supposed his friend attractive to some women. Not in his own league, of course, but vicars were often the target for lonely spinsters, especially the unmarried ones like Bernard. He could understand it, he supposed.

He thought about Dorothy as he wandered up the road to the church hall. They had really hit it off, and he had already asked her out again. They had made a date to go to the pictures, and he was looking forward to it. But something was niggling at him. Although he didn't think Bernard was as attractive as himself, it was obvious that Lucy liked him and, try as he might, he couldn't forget the spark of something that seemed to pass from Dorothy to Bernard when they were introduced to each other. It was just his imagination, he told himself, but he couldn't quite dismiss the suspicion that there had been an instant rapport between them. It wasn't just that she obviously liked him, Bernard was easy to like. There was something deeper going on, and that was what was troubling him.

He reached the church hall at about five minutes past twelve to find the door open. He entered tentatively and saw, with a sinking heart, several ladies bustling about, still in the process of clearing up the remains of the previous night's festivities.

"Hello," he called. "How are you ladies doing?"

Mrs Harper, who was briskly sweeping up the pine needles from under the Christmas tree, looked up as he came into the hall. "Hello, Doc. Nearly done. The vicar told me to expect you. Give us another 'alf an hour."

She carried on sweeping up the pine needles, and Robbie fervently hoped she wasn't sweeping up the children with them.

"Thank you, Mrs Harper. I'll go and talk to Bernie for a bit, then. Is there any tea going?"

Mrs Harper stopped sweeping and put her hand on her hip. "I can't be in two places at once, now can I?" she said crossly. "I've just brewed a pot for 'is nibs, so there may be some left if you hurry. I can't vouch for the biscuits, though."

"I'll go and see him right away."

He found Bernard happily crunching his way through Mrs Harper's home-made biscuits and was just in time to claim the last one. The tea was good, though, piping hot and well brewed.

"How is Mrs Carter this morning?" Bernard asked, a trace of nervousness in his voice.

"A little the worse for wear, I should say," Robbie replied, smiling wryly. "I think she's a bit ashamed of her behaviour last night. I reckon she owes you an apology, Bernie. I could see she was trying to flirt with you."

"Well, she *was* very intoxicated," observed Bernard, sipping his tea thoughtfully. "I just hope that's all it was."

"Oh, I'm sure it was. She must be lonely, having lost her fiancé in the war. We mustn't be too hard on her."

"No, indeed," said Bernard. "There are so many lonely women since the war. That's why single, able-bodied men like you and me are prime targets, I suppose. We'd be safer if we were married." He gave a laugh.

"Well, I for one am glad I'm not," said Robbie decisively. "I wouldn't be able to take out Dorothy if I was. That'd leave the field open for you," he added knowingly, carefully watching his friend's reaction to this comment.

He saw the colour rise in Bernard's cheeks and knew he'd got the answer he was expecting. His friend had obviously been smitten.

"I – I don't know what you mean," said Bernard, unconvincingly.

"I think you do," Robbie replied, a little sadly.

Bernard bridled. "I don't, I tell you."

"Look, it's okay if you like Dorothy too. I don't blame you. All's fair and all that. May the best man win, et cetera. We won't let it spoil our friendship, will we?"

Bernard relaxed into a smile. "No, nothing can do that, Robbie. Yes, I do like Dorothy, but you saw her first. Anyway, I'm sure she prefers you."

"I'm not sure she does. I saw the way she was looking at you last night."

"Oh, you must be mistaken," protested Bernard, unsure whether to be pleased or not by this. It was true he had felt a connection with Dorothy, but he didn't have the confidence to think it meant anything very significant. Robbie was tall and handsome, just the kind of man women went for. He, on the other hand, was at least six inches shorter and, while not exactly Quasimodo, wasn't any woman's idea of the perfect male specimen.

"Have it your own way. Anyway, we're seeing each other tomorrow night," said Robbie, standing up. It was time he was in the church hall. The cleaning up must be finished by now, he thought.

Bernard gave one of his nervous coughs. "Er, yes I know. She asked me to come too."

Robbie felt his stomach plummet at this. "When did you make that arrangement?" he asked, almost with a snarl in his voice.

"She called me earlier this morning. We were just chatting and then she mentioned she was going to the pictures with you and asked me to come too."

Was it true? Robbie wondered. Had Dorothy asked Bernard, or had it been the other way around? Without another word, he left the room and headed out of the vicarage to the church hall.

❧

He turned up at the hall just as Mrs Harper was leaving it, and she handed over the key to him. "Don't know what you want to get up to in there," she sniffed. "But make sure you leave it as you found it. We've been working very 'ard this morning, and we don't want any Tom, Dick or Harry mucking it up."

"No, Mrs Harper, of course not." He pocketed the key.

"And make sure you lock up when you leave," she told him.

"Yes, ma'am," he said, doing a mock salute at her retreating back. Bloody woman, he thought to himself. Doesn't she ever smile? Not at him, obviously.

Anyway, that wasn't his concern right now. He stared at the Christmas tree. Despite its decorations, it was beginning to look quite threadbare, with many of its needles littering the floor. Mrs Harper's broom had still a lot of work to do. Every time he moved near it, more pine needles hit the floor. Was this the tree under which he had seen those poor children?

He drew up a chair near to it and sat down, trying to clear his mind of all thoughts. They were cluttered with visons of Dorothy and Bernard dancing together, kissing, and he knew no spirits could get through that muddle.

Armed with pen and paper, ready to write down as carefully as he could what the children might say, he made himself comfortable, prepared to wait as long as necessary. He had seen one of the children the night before, he was certain now, and he was also certain that they would try to contact him again. He just had to be patient.

It was now nearly one o'clock, and he realised he was hungry. He almost wished he'd had his dinner before coming to the hall, but he had been too eager to see the children again. As he continued to sit there, staring at the tree, he began to feel a little foolish. What man in his right mind spends his afternoon staring at a Christmas tree, no matter how pretty it is?

After about twenty minutes, he suddenly felt a draught of cold air. He turned swiftly, thinking that someone had come into the hall. But there was no one. He turned back to the tree to see a little blond-haired child standing there, looking at him with a soulful expression.

The little boy started to speak, and Robbie tried to write it down, but he was going too fast for him. He gestured with his hands, indicating that he wanted him to slow down. Halle stopped mid-flow, watching the doctor's hands move in and out, looking puzzled. Suddenly, there was a little girl beside him. She couldn't have been more than five or six and, she was so pretty, Robbie wanted to cry.

The two little children chatted together for a moment or two, then Halle turned back to Robbie. It seemed he and the little girl realised what he meant, because the boy began speaking very slowly now. Robbie still struggled to write it all down, holding up his hand every so often to indicate he wanted the child to stop so that he could catch up, but he managed it to get it all down at last.

As the boy finished speaking, he took his little companion by the hand, and they both smiled at Robbie. He smiled back at them, wishing he could reassure them that he was going to do everything in his power to help them. But, somehow, he knew they understood. He looked down at his notepad and the incomprehensible writing, wondering if it would be intelligible to someone who knew the Norwegian language. He fervently hoped so. He closed the pad and put it in his pocket, looking up to find the children were no longer there.

After his three-course dinner of tomato soup, steak pudding and apple pie, Bernard was sitting in his study, feeling pleasantly full, sipping a postprandial sherry. He was mulling over his conversation earlier that day with Robbie. It would be nice, he thought, if Dorothy *did* like him better than Robbie. He would feel sorry for him, of course, but it was up to Dorothy whom she liked, wasn't it? Bernard was sure that, if the boot was on the other foot, his friend wouldn't hesitate to snatch her away from him. She had asked him to go to the pictures with them both, and she wouldn't have done that if she wanted to be alone with Robbie. He smiled to himself. Dorothy was certainly very pretty. Lovely, in fact. He could almost see her sitting there opposite him, knitting him a pullover.

"The bloomin' lavatory's packed up again." These words broke into his reverie and he was back to earth with a bang.

"What did you say, Mrs Harper?"

"The chain 'as broken off again, and the bowl's flooded. I'll 'ave to get that no good Gilbert 'Ardcastle back, I suppose. I don't think 'e knows what 'e's doing."

"Whatever you say, Mrs Harper. It sounds urgent now. Perhaps we should just get a completely new cistern; otherwise, we'll keep having problems. Don't you think so?"

She sniffed. "It's up to you, Vicar. But new cisterns don't come cheap."

"No, I suppose not. But we can't go through Christmas with a flooded toilet, can we?"

Mrs Harper shrugged. "We could always go next door or across the road. They won't mind. I'm well in with all the neighbours."

"I'm sure you are, but I don't think that would be very convenient – no pun intended – either for them or for us, do you?"

"You're the boss, Vicar. So, I'll ask Gilbert 'ow much a new one'll cost, then?"

"Yes, please do, Mrs Harper. Thank you. Can I have some coffee, by the way?"

Bernard tried to get back into the mood of his earlier thoughts, but the fate of the vicarage's sanitary arrangements took over. He hoped a new cistern wouldn't cost too much. Whatever the cost, it would probably be beyond his meagre stipend. Maybe he could use some of the proceeds from the dinner dance... He banished the thought immediately. The old folks' Christmas dinner came first, he told himself severely.

Mrs Harper returned with a tray of coffee and two cups, Robbie right behind her. "Your friend's 'ere, Vicar," she said. "I think 'e thinks 'e lives 'ere. Anyway, I brought another cup."

"Thank you, Mrs Aitch."

"By the way, Gilbert says 'e'll be over in 'alf an hour with some prices," she said, as she left the room.

"Prices for what, old boy?" asked Robbie, sitting down by the fire opposite his friend.

"It's the blessed toilet again. It's broken for good this time. Well, it's the cistern, actually. The toilet bowl itself is salvageable, I think – I hope. I'll have to invest in a new one. It's not going to be cheap, according to Mrs Harper."

"Not cheap, but a necessity," said Robbie wisely. "Anyway, do you want to hear *my* news?"

"Gosh, yes. How did you get on? Did you see the children again?"

"I certainly did. A little boy and girl. I saw them quite clearly this time. They are very young and the girl, especially, is very pretty. They are definitely dead. They must have been murdered by the same killer who did for their mother, poor things."

"So, did they talk to you?"

"Yes, but of course it was in Norwegian. I wrote down exactly what I heard though. Here ..." Robbie showed Bernard the page of indecipherable writing he had managed to produce.

"Looks like double Dutch to me," observed Bernard, pouring out the coffee. "This is of no help, whatsoever, Robbie. You know that, don't you? Why don't you give it up as a bad job?"

"I can't do that, Bernie. I keep telling you. It was meant for me to help them. They appeared to me for a reason. I would have given up – *had* given up, but now that I've seen them again, I just can't."

"But what's the good if you can't speak their language? It's not as if it's a more common language like French or German. There's probably lots of people can speak those. But *Norwegian*? I wouldn't have a clue."

"I'll put a call through to Edinburgh University later on – you know, Carl's old college. They've got an excellent linguistics department there. I'm sure someone will be able to help me, especially if I mention I was a former student there as well as a friend of poor Carl."

"Very well," said Bernard slowly. "I suppose that might work. But I doubt you'll get anyone to come down before Christmas."

"You're probably right there," said Robbie dolefully. "I think I could do with a tot of whisky, Bernie," he said, "you know – to help me get over the disappointment."

"Any excuse," smiled Bernard. "You know where it is. Get me another sherry while you're about it."

As Robbie was pouring the drinks, Mrs Harper knocked on the door and entered without waiting for permission, closely followed by Gilbert Hardcastle.

"Oh, not now, Mrs Harper," said Bernard huffily. "Can't you see I've got company? Robbie and I want some privacy."

Mrs Harper sniffed very loudly. "I think the toilet comes before privacy," she said firmly. "Gilbert's a busy man. Especially as it's Christmas. We're lucky to get 'im 'ere so quick. So, what about looking at these prices?"

Bernard sighed a long-suffering sigh. "Very well, Mrs Harper. What sort of cost are we looking at? Just a basic cistern, that's all we want."

Gilbert stepped forward and handed him a piece of paper. On it was written a list of prices that started high and ended up going through the roof.

"Oh dear," he said. "I can't afford any of these. Are you sure there's nothing cheaper?"

Mrs Harper took over. "Look, I've told you before, Gilbert 'Ardcastle. Don't come the old acid. These prices," she said, snatching the paper from Bernard's hands, "are pure science fiction, you toe-rag. I suggest you go back and try again."

Gilbert looked askance at her. "You drive a hard bargain, Nance," he protested. "I've got to make a living, you know."

"Yes, but not on the backs of others, you don't," she said. "Now get along with you and come back when you've rubbed a few noughts off the end of these figures."

Gilbert turned to go, but as he did so his eye caught sight of Robbie's writing pad on the table. "That looks like Norwegian," he said, as he walked out.

Robbie stared after him and then looked at Bernard. "Gilbert!" they yelled in unison. "Come back!"

❧

But it was no use. Gilbert Hardcastle moved very fast for a slow-witted man.

"Didn't he hear us?" asked Bernard crossly.

"Obviously not," said Robbie.

"Mrs Harper!" Bernard called after her departing back. "Has Gilbert left the vicarage?"

"Yes, Vicar. He ain't getting a cup of tea out of me until 'e comes back with more reasonable prices. I told 'im straight."

"Can you come here a minute, please?"

Bernard stood on the landing, watching his housekeeper bustle back up the stairs. She didn't look too pleased.

"What is it, Vicar? I've work to do."

"Just a tick, please," said Bernard as ingratiatingly as he could. "Come in."

"Well?" she questioned, arms folded belligerently.

"This Gilbert, Mrs Aitch," said Robbie, standing up and beginning to pace up and down the study. "He seemed to know that this writing – here." He showed her his pad, open at the page of Norwegian writing.

"Looks like a load of gobbledegook to me," she observed.

"Yes, and to most people that is exactly what it does look like. But Gilbert recognised it as Norwegian. How on earth did he know that?"

"Oh," said Mrs Harper, smiling now. "That's easily explained. Gilbert's 'alf Norwegian, didn't you know?"

"How would I?" said Robbie, now very animated. "He seems an Englishman through and through to me, especially with a name like Gilbert Hardcastle."

"'Is mother's Norwegian, that's why. She married an Englishman. I think 'e's dead now. Anyway, Gilbert's real name is Gils, I think, something like that. Does that answer your question?"

"It very much does, Mrs Harper," said Robbie gleefully. He was almost dancing a jig.

"Be sure to send him straight up here as soon as he comes back with the revised prices, Mrs Harper," Bernard instructed, smiling.

"You seem very interested in 'im all of a sudden," observed Mrs Harper, eyeing both men with suspicion. "Can't say I see the attraction, myself."

"Never you mind, Mrs Harper," said Robbie, escorting her to the door. "Just send him up when he comes back."

"Whatever you say," she said.

"Well, there's a turn up for the books, eh?" Robbie sat back down and lit his pipe.

"You know, Robbie, all along I've been sceptical and unhelpful over this business, but I'm with you completely now, and I'll back you up and help in any way I can. These children's bodies must be found and given a Christian burial." An evangelical light was in his eyes.

"Absolutely," agreed Robbie. "Thanks, Bernie."

"More whisky?" asked his friend, grinning.

❧

Later that afternoon, Gilbert Hardcastle returned to the vicarage armed with a new price list. Before he could be shown up to the Vicar's study, however, he had to get past Mrs Harper, who stood in the hall, arms akimbo.

"All right, Gilbert," she said. "Let's 'ave a look at that list now. I won't 'ave you diddling the vicar, I've told you that before."

"Here you are," he said, shoving the sheet of paper at her. "Pick the bones out of that."

"No need to be rude," she told him, as she cast her beady eyes over the new price list. "There's other plumbers, you know."

"Not one you could get to come before Christmas, though," Gilbert pointed out, with a smug look on his sallow face. "Well? Are these prices more what you're after? That's as low as I can go."

He watched her carefully, ready to complain if she started to quibble again. "I haven't got all day, you know. And if his worship wants the cistern installed before Christmas he'd better let me know soon, as me and the missus are going to stay with my mum in a few days."

"So?" said Mr Harper, still scrutinising the paper. "Can't you come and fit it even if you're staying with your mum?"

"Not easily, no," smiled Mr Hardcastle wanly. "She lives in Norway."

Mrs Harper looked up at that. "But I thought she only lived in Tooting?"

"She used to. But when my dad died, she went back to live with her sister, who's a bit gaga these days."

"Oh, I didn't know that. Well, I can't see the vicar objecting to these prices. I think 'e'll agree to this one." She pointed to the cheapest on the list. "I'll let you know later."

"Okay, thanks." Gilbert turned to go, but Mrs Harper remembered just in time.

"Oh, I forgot. I think the vicar wants to see you about something else," she said. "Can you wait a minute, while I tell 'im you're 'ere?"

"Well, hurry up then. I've got a sink to unblock before five."

"'Old your 'orses," she said, climbing the stairs. "It won't take a minute."

A few moments later, Gilbert was standing in the study, cap in hand, wondering why these two professional gentlemen seemed so pleased to see him. He knew he was good at his job, but his arrival in people's homes had never warranted such euphoria before.

"You, er – wanted to see me? I've given Mrs Harper the prices for the new cistern," he said.

"Thank you, Gilbert," said Bernard. "But that's not why we wanted to see you. Please – sit down."

"I haven't got much time," he told them, reluctantly taking the seat that was offered. "I've got a sink to unblock. I told her downstairs that..."

"Nonsense, man," interrupted Robbie. "You've got time for a chat, surely?"

"Well, I ..." Gilbert was even more puzzled.

"Good, good," said Robbie, rubbing his hands. "Now, I understand from Mrs Harper that your mother is Norwegian. Is that correct?"

"Well, yes. But I don't see... I mean, I was born here, you know. I'm not illegal or anything."

"Shut up, man, and listen. You looked at this piece of paper when you were here just now and recognised the writing on it, didn't you?"

"Well, yes, I thought it looked like Norwegian. My mum taught me when I was little and, somehow, I never lost the knack. I can speak a bit of French, too," he added proudly.

"Bother French!" expostulated Robbie. "But the fact that you understand Norwegian is of great interest to us."

"It is?"

"Yes, Gilbert, it is. You don't know what a godsend you are." Saying this, Robbie handed him his attempt at writing Norwegian. "So, you think you can translate this?" he asked.

"I don't understand," said Gilbert, taking the notepad and staring at the page of squiggly writing. "Where did you get this from? Who wrote it? The spelling's all wrong."

"*I* wrote it, Gilbert, so I'm quite sure the spelling's all wrong. But can you translate it, do you think?"

Gilbert scratched his head. "I think I can tell you more or less what it says," he said slowly.

"That's all I need to know," said Robbie. "Would you like a whisky?"

Gilbert's naturally sullen features lit up at this. "Well, that would be ..." Robbie was on his feet and pouring him a generous measure before he could finish his sentence.

"Do you want me to read what I *think* it says? It's rather badly written so I might not get all the words right."

"I did my best, man. Not easy when you don't speak a word of the language."

Gilbert wondered why an English doctor should suddenly start writing Norwegian, especially as he was obviously no good at it. He wisely refrained from saying this, however.

"Anyway," prompted Robbie, "just give us the gist of it."

"All right. Here goes then." He cleared his throat. "It says: 'My name is Halle Dahl, and this is my sister Birgitta. Our mother was shot dead by a man called

Baldur. We don't know his last name. He used to help out on the farm. He then'..." Gilbert paused, trying to decipher the next word. "I think it says 'killed'." Gilbert looked up enquiringly.

"Yes, yes. Go on, man," Robbie said impatiently.

"...killed me and my sister and buried us in the wood. We were underneath the tree that is in your hall now. We came here with it. We need to be found. We can't rest until then. The man who killed us is still free. He used to live in the town. We don't know anything more about him. Please help us."

Gilbert finished reading and gave the pad back to Robbie. "What's it all about?" he asked. "Is it some sort of a joke?"

"Far from it, man," said Robbie. "Does it sound like it?"

"My mum wrote to me about the murder of a woman called Dahl," said Gilbert. "She said it caused quite a stir at the time. Her two children went missing and, according to Mum, they still are. The police never found them or the murderer."

It was Robbie's turn to be surprised. "So, your mother's in Norway now?"

"That's right. She moved there to live with her sister when my dad died last year. My aunt's not got all her marbles, and she needs looking after. She never married and hasn't got any kids to help her."

"I suppose it was headline news once," said Robbie. "Does your mother think the police are still trying to solve the case?"

"I don't know. I'll ask her, if you like."

"Please do, Gilbert."

"So, how come you seem to have got this information?"

"It's a long story," said Robbie. "But I'll tell you this. I intend to find those poor children's bodies. With your help, Gilbert."

"I don't get any of this," he said, scratching his head. "But I'll do anything I can, of course. Poor mites. My mum'll be ever so pleased to hear what you say when I see her next week."

"You're going to stay with her?" asked Robbie, escorting Gilbert to the door.

"That's right," he replied. "The missus is really looking forward to it. She's never been abroad before. I've been to loads of places – the war and all that, but this'll be the first time for me in Norway."

"Whereabouts in Norway does your mother live, Gilbert?"

"Bergen. Not all that far from the farm where that woman was murdered."

When Gilbert had gone, Robbie turned to Bernard and smiled. "Can you believe it?"

Bernard, who had sat silently for a while, taking it all in, nodded. "It's amazing – the coincidences that keep happening. The fact that Gilbert's mother is Norwegian and is living in Bergen, of all places. Do you realise that, if my toilet hadn't broken, we'd never have known any of this?"

"Yes," Robbie agreed. "Thank God for your dodgy plumbing."

"Well, I wouldn't go that far," said Bernard. "It's been very inconvenient for me – and Mrs Harper, of course. But, as you say, thank God for it."

Meanwhile, Mrs Harper, unable to contain her natural curiosity, which some uncharitable people among her acquaintances termed nosiness, invited the departing plumber into the kitchen for a cup of tea and a slice of upside down cake.

The following evening, Bernard, Robbie and Dorothy were sitting in the Bricklayer's Arms, having sat through a seemingly endless western in vivid Technicolor. They had each been engrossed in their own private thoughts, and not in the least interested in the antics of John Wayne on the screen.

"Same again?" asked Robbie, looking at the empty glasses.

While he was at the bar, Dorothy leaned towards Bernard and put her hand gently on his. "Bernard?"

"Dorothy," he replied, his eyes staring at her, like a rabbit caught in the headlights of an oncoming car.

She withdrew her hand as she saw Robbie returning with the drinks and made a pretence of looking for something in her handbag as he handed them out.

"So, as I see it, we need to brief Gilbert carefully," said Robbie, continuing the conversation they had been having before he'd gone to the bar. He was seemingly oblivious to the little scene that had ended abruptly with his return.

"Yes," said Dorothy, recovering her composure a little.

"Yes," echoed Bernard.

"We need to tell him to get the Bergen police to search the area where I found the gun, if they haven't already done so," Robbie continued, undeterred.

"Yes." Bernard looked ill at ease as he sipped his second sherry of the evening.

Robbie continued to talk, even though his companions seemed distracted and talking only in monosyllables. "And we know that the killer's name is Baldur."

"But that's probably a common name in Norway," Dorothy pointed out. She was looking at Bernard as she said this, and he nodded in agreement.

"Probably, but we've nothing else to go on," Robbie said, at last beginning to sense an atmosphere between his two companions. He made short work of his whisky, placing his empty glass down carefully.

Looking from one to the other, he cleared his throat into the strained silence. "Right," he said. "I think I'll get off home now. Do you mind if I leave you two alone together?"

"Actually," said Bernard, "I think it's about time I went home too. It was a long film, wasn't it? Shall we all leave together?"

"All right," said Dorothy, standing up. "Can you at least wait until I've been to the ladies?"

She walked off towards the facilities, leaving them in no doubt that the evening, for her, had ended too abruptly.

Robbie smiled at Bernard. "I think she wanted to be alone with you, Bernie."

"No – I just think she wanted us both to stay a bit longer."

"You don't believe that any more than I do."

Bernard looked embarrassed but didn't try to deny it.

Bergen, December 1948

Gunda Pedersen let herself into the apartment, shaking the snow off her boots as she did so. Berthina Hardcastle called out to her from her sister's bedroom.

"Is that you, Gunda?"

"Yes, Mrs Hardcastle," she replied, hanging up her coat. "I let myself in like you told me. Where do you want me to start?"

"In the front room, please," came the reply. "Liv wasn't too well in the night, and I've sent for the doctor."

"I'm sorry to hear that. Shall I make us some tea first?"

"Yes, please. Thank you, Gunda."

Five minutes later, Gunda and Berthina were sitting together at the kitchen table, the tea mashing in the pot.

"You should have your sister properly looked after, you know," said Gunda sympathetically. "There's homes for people in her condition. You can't cope on your own. What with your son and daughter-in-law coming to stay, as well."

"I suppose you're right," replied Mrs Hardcastle. "But I can't let her go to one of those places. I've heard nightmare stories about the way they treat the inmates. Worse than being in prison."

"They're not all as bad as that," said Gunda. "You just have to go and look around a few."

"Maybe." Berthina had been thinking along the same lines for some time now, as she continued to witness her sister's rapid decline into dementia. But to put her in a home seemed a callous thing to do.

"Anyway, Gunda, how are you?" she asked, fishing out a packet of cigarettes from her skirt pocket and offering her one.

"Oh, I'm fine," she replied, accepting a cigarette gratefully. "Thanks. Baldur doesn't like me smoking."

Berthina lit her cigarette for her and smiled. "Men! They can smoke like chimneys themselves, but if the 'little woman' decides to do the same – well."

Gunda nodded in agreement, enjoying the feel of the smoke at the back of her throat. "Still, he's not so bad, my old man."

"I'm glad you've found someone," said Mrs Hardcastle. "How long have you been together?"

"Oh, not long. Just about a month," said the younger woman. "He's not my Björn, but he's kind, and works hard. In fact, he doesn't like me working, says he earns enough at the lumber jacking. But I like coming here, and all the others. It would be lonely for me stuck at home all day, otherwise."

Berthina smiled as Gunda poured out the tea. "That's men for you. Still, as long as he's decent and honest, that's all that matters."

"Oh, yes. Baldur's a good man, if a little rough around the edges." Gunda smiled back at her, passing her a mug of hot tea. "And, anyway, beggars can't be choosers. Isn't that what they say?"

"Don't put yourself down," admonished Berthina.

"I bet you're looking forward to seeing your son again," observed Gunda. "It's been a while, hasn't it?"

"Yes, I haven't seen him for almost a year, not since I left England at the end of last year. Gils has never been to Norway before, nor has Marjorie – his wife. She's very nice, I like her very much."

"Are there any grandchildren?"

"No. I think they've given up trying. I don't think they'll be blessed now. Marjorie's nearly forty."

"That's a shame. I always wanted children myself, but it wasn't to be. Björn was very sad about it."

They continued to chat for a while, Berthina enjoying the company of Gunda more than she cared to admit. Her poor sister, Liv, had her lucid moments, but they were fewer and further between lately.

Eventually, Gunda stood up and stubbed out her cigarette. "Dear me, look at the time," she said. "Must get on," she said. She took the empty mugs to the sink and left the kitchen.

Berthina wondered about her cleaner's new man. They seemed to be pretty thick together after a relatively short space of time. She had asked Gunda about him more than once, but she seemed to know very little about his past life, which was strange and a little worrying. Still, Berthina supposed, it was none of her business, and if he made Gunda happy, who was she to interfere?

London, December 1948

Bernard was in his study, dozing. It was just under a week till Christmas, and the sermon he had been writing had slipped to the floor. He was jolted awake by the voice of his housekeeper announcing that "a Miss Plunkett" was downstairs, wishing to see him. Bernard was thrown into a panic. What could she want to see him about? he wondered. After that embarrassing evening in the pub, he thought she would stay away, and he certainly wouldn't have blamed her if she never spoke to him again. But now, here she was, wanting to see him.

Oh dear, he thought. He wasn't ready for a confrontation, which he was sure it was bound to be. But he couldn't leave her downstairs to the mercies of Mrs Harper, either. "All right, Mrs Aitch, please show her up," he said finally.

"Are you sure, Vicar? I could tell 'er you're too busy." She could see he looked flustered.

"No, no, Mrs Aitch, I'll see her, of course."

"As you like," she sniffed.

Bernard was waiting for her at the top of the stairs and shook her formally by the hand, hoping to set the tone for the rest of the meeting.

"I suppose you'll be wanting tea," said Mrs Harper, standing aside to allow Dorothy to enter the study.

"Er, what can I do for you?" he said, keeping up the formality. "Is it still snowing?" It was a silly question, as he could see the evidence quite clearly on her coat, hat and fur-lined ankle boots.

"As you can see," she said, smiling.

"Come and sit by the fire and get warm," he said. It was the least he could do. The poor woman looked frozen.

She did so, removing her coat and hat.

"Didn't my housekeeper take your things? She should have done."

"I wasn't sure if I was stopping. Am I stopping, Bernard?"

"It's all very awkward – there's Robbie to consider," he said. It was useless to go on with the charade, he thought. It was time they cleared the air.

"Don't you think I know that?" Dorothy fumbled for her hanky as her tears started to fall unbidden.

Bernard was now thoroughly distraught. Luckily, Mrs Harper entered at that moment, bearing the tea tray, and sizing up the situation at once.

"There, there," she said, placing the tray down and patting Dorothy on the shoulder. "It's all right. What 'as the bad man been saying to you?"

Bernard had never seen his granite-like housekeeper so 'mumsy' before. He didn't know she was capable of it. Despite the situation, he felt like laughing. In amongst this confusion, the doorbell rang, and Bernard was relieved to be able to leave the room to answer it. He wasn't relieved when he saw who it was, though.

"Robbie!" he exclaimed. "What are you doing here?"

"What a greeting, man," Robbie laughed. "My morning surgery finished early today, and I wanted to talk some more about our plans for Gilbert's Bergen trip." He was quite taken aback at his friend's attitude.

"It's – it's not very convenient right now," burbled Bernard. "You see, I've got my Christmas day sermon to write ..."

Robbie remained where he was on the doorstep, covered in snow, while Bernard debated what to do. He couldn't let his friend find Dorothy in his study crying, could he? He'd very likely punch him on the nose.

"Aren't you going to let me in, Bernie?" Robbie had one wellington booted foot over the threshold.

"Er, as I said, not right now," said Bernard, trying his best to appear normal. "Just need to get on. Let's meet later. Come over this evening."

Robbie looked thoroughly rattled now. "Don't bother. Let me know when you've got time for an old friend." He turned and walked back through the fast falling snow to the vicarage gate. He opened it and looked back to see the door closing.

It had been the hardest thing Bernard had had to do for a long time. How could he ever have closed the door on Robbie? But what choice did he have? He couldn't let him see Dorothy in that state, he just couldn't.

He returned to the study to find Mrs Harper handing a much more composed Dorothy a cup of tea.

As Bernard entered, his housekeeper gently pushed him back onto the landing and closed the study door.

"She's feeling better now," she whispered. "What 'ave you done to her?"

"N-nothing," he stammered, "that I can think of. I think she's taken a fancy to me, that's all."

"More than just a fancy, I should say. You'd better let 'er down gently – that is, if you don't feel the same way?"

"I – I like her very much, but so does Robbie. And he saw her first."

"What are you talking about?" said Mrs Harper in astonishment. "It's not some kind of a competition. The woman can't 'elp 'er feelings and she likes you best, though God knows why. Your friend will 'ave to like or lump it. The most important thing *is 'er* feelings. Tell me, 'ow do you really feel?"

"I – I'm not sure," said Bernard, dithering. "I don't want to hurt Robbie. This will spoil our friendship."

"So, your friendship with the Doctor is more important than any feelings you 'ave for that poor heartbroken woman in there?"

"Well – not if you put it like that. I don't want to hurt either of them."

Mrs Harper sighed. Just then, the doorbell rang again. "That'll be Gilbert with the new cistern," she said. "I'd better go and sort 'im out. You go and talk to 'er. And, mind what I said, let 'er down *gently*."

Bernard returned to Dorothy, who was looking almost cheerful now. "I – I'm sorry," he began.

"No – it's my fault. I'm the one who should apologise. Putting you on the spot like that. But whatever you feel about me," she said, putting her cup down, "if you're holding back because of Robbie, there's really no point. If you don't feel as I do, then that's fine. At least I'll know and can move on – go somewhere else. It might be best, before I get too settled here."

"But you've only just moved here!" remonstrated Bernard. "You can't just up and leave like that."

"Well, I'll have to if you don't want me around," she said. "It'd be too painful for both of us."

"That's not fair," said Bernard, sitting down and giving the fire a poke to hide his confusion. "I like you very much and I want you around. So does Robbie. Perhaps we're all moving too fast. I'm just not ready for any commitment at the moment. Maybe in time ...."

Dorothy sighed and got up to leave. "You're absolutely right. I'm pushing you too hard. Let's at least be friends though?"

"Of course," said Bernard, standing up and taking her hand. "I hope we'll always be that."

"Thank you," she said demurely. "Goodbye."

She left the room, closing the door quietly. Bernard stared at it. She was gone. She had understood how he felt and accepted it. That's what he wanted, wasn't it? Wasn't it?

❧

Robbie decided to go straight to the pub from the vicarage. There was still half an hour before nearly closing time, thank goodness.

He couldn't begin to comprehend why Bernard was behaving so oddly towards him, but at the back of his mind he suspected that Dorothy had something to do with it. Well, that was it, as far as he was concerned; if a woman could come between them as easily as that, then their friendship was a very fragile thing indeed. He cared a great deal for both of them, but when the chips were down, it would be Bernard every time.

He ordered a double whisky and went and sat in the corner to cogitate, his mind in a turmoil. Not only was there the Dorothy and Bernard problem, but also the poor Norwegian children to consider. He knew there was little more he could do until Gilbert had seen his mother and found out exactly what was happening, but it made him feel so impotent.

As he sipped his whisky, his thoughts inevitably reverted to Bernard. He'd been invited over to the vicarage that evening and had more or less decided not to go. Bernard's treatment of him just now had hurt him more than he cared to admit. It seemed that, ever since Dorothy had come on the scene, things hadn't been right between them. Carl had nearly caused a rift, too. Surely they could each have other friends, without falling out over them?

He went to the bar and ordered another double just as the landlord called time and returned to his seat. He had been bowled over by Dorothy from the first, but he knew she didn't feel the same way about him. He just had to get over it. Downing his second drink, he left the pub and decided to take a walk in the park before it got too dark. The nights were drawing in very quickly. December was always a dismal time of year, he thought. 'Dark days before Christmas' had been a saying he'd heard all his life, not quite understanding what it meant until now. The snow lay underfoot and cast a pale glow as the street lights came on.

As he turned into the park, he bumped into Dorothy who was just about to leave it. She was the last person he expected to see at that moment, and he wasn't sure whether he was pleased or sorry.

"Oh, hello," she gasped, obviously disconcerted to see him there.

"Hello, Dorothy," he said, regaining his composure quickly. "How are you?"

"I'm well," she said, smiling weakly.

"Not getting any more headaches?"

"No, no," she said dismissively. "Anyway, we both know the reason for those now, don't we? I haven't been near that Christmas tree since the night of the dinner dance."

"Of course," said Robbie. He was at a loss what to say next. Small talk seemed pointless under the circumstances.

"Look, Robbie, it's nice to see you, but I'm in rather a hurry." She was avoiding his probing blue eyes.

"Of course," said Robbie. "Well, goodbye. Look after yourself."

"I will, thank you," she replied, hurrying past him.

She was the second person today who didn't want his company. Maybe he was wearing the wrong eau de cologne, he thought bitterly.

❧

Later that afternoon, Bernard picked up his half-finished sermon, knowing full well that he wouldn't be able to write a word. All he could think about was his imperilled friendship with Robbie, and how Dorothy fitted into the picture. If, indeed, she did. It was all such a mess.

He wondered if Robbie would come back later. He wouldn't blame him if he didn't. He tried to gather his wits as he stared at his sermon, but it was useless. His eyes began to feel heavy and he was just drifting off when the door opened, and Robbie strode in, bringing what seemed like half a hundredweight of snow with him.

"Is it all right for me to come in now?" he asked.

Bernard jumped up and grasped him by the shoulder. "Of course, it is! I'm so sorry about earlier, I was busy with my sermon."

Robbie looked at the page on the table beside Bernard's armchair. "I see you haven't got very far," he observed.

"No, well, I keep falling asleep," said Bernard with a rueful grin.

Robbie sat by the fire opposite him and gave him a stern look. Bernard returned his stare as bravely as he could.

"What exactly is going on, Bernie? I think I have a right to know."

Bernard couldn't bring himself to lie glibly. He had never been any good at lying, even when it was in a good cause. And he certainly couldn't lie to his best friend. So he took a deep breath and told him all about Dorothy's visit that afternoon.

"I thought so," said Robbie, a wistful smile on his handsome face. "But you shouldn't have sent me away like that, Bernie. I thought she preferred you anyway. It wouldn't have come as a shock."

"But you like her so much," insisted Bernard. "It doesn't seem fair."

"Maybe it isn't. But I'll get over it. And I don't want to lose your friendship over it."

"No, no. Absolutely not," said Bernard emphatically. "That's the last thing I want too."

They sat in silence for several minutes. Bernard got up and fetched the whisky bottle. "Here, Robbie, help yourself," he said.

"Thanks, old boy," said Robbie, doing just that. "I saw Dorothy this afternoon – in the park," Robbie told him, taking a long swig of Bernard's whisky.

"Did you? How did she seem to you?"

"Well, it makes sense now. She'd obviously just been to see you, so she wasn't really herself. I thought she had another of her headaches."

"I feel so sorry for her," said Bernard, pouring himself a sweet sherry.

"What's the matter with you, man?" said Robbie impatiently. "You don't have to marry the woman, for God's sake. Just go for a drink or a meal, maybe the pictures. Just enjoy her company."

"Well, if it really *is* all right with you, Robbie," said Bernard thoughtfully. "I'd like to take her out sometime."

"It's nothing to do with me," said Robbie. "I'll probably be jealous, but we aren't going to fall out over it. We've already agreed on that."

"Thanks, Robbie," said Bernard gratefully.

The following day dawned crisp, bright and cold, the snow in evidence everywhere. No further falls had occurred overnight, but the sub-zero temperatures ensured that what had fallen the day before remained crisp and white. It was the perfect day for a walk to the park, and Bernard decided to do just that. He was feeling very cheerful this morning, now that he and Robbie were friends again. He was also feeling doubly pleased with himself as he had managed to finish writing his sermon before leaving for the park.

As he set off, he looked up and saw a vivid blue sky without a cloud in sight. The leafless trees provided a stark contrast as they bent in the stiffening wind. He breathed in the sharp, clear air, filling his lungs; it made him feel strong and healthy. He suddenly realised he wanted to see Dorothy very much. Perhaps he would phone her later and ask her out.

He wondered what she would be doing for Christmas. He realised he didn't know anything about her personal life: whether she had parents living, or siblings, and, if so, where they lived. He suddenly wanted to know all these things very much. How could he have been so stupid as to repel her advances like that? Robbie was right. He should at least have listened to his own heart in the matter, and not worried about what his friend would say.

As he was thinking these thoughts, he sat down on a cold, hard bench, wishing he'd put on his overcoat to protect him from the biting wind gnawing at his vitals. But, as he didn't want to go back to his cosy study fire just yet, he sat on bravely, facing the elements.

Suddenly he felt a nudge in his ribs. He turned to his right and saw, with dismay, Diabol sitting beside him. Not him again! Who was he after now?

"Hello," said Diabol with a grin as wicked as, no doubt, the man himself. "Remember me?"

"You're not exactly easy to forget," observed Bernard cuttingly. "What do you want this time?"

"I need to find a Dorothy Blunkett," said the little man, grinning impishly at him. "I only need a couple more to get my horns. I've been escorting people downstairs for two years now, and at last I'm getting the hang of it. But I'll be glad of a rest."

"Dorothy Plunkett?" screamed Bernard. "You don't mean to take *her*, do you?" He was desperate. This couldn't be happening.

"'Fraid so," said the little man, almost as if he cared. "I've got a nice warm spot all ready for her. But you needn't worry, you know. It's not all fire and brimstone down there. That's just a myth. It's quite a gay place at times. To be honest, upstairs is a bit boring. Most people, if they get up there, opt to go down below after a few days. It's like one long Sunday – it goes on forever. All right for some, but most people like a bit of life – even if they're dead."

Bernard tore at his hair. "Shut up!" he yelled at him. "Shut up! You can't take Dorothy – you just can't!"

"I've got no choice. You see, she's the second from bottom on my list. Look." And he showed Bernard his clipboard.

Bernard hardly glanced at it. He didn't care how many times she was on his list, he wasn't going to let him take Dorothy. He grabbed the little man by the collar, but found he was only grabbing thin air. Bernard looked around frantically, but he'd vanished.

"Don't do that again," said a voice beside him. The man was back again, this time sitting on his left side. Bernard turned to face him.

"Look, I'm sorry," said Bernard. "I suppose you've got your job to do, but Dorothy means a lot to me. I've hardly got to know her yet, and you come here telling me you plan to take her from me forever."

Diabol simply shrugged. "I understand you know where I can find her."

Bernard glared at him. Hadn't he heard what he'd just said? Was there no humanity in the man? Then, he supposed, he wasn't really human, was he?

"Come on, I haven't got all day. Where can I find Miss Blunkett?"

Bernard's ears pricked up suddenly. Had he heard him correctly? He said 'Blunkett' not 'Plunkett'.

"Did you say *Blun*kett?"

"Yes, I keep telling you. Dorothy Blunkett."

"Let me look at that list again," demanded Bernard.

"Here," said Diabol, handing it to him.

There was no doubt: the list said 'Blunkett' not 'Plunkett'. Bernard's heart sang.

"You've got it wrong again!" said Bernard, almost laughing. "I know a Dorothy *Plun*kett not *Blun*kett."

"Oh, bother," said Diabol with a jerk of his elbows. "Don't tell me I've cocked it up again. Do you know – I made a mistake about that Carl Oppenheimer as well?"

"What?"

"Yes. It wasn't Carl Oppenheimer with a 'C', but Karl Oppenheimer with a 'K' I should have taken. I got into a big row about that, I can tell you."

Bernard could hardly believe his ears. "Do you mean to tell me that Carl shouldn't have died, after all?"

"Not *your* Carl, no." The impish man grimaced. "That's why it's taking me so long to get my horns. It's all these funny names I have to deal with."

Bernard felt like strangling him but realised that he would just do another vanishing trick if he tried. "So," he gulped, "does that mean that *your* Karl Oppenheimer is still alive then?"

"Yes," he replied. "He's ninety-nine and very frail. Still, I'll probably get him on my next trip."

"You're mad," said Bernard, still feeling relief that Dorothy wasn't going to be taken from him, after all.

"Let me get this straight," said Diabol, ignoring Bernard's insult. "Am I to understand that you don't know this Dorothy *Blun*kett, then?"

"No. I keep telling you. I only know a Dorothy *Plunkett*."

"Bother, so you've no idea where I can find this Blunkett woman?"

"None in the world. I've never heard of her. Go and bother someone else."

"No need to be rude. You have no idea how difficult my job is."

"And you've no idea what a blow the death of Carl Oppenheimer was to my friend. You can't bring him back from where you've taken him, can you?"

The little man only shrugged again.

"You're a menace, you are," snarled Bernard. "Will you please stop annoying me? I never want to see you again."

Just then he heard a burst of birdsong and realised the little man had done his bidding and disappeared. Bernard was back in the real world, with people passing by and the sounds of distant traffic; everything normal again.

But, now he had another problem: the fact that Carl Oppenheimer needn't have died when he did. But what would be the point of telling Robbie? It would only upset him, and that would be putting it mildly. And, anyway, nothing could bring the professor back. He only hoped he was enjoying the high life down below.

He stayed on the bench for another half an hour, feeling the bitter wind whip round him, but ignoring it as he thought these sombre thoughts. The more he saw of life, the less he understood it. And the mysteries of the occult were well beyond him, even experiencing such things firsthand.

At last, he began walking slowly out of the park, his thoughts back on Dorothy again, relieved that Diabol hadn't come for her, after all. He felt sorry for this Dorothy Blunkett woman, though, whoever she was. But it was an ill wind. At least he knew he had to make every moment count now, lose no time in asking her out, before Diabol came back for her another time.

"Vicar, there's a call for you – says she's your mum." Mrs Harper was standing in the doorway of Bernard's study.

"Oh dear," he said. "Did you tell her I was at home?"

"Yes, why? Don't you want to talk to the woman who suffered to give birth to you?"

Make me feel guilty, why don't you? thought Bernard miserably. But the truth was he *didn't* want to talk to her. Being his mother, he supposed he loved her. But he didn't always like her. The inescapable fact was, she was an interfering, overbearing snob.

"Yes, of course. I do," he said, reluctantly, descending to the hall where the telephone was situated. He expected she was probably calling him about Christmas, under the impression he was going to join the family for the festive season. Well, he would have to put her right about that. Didn't she realise that Christmas was his busiest time in the parish? She could hardly expect him to trek up to Wakefield when he had the most important events in the Christian calendar to supervise. Or could she? Knowing his mother, she probably could.

"Hello, Mum, how are you?" he enquired, trying to drum up some filial affection.

"How do you think, when I don't hear from you from one year's end to the next?" came his mother's querulous reply.

"Didn't you get my flowers last birthday?" he asked.

"Oh, yes. They were half-wilted by the time they arrived, of course," was her ungrateful response. "Anyway, that's by-the-by. I presume you're coming home for Christmas? Caroline, George and the twins are coming, naturally."

Bernard smiled ruefully. Saint Caroline would always do exactly as her mother wanted. She had always been the favourite. Bernard was five years younger than his sister, and they'd never got on.

"Look, Mum..." he began.

"*Mother*, please! 'Mum' is so common."

Bernard sighed. "Sorry, *Mother*. I can't leave my parish at this time of the year, you must understand that. I haven't been here a year yet, and I need to get to know all my parishioners. The best time to do that is at Christmas, when most people come to church."

"I see," said his mother. He could tell she wasn't prepared to accept this excuse, however.

"You must be allowed *some* time off, surely?"

"No, Mum – er, Mother. Not at this time of the year, as I just explained. Tell you what, I'll try and get up for a few days in the New Year. How about that?"

"Your father will be disappointed," she said, obviously trying a bit of emotional blackmail.

"I'm sorry about Dad," he said. Poor Dad, he thought. He was a dear old soul, but well and truly under Mrs Paltoquet's thumb. "But I really can't get away just now. Give him my best love, though."

Bernard hoped the conversation was now over as it was cold in the hall. The leaky radiator gave off hardly any heat and made a clanking sound every few seconds. He would have to get Gilbert in to look at it after Christmas.

"Very well," said his mother, defeated at last. "I'll send your present by the next post. Merry Christmas, Bernard."

"And to you, Mother. Give my regards to Caroline."

He replaced the receiver gently, sighing with relief. That went better than he he'd expected. His mother must be mellowing in her old age.

Now he could think about his *own* Christmas. Mrs Harper had already told him she wouldn't be going anywhere. She had no family to speak of, apart from a niece. Both her parents were dead, and she was an only child. Her niece, Mandy, had just got married and was living in Norfolk, but she had no intention of 'trekking all the way out there', as she put it. That meant she would be at home to serve him his Christmas dinner, which would be wonderful if it was up to the standard of the rest of her cooking. And he could see no reason why it shouldn't be.

Then there was Robbie. Robbie had a mother living somewhere, but apparently, he didn't get on with her, so, hopefully, he would be able to join him for Christmas dinner. He wondered again what Dorothy would be doing. He knew that all he had to do was pick up the telephone and call her. He would think about it.

The carol service was arranged for the last Friday before Christmas itself. It had started to snow again, and Bernard stood at the church door, welcoming his parishioners as they arrived. Everyone looked happy, enjoying the festive season and looking forward to singing their hearts out.

He kept his eyes peeled for Dorothy, but it was well past three o'clock when the service was due to start, and she hadn't appeared. Just as he was about to close the doors, however, she came running through the church gate.

"Oh, thank goodness," she puffed, as he took her hand and led her into the church. "I thought the service would have started by now."

"You're just in time, Dorothy," he smiled. "Can we have a chat afterwards?"

"Yes, I wanted to talk to you too," she replied, smiling back at him. His heart gave a lurch.

"Ah, there's Robbie," she said, as she saw the doctor wave to her from the second pew from the front. "There's an empty seat beside him. Good."

Bernard watched her run down the aisle to join his friend. He felt so jealous, he could have screamed. But he kept the beatific smile firmly fixed on his face and made his way to the lectern.

"Good afternoon, everyone," he said. "It's good to see so many of you here today. Some of your faces are unfamiliar to me, but I hope to rectify that soon. We'll begin with *While Shepherds Watched*, which is number five in your carol sheets. Please stand."

There was a rustle and clatter as people found the words to the familiar carol and stood up. Old Mrs

Wilberforce struck up the creaky organ, and the air was filled with the sound of human voices singing with gusto. Bernard, for the first time, felt like it was really Christmas as he joined in. The snow was falling heavily outside the windows, and all the candles were lit. It was a truly magical scene.

His eyes wandered over to Dorothy, who was singing heartily, sharing Robbie's carol sheet. He tried not to mind this, but he did. He felt like handing her his own carol sheet so that she didn't have to stand quite so close to him.

But the thought of their confidential chat after the service cheered him, and he conducted the rest of the service with enthusiasm, feeling a warm love that encompassed the whole congregation, not just Dorothy Plunkett.

When the church had emptied at the end of the service, Bernard saw that Dorothy and Robbie were waiting for him by the door. His heart sank. Why was Robbie still here? he wondered. He was expecting just Dorothy to remain for their promised chat.

"That was a wonderful service, Bernard," said Dorothy. "I feel all warm and Christmassy now."

"Me too," said Robbie, smiling in agreement. "I think everyone enjoyed it. Thank you, Bernie."

"My pleasure," Bernard replied, collecting the last of the carol sheets into a neat pile. "Are you off to evening surgery now?" he asked, hopefully.

"Not yet, old boy," Robbie replied. "It's only half-past four. Anyway, Dorothy has asked me back to her place for afternoon tea. You're invited too."

This was even worse than he expected. He looked at Dorothy, who was avoiding eye contact with him. So it was a chat not just with him, but Robbie too. Now he wouldn't get the opportunity to ask her out properly and put their relationship on a more romantic footing. Why had he waited?

"Yes, dear," she said to Bernard. "I wanted to talk to *both* of you, so I've prepared a nice tea. There's some homemade cakes too."

"That's nice," said Bernard, glaring at Robbie, who was smiling back at him. The three of them left the church five minutes later and headed towards Dorothy's home. They were soon led into a cosy maisonette where a fire was banked up in the parlour, giving off much welcome heat after their walk through the heavy snow.

Once they had removed their outer garments, the three of them sat down together in front of the fire, with Dorothy in charge of pouring the tea from an ornate silver teapot. Probably a family heirloom, thought Bernard distractedly.

"Help yourself to the cakes, please," she said, as she passed round the cups.

Bernard had found he'd lost his appetite; he didn't care if he ever saw another cake. Robbie, on the other hand, was tucking into a squelchy cream bun with obvious delight. "Hmm," he said, "this is delicious. Did you make them yourself?"

"No, I have to confess I didn't," laughed Dorothy. "I've got a part-time cook-cum-cleaner who does all that. She even made the tea before she left. I told her roughly what time I'd be back, so it's just brewed."

"That's very handy," said Robbie, helping himself to another cake. "Come on Bernie, they'll all be gone at this rate."

Bernard selected a Chelsea bun and started to nibble on it without much enthusiasm.

"Well, boys," said Dorothy, when the tea and cakes had been more or less despatched, "the reason I asked you both here today was to tell you that I'm leaving Wandsworth."

"You're leaving?" uttered Bernard, putting his half-eaten bun back on the plate. "But, why?"

"Yes, why, Dorothy, dear?" echoed Robbie.

"Well, it's partly to do with the situation here – with you two," she explained, "but it's not the main reason." She said this quickly as she saw both men were about to protest. "It's my mother. She hasn't been too well lately, and my father rang me last night to tell me that the doctors have said she might have only a few weeks."

"I'm sorry," said Bernard. "But that's no reason to leave here altogether, is it?"

Dorothy gave him a look he couldn't quite interpret. He only knew it made him feel uncomfortable. Shut up Bernard, he said to himself, realising how insensitive he was being.

"Well, it does, really," she continued. "I need to go back home to look after her. My sister has a family, so it's down to me, as a single woman, to bear the brunt of it. Then, when my mother goes, my father will need looking after, too. He's quite frail, himself. Emphysema, so the doctors say."

Bernard felt like saying that, when they're both dead, you can come back then. But he wisely didn't.

Robbie reached out for her hand. "Oh, Dorothy, dear, I'm so sorry," he said, looking genuinely moved. "Where do your parents live?"

"Exeter," she replied.

"Oh, yes, I believe you mentioned that you came from there," said Robbie, still holding her hand.

Meanwhile, Bernard's heart had sunk even further. Exeter was a long way from London. Not easy for a casual visit. He feared he might never see Dorothy again, and realised he couldn't bear the thought of that. "Are you going soon?" he asked.

"Tomorrow, actually," she said, giving him a sad smile. "It's all happened rather fast. But I wanted to give you your Christmas presents before I go." Saying this, she got up and left the room.

The two friends stared at each other. Neither of them had thought of Christmas presents. It was all too much. Losing their beloved Dorothy, and not even giving her something she could remember them by.

She returned with two gaily wrapped parcels, passing one to each of them. "Now, don't open them until Christmas day," she instructed.

"But we haven't got you anything, Dorothy," said Bernard, turning his parcel over with interest. What could it be? he wondered. He hoped it wasn't something as unromantic as socks.

"Don't be silly," she admonished. "You didn't know I was leaving, did you?"

"But we'll see you again soon, won't we?" asked Bernard, tears starting to prick his eyes.

"Of course, Bernard, dear," she said. "I'll come and see you sometime."

Sometime, thought Bernard. That meant – what? He must try to see her alone before she went. "Can I see you off?" he asked. "Come with you to the station?"

"No, Bernard," she said, firmly. "I'd rather go alone."

He knew when he was beaten. He had to let her go.

"Now," she said cheerfully. "I have a rather superior brandy somewhere. How about we drink a farewell toast to each other?"

Bergen, December 1948

Gunda and Baldur were sitting in the local bar, enjoying the festive atmosphere and drinking their third pint of lager. It was very busy, full of happy crowds, and they sat together, watching them. Baldur had always avoided joining in with crowds, and Gunda was also used to her own company. They were outsiders, but they didn't care. They had each other now.

"I'm looking forward to Christmas," said Gunda, smiling and holding Baldur's hand under the table. "Waking up with you on Christmas morning and everything. It will feel almost magical, like it was when I was a child. Although the toy I'll be unwrapping will be you!" She laughed happily.

Since she had met Baldur, her life had changed considerably. Within two weeks of their meeting, he had moved in with her. She rented a well-furnished apartment in the city centre, and he was enjoying all the home comforts missing so long from his lonely life. Being with him had given her a new lease on life too and had radically improved her looks. She seemed less haggard and the extra weight she had since gained had softened her appearance. Baldur's dark looks had also improved. He was still a 'big brute of a man' but, somehow, he didn't seem quite so menacing now.

But, despite the positive aspects of their burgeoning relationship, it wasn't all plain sailing. Gunda, for the most part, was well pleased with her new lover. But, occasionally, he showed her a side of his nature she didn't entirely approve of or trust. It wasn't that he was cruel to her, but sometimes a frown would appear that seemed to knit his hairy eyebrows together, and he would start picking an argument for no apparent reason. And, once, he had even clenched his fist at her, as if he was about to strike her. She tried not to dwell on these moments, though, as the rest of the time they were perfectly happy together. After all, she reasoned to herself, no relationship is hearts and flowers all the way. And she thought of her late husband. He had been a wonderful man, but he, too, had had his off-days. Life was like that.

Baldur, for his part, liked her well enough, but sometimes couldn't help comparing her to Marianne Dahl, hankering after what he knew he could never have. It gave him no comfort to know he had been the one to irrevocably cut off that route to his happiness by killing her. Was it true that, according to the song, "you always hurt the one you love"? he wondered. He supposed that's what had happened between him and Marianne, except the lyric had been slightly amended in their case to "you always *kill* the one you love".

But he had met Gunda and, although she wasn't anywhere near as pretty as Marianne, he liked her well enough and she obviously liked him too. He had even begun to think he might marry her one day. After all, it was time he settled down, he wasn't getting any younger. And it would give him some status in the neighbourhood, an air of respectability that would help remove him even further from the events of last March.

He still had sleepless nights about the children, but no amount of remorse could bring them back. He would never be free of what he had done, he knew that. Retribution would catch up with him one day, and he was constantly looking over his shoulder at some shadow that only he could see. For now, though, he was safe. There was no more talk about the murder of the farm widow, and virtually nobody mentioned the missing children anymore.

They left the inn as the clock struck midnight, surrounded by other happy customers, many of them the worse for drink. They called 'goodnight' as they passed them, and Gunda put her arm in his as they slowly walked together the few blocks to her apartment.

"I'm glad we found each other," she said, stopping to give him a kiss. She looked at the hulking brute beside her and smiled up into his eyes. "I never thought I'd be happy again but, thanks to you, I am. I don't deserve you, I really don't."

Which was true, thought Baldur wryly, as he gripped her tightly in an urgent embrace. She didn't deserve him at all; she deserved someone much better.

London, December 1948

Christmas day was to prove a less than happy time for Bernard and Robbie following Dorothy's departure to Devon. She had promised to write to them and let them know how things were going, which was something, they supposed.

When it was time for Mrs Harper to serve them their Christmas dinner (Lucy had gone home to her parents in Chichester), both men sat down at the table, looking miserable and barely uttering a word. Bernard's long-suffering housekeeper served it up as cheerfully as she could under the circumstances, even wearing a paper hat from a Christmas cracker she had pulled with the milkman that morning. There were crackers beside the two diners' plates, but neither man had even noticed them. They just lay there looking less and less festive as the meal went on.

Knowing the reason for the pair's depression, she tried her best to chivvy them up, but to no avail. Even her flaming brandy pudding did little to lift their gloom.

"Come on, the pair of you," she said with impatience, as the rich pudding sat uneaten on their plates. "I've 'ad more fun at a funeral. It's supposed to be Christmas!"

Bernard tried a smile, but it wasn't a success. Robbie's was a little more convincing, but not much.

"Sorry, Mrs Aitch," said the doctor, "your food's delicious, as always. It's just that we haven't got much appetite today."

"What a day to lose it," she said, gathering up the plates. "I'm sorry your Miss Plunkett's gone off, but that ain't no reason not to be cheerful on Our Lord's birthday, is it?"

"Isn't it?" asked Bernard. He'd conducted the service that morning like a robot. The congregation must have noticed he wasn't getting into the spirit, but he hadn't cared. He wished them all a merry Christmas as they left, but not one of them had believed he'd meant it.

"Are you going to listen to the King on the wireless?" Mrs Harper asked them.

"Suppose so," said Robbie, switching it on.

Later on, they opened Dorothy's presents together. They were both the same: thick, woolly scarves: red for Bernard, blue for Robbie. Not so bad as socks, but very nearly, thought Bernard miserably.

London, January 1949

As December turned into January, Bernard went about his daily routine on automatic pilot. Robbie, too, had lost all his zest for life, causing several of his patients to ask ironically after *his* health.

The Christmas tree remained in the church hall into the New Year, as Robbie wanted to extend its life until Gilbert returned in the second week of January. "I want to make sure they've been found and been given a Christian burial before it's destroyed," he said.

The weather continued bitterly cold. More snow fell, covering everything in a blanket of white, much to the delight of the neighbourhood children who could be seen dragging toboggans behind them, when not hitting each other with snowballs or building snowmen. Bernard, watching from his study window, saw their happy glowing faces and wished he was a boy again, able to take delight in such innocent pleasures.

But, although he was happy for the children, nothing really helped his mood. Every time Mrs Harper brought him the post, he scanned the envelopes eagerly for a Devon postmark, only to be continually disappointed. He sighed, as he riffled through the post several times to make sure he hadn't missed anything. It didn't occur to him to initiate a letter to Dorothy himself, even though she had furnished him with her address for that very purpose. Robbie, too, looked forward in vain to a letter. He, like Bernard, didn't think about writing to her first. So, all they could do was drown their sorrows and bemoan their lot. Mrs Harper, finally, had had enough of it.

"What's the matter, Vicar?" she asked one morning, after Bernard had searched the post in vain for the umpteenth time. "Are you expecting a special letter or something?" As if she didn't know.

Bernard reddened with embarrassment. "Er, not exactly, Mrs Harper," he said.

"What does that mean?" She put her hands on her ample hips and looked at him quizzically.

"It's sort of, well, complicated."

"Hmm," she muttered, "it must be. Can I 'elp at all? Do you want me to chase Charlie for you? 'E may 'ave some letters buried at the bottom of 'is sack. 'E's not all that thorough, you know. I got a postcard from Ada nearly three months after she sent it to me. 'E'd 'ad it in 'is sack all the time, but 'adn't found it until 'e 'ad to turn it out because someone else complained that they 'adn't received a letter they was expecting."

Bernard perked up slightly at this. Was it possible that there *was* a letter from Dorothy buried in the seemingly 'not all that thorough' Charlie's sack?

"Er, well, maybe you could just check with him for me?" he said. "I mean, it's not that I'm expecting a letter *definitely*, but I think there's a strong possibility that there may be one."

Mrs Harper wasn't in any doubt who he was expecting a letter from. She would have to be deaf, dumb and blind not to know which way the wind was blowing in that quarter. "Right you are," she said. "Leave it to me."

She was about to leave the study when she remembered. "Oh, Gilbert's back, by the way. I met Marjorie in Woolworths yesterday. She said they'd 'ad a nice time, although Gilbert was worried about 'is mother 'aving to look after his aunt. She's very 'ard work, apparently. Lost 'er marbles, so she said. It's a shame when they get like that, ain't it?"

"Yes, it is," said Bernard. "Did she say anything about what Gilbert was going to tell his mother, about what Robbie wanted him to do?"

"Oh, you mean about the murdered children?" said Mrs Harper.

"Oh, so you know all about it, do you?"

"'Course. Gilbert told me. 'E said you two were trying to find out what 'appened to them and to find out who did it, like."

"I see, Mrs Aitch. Nothing gets past you, does it? Anyway, did she say he had anything to report?"

"All Marge said was, 'e was going to see the Doc today, and that 'e 'ad some good news."

"Really?"

"Yes, that's what she said. Now I'd best get on."

"Of course, Mrs Aitch. Thanks."

As she left the room, she was pleased to see he had a smile on his face at last.

∾

Bernard rushed down the stairs to the telephone and asked the operator to put him straight through to Robbie. As predicted, the news as relayed by Mrs Harper was received with delight by his friend.

"Get him round to the vicarage, Bernie," he said. "I'll be over as soon as morning surgery's finished. Can you see if he can get there then?"

"I'll do my best," said Bernard, "although he might be working, of course."

"Oh, well, as soon as possible, then," said Robbie, a slight irritation creeping into his voice. "After all, the fate of these poor children is slightly more important than a blocked drain or a leaky radiator."

Bernard thought that it probably wouldn't feel that way to someone with a blocked drain or a leaky radiator, but wisely refrained from pointing this out.

"Okay, Robbie. Come over when you're free, anyway. We'll wait for him together. Tell Mrs Carter you're having your dinner with me today."

"Righto," said Robbie, slamming down the receiver.

Gilbert arrived shortly after two o'clock. He was wearing a very uncustomary smile, as he was shown into the study by Mrs Harper.

"Hello, Gilbert," Bernard greeted him. "Did you have a good holiday?"

"Yes, thank you. But my mum's having a lot of trouble with Auntie Liv. She needs to be in a home, but she won't hear of it."

"Very sad," said Bernard, offering Gilbert a chair.

Once he was settled, Robbie asked him the obvious question. "Have the bodies been found, Gilbert?"

Gilbert smiled again. It was quite alarming to watch his usually doleful features transform into an almost rictus grin. "They have," he declared. "And you've got my mum to thank for that."

"How come?" asked Robbie.

"She's well in with one of the Bergen policemen," Gilbert explained. "In fact, he wants to marry her, but she won't while she's got to look after my Auntie. Anyway, this policeman is close with the Politimester himself, so it was easy to get him to order another search of the woods around the Dahl farm."

"Well done, your mother," said Robbie, happily. "I think this calls for a toast. Let's all raise our glasses to Mrs Hardcastle."

"I would like to send a thank you gift to your mother," said Robbie a few minutes later, getting up to replenish the glasses.

"There's no need," said Gilbert, holding out his glass, eagerly.

"But I'd like to," Robbie replied. "She has saved those little children's souls. They can rest in peace now. Your mother deserves a medal, never mind a box of chocolates. Anyway, give me her address, please."

"Of course." Gilbert wrote it down on the back of an envelope he took from his pocket and handed it to him. "The discovery of the bodies caused quite a stir," he continued. "The police are basking in glory now."

"But they were totally incompetent!" said Robbie. "They hardly lifted a finger to find those poor mites."

"I know," nodded Gilbert. "But what can you do? Most people don't really believe in ghosts and stuff like that, do they?"

"I don't care for myself," said Robbie, "but your mother deserves some recognition for her help, at least."

"You would hope so, wouldn't you?" agreed Gilbert.

"Never mind, it's still the children that are most important in all this. Did your mother get anywhere with the police about looking for this Baldur bloke?"

Gilbert's expression was back to normal now. "'Fraid not," he said dourly. "They said it was virtually impossible to start a search for a man called Baldur, given that there were so many of them knocking about. They used the excuse that the man could be anywhere by now, and they wouldn't know where to start looking. Then they said they didn't have enough resources to mount a search, anyway."

Robbie nodded. "Hmm. I suppose I can see their point. It's like asking the police in this country to start looking for someone called John."

Gilbert finished his second whisky and placed the glass on the table. "Yes, that's about the size of it. They might do a house-to-house in Bergen but he's probably not even there now. If only they had a surname to go on."

"If only," echoed Robbie.

Bergen, January 1949

Gunda was reading the morning paper as Baldur entered the kitchen in search of his breakfast. He always started with a large one as his work as a lumberjack was physically demanding and he was usually starving by mid-morning. So there was always a satisfyingly filling repast awaiting him in the morning, as well as a stack of sandwiches to take with him. She knew how to look after her man.

"Have you seen this, Baldur darling?" she greeted him, showing him the paper's headline. "They've found those poor kiddies' bodies – you know, whose mother was killed on her farm last year. You remember?" She put the paper down to pour him a large mug of tea.

"What bodies?" he asked, already on high alert. It couldn't be, could it? The children he killed in cold blood last year? Found after all this time? Still, he couldn't possibly be connected with them now, he reassured himself. He slurped his tea, as Gunda relayed the information contained in the newspaper.

"It says here that their bodies were found in some woods, on the outskirts of Bergen. They haven't been formally identified yet, but the police are definitely linking them with the murder of Marianne Dahl," explained Gunda, totally unaware of the look on her paramour's face. "For one thing, they were found close to the Dahl farm. They're always so cautious in telling the news, aren't they? It's obvious it's those poor Dahl children the police have found."

"They must have been buried deep," said Baldur, trying desperately not to look shifty, "for them not to have been discovered sooner."

"They don't say they were buried at all," said Gunda, puzzled, "just that the bodies have been found. Why should you think they'd been buried?"

He realised at once he'd made a blunder. Had he given himself away? But he regained his composure quickly. "Well, it stands to reason, doesn't it?" he said in a distinctly belligerent tone. "Otherwise, why wouldn't they have been found sooner?"

"Suppose so," agreed Gunda, going back to her paper. "But those woods near the Dahl farm aren't exactly well used, are they? Not that many people go there, so they could have lain unnoticed for ages. It says here that it was only through a tip-off – they don't say from who – that they were able to trace the bodies at all. But it was probably easier, because a lot of the trees had been cut down."

Baldur was naturally aware of this, considering he'd help to cut down those trees himself. He couldn't even quite remember where he'd buried the children, himself, so it was a wonder that the incompetent Bergen police had managed to unearth them at last. But why should he worry? Finding the bodies wasn't going to yield any clue to their murderer. He was in the clear.

Finishing his breakfast, he took up his sandwich pack and put it in his knapsack. "See you later, then, love," he said, kissing the top of her head. "You working today?"

"Yes. I've got Mrs Hardcastle's today. It's the first time I've been there since Christmas, so it'll probably need doing. She's got her hands full with that poor sister of hers."

"Oh, the nutty one, you mean?"

Gunda bridled. "Don't call her that," she said crossly. "She can't help being like that, poor thing. You'll be old one day."

"And so will you, my pet," he grinned and kissed her again. "See you later," he said.

London, January 1949

Robbie was back to his old ebullient, friendly and happy self now that he had been successful in his quest to save the children. Bernard was almost as glad, especially for his friend. It had been quite a saga, but now all his efforts had been vindicated. There was just one more thing Robbie had to do.

"So, you just need a few hours to yourself in the hall, right?" asked Bernard, the day after Gilbert had brought the glad tidings.

"Yes, old boy, just to make sure the children have really gone."

"Okay. Here's the key. You'll be undisturbed."

Robbie let himself into the hall, which was bare now except for the Christmas tree. Pine needles still littered the floor beneath it and, without the baubles and tinsel, it looked very sorry for itself. He wondered if it would revive if they planted it in the churchyard, rather than just throw it away. He somehow didn't like the idea of getting rid of it altogether. If it hadn't been for the tree, the children wouldn't have been found, so it deserved preserving, in his opinion.

He sat down in front of it and took out a flask of tea from his inside coat pocket which Lucy had thoughtfully prepared for him. After about an hour, he began to think that the children had really gone at last. He had finished the last of the tea, which he had spiced up with whisky from his hip flask, as usual. He was feeling contented and mellow and was inwardly congratulating himself on his success.

However, just as he was about to leave the hall, convinced his job was done, he heard a little voice saying something unintelligible. He looked back at the tree and saw, to his dismay, the two little Norwegian children standing underneath it. What could they want now? he wondered. They'd had their Christian burial, hadn't they?

He signalled for the little boy to slow down as he fumbled in his pockets for a piece of paper and a pen. He pulled out his new diary and turned to the blank pages at the back. He managed to find a stub of pencil; that would have to do. He cursed himself for not having the foresight to prepare himself properly, but he had been so sure the children wouldn't reappear.

So, once again, he struggled to write down what the boy was saying. He was at least sure that he could get a reliable translation from Gilbert, that was one good thing. When the boy had finished speaking, he closed his diary and replaced both it and the pencil back in his overcoat pocket.

The children had vanished in the time it took him to gather up his belongings, ready to leave. He wished he could answer them, to reassure them that he was doing everything he could to help. They had realised he didn't understand their language, of course, but did they at least have some idea that he was getting help on their behalf? He hoped so.

Bernard was surprised to learn that the children had not left the tree, after all. "But we can't leave it there much longer," he told Robbie. "There's nothing left of it, as it is. Mrs Aitch wants to do a thorough clean of the hall and she keeps asking me to get the tree removed. The pine needles are driving her nuts – so she says."

"Well you'll just have to tell her she'll have to wait a bit longer, now," said Robbie irritably.

"All right, I'll make sure she's kept sweet. But let's hope this is all resolved soon. There's a sixtieth birthday party booked for Wednesday next week. It'll have to be gone by then."

"Bernie, I've been thinking," said Robbie, "why don't we plant it in the churchyard, then it can stay there as long as it likes."

Bernard thought for a moment. "We could, I suppose, although it's hardly very picturesque." He gave a hollow laugh. "People will wonder why it's there, looking practically dead as it does."

"Who cares what they think? The children's fate is much more important, surely?"

Bernard agreed, if somewhat reluctantly. "All right," he said. "We'll leave it where it is for now, but if, by Wednesday, the children haven't gone, we'll do as you say and plant it in the churchyard."

"That's the ticket," said Robbie, relieved. "Now, where's that Gilbert Hardcastle? I've got another translation job for him."

Bergen, January 1949

Gunda let herself into Berthina Hardcastle's third floor Bergen apartment at nine o'clock, stamping on the wire matting to knock the snow off her boots. She knew she would need to spend at least three hours getting the place spick and span as she hadn't been there since three days before Christmas. She removed her outer garments and hung them on the hall peg, calling out to her employer as she did so.

"Hello, Mrs Hardcastle, it's Gunda. Happy New Year!"

Berthina came out of her sister's bedroom looking grey-faced. There were dark rings under her eyes, as if she hadn't slept for days. "And to you, dear," she said.

"Are you all right, Mrs Hardcastle?" Gunda asked her. "You look very tired. Did you have a good Christmas with your son and daughter-in-law? How's your sister?"

"Thank you, Gunda, it was good to see my son again," she replied, "but Liv is being extra difficult at the moment. She went out in the middle of the night again last night, just in her nightdress. When the policeman brought her back, she said she'd been going shopping – said she'd realised she hadn't any carrots. I don't mind telling you, it's not easy looking after someone in my sister's condition. The doctor's with her now. I know he'll tell me to put her in a home. Again!"

"Come into the kitchen," said Gunda, taking charge. "I'll make a cup of tea. Come and sit down, you look worn out."

"You're very kind," said Berthina, and allowed her to lead her into the kitchen. Once the tea was brewed, Gunda broached the subject again.

"Don't you think it would be best for everybody if you considered a home for her? They're not all such bad places. I'm sure the doctor could recommend one."

Berthina sipped her tea, and Gunda could see her hands were shaking. "I really don't want to discuss it, if you don't mind," she said, tears standing in her eyes.

"But it's just not right you should have to shoulder all the responsibility for her at your time of life," she persisted.

"Anyway, Gunda," said Berthina, deliberately ignoring what she had said. "How was *your* Christmas?"

"Oh, quiet, you know ... just me and Baldur. But we enjoyed it."

Something clicked in the back of Berthina's mind when Gunda mentioned his name. Baldur. Where had she heard that recently? "Did you get any nice presents?" she asked, racking her brains trying to remember where she had heard it mentioned before.

"Baldur bought me a box of lace hankies," she answered, looking proud. "They're beautiful. So delicate – hand finished, with my initial on them and everything. They must have cost him a lot of krone."

"Yes, I'm sure," said Berthina. "I'm glad he's looking after you." She paused. Suddenly she remembered where she had heard the name –her son had mentioned it in connection with the Dahl murder.

Gilbert hadn't really explained how he knew the children were dead. After all, no one had seen them all these months, but they could have been abducted. But he had been convinced and had convinced her to ask her policeman friend to bring pressure to bear, and it had led to their bodies being discovered at last. It was closure for the grandparents, she had thought, although they would never really be able to rest until their murderer had been caught. The Heglunds now knew that some evil bastard had killed not only their daughter, but their little grandchildren as well. She just couldn't imagine what they were going through.

She cleared her throat. "Is – is your husband kind to you *always*, Gunda?" she asked tentatively. It was silly to even suspect him. Baldur was a common enough name.

"What do you mean?" Gunda turned back from the sink to look at her employer. There was a wary look on her face.

"Well, I mean, is he ever moody? Angry with you sometimes, that sort of thing?"

"Why on earth do you ask that?" Gunda continued with the washing up, splashing water over the draining board and slopping soap onto the floor.

"Oh, no particular reason," Berthina replied, more worried now. It was clear she had touched a nerve, judging by the mess she was making of the washing up. She carried on, however. "You sometimes hear of husbands beating their wives. There are a lot of disillusioned men about since the war; some of them turn violent. I've heard stories and read about them in the paper."

"Well, my Baldur isn't one of them," Gunda lied. The truth was, however, he was getting more unpredictable lately. He seemed to pick rows at every opportunity and had grabbed her roughly several times. He had even hit her once, but at least the bruising had more or less faded now.

Just then, the doctor knocked on the kitchen door and entered the room. "Might I have a word with you, Mrs Hardcastle?" he asked.

"Of course, Doctor. Please sit down. Would you like some tea? I think there's still some left in the pot."

"That would be very kind – thank you." He sat down at the table, while Gunda excused herself, saying "she must get on".

"How is she, Doctor?" asked Berthina, pouring his tea.

"She seems very agitated today," he replied, spooning sugar into his cup. "She keeps talking about an article in the newspaper she's been reading. Did you give her today's paper, Mrs Hardcastle? You really shouldn't, you know. Bad news upsets her too much."

"Oh dear," sighed Berthina. "She asked me for it, and I didn't like to refuse her, it seemed such a little thing to ask. I know she keeps on about those poor children whose bodies have at last been found."

"Yes, but there's something else about that," continued the doctor.

"Oh?"

"It seems that she imagines that she saw the murderer on the night it happened."

"Oh, but that's impossible!" exclaimed Berthina, "How could she?"

"Well, she obviously didn't, but she is very insistent."

"Look, I'll try and calm her down, Doctor, and I'll remove the paper. Give her a nice novel or something, instead. I've got to return her library book today, anyway."

"That would be good." The doctor looked as if he was about to say something else.

"What is it?" she asked.

"Well, it's silly, I know, but is there any chance that she could be speaking the truth? About being there and witnessing the murders?"

"Of course not," said Berthina dismissively. "The very idea!"

"Yes, it does seem crazy," he ventured, "but she has been known to go wandering off on her own at night, hasn't she? I mean, she did so last night, you told me."

"Well, yes, but I don't think she ever got as far as the forest. It's at least five kilometres from here."

"I think you underestimate her," smiled the doctor. "Didn't you say the police have brought her from further away than that?"

"Once, yes," Berthina remembered. "But, really, I'm sure she would have told me at the time if she'd witnessed any murders."

"Not necessarily," said the doctor. "Her memory is not what it was. She can remember things from her early childhood with crystal clarity, but things that happened yesterday, for example, she will have no memory of at all. If she did see the murders, she could have forgotten by the time she was brought home."

"Right," said Berthina slowly. "So, why do you think she would remember it now – if what you say is true?"

"It's difficult to explain," said the doctor, "but probably the newspaper article triggered it. She saw the pictures of the little children, and she was crying, saying she saw the man do it."

"So, if she's speaking the truth, she's a material witness then?"

"No. Not at all. Her mental condition would preclude her being called upon to give evidence in court. What she said would be viewed as completely unreliable."

"Oh, I see. Poor Liv. I'd better go and see her right away."

"She's all right for the moment, I gave her a mild sedative. When she wakes up, she may well have forgotten all about it again. See how she goes. Now, I'd better be going, I've got quite a few patients to see – this current flu epidemic is keeping me busy, I can tell you."

After he'd gone, Berthina sat for a while in the kitchen mulling over what the doctor had told her. Was it remotely possible that her sister had witnessed the murder of these children? She didn't really believe it but couldn't quite dismiss it from her mind. But one thing she was resolved to do, and that was lock the front door at night from now on. She couldn't have her sister keep wandering about on her own at night. If she had seen the murders, and the murderer had seen her – well! She went quite cold thinking about it.

London, January 1949

It was just after ten o'clock in the evening when Gilbert Hardcastle turned up at the vicarage. Robbie had left a message with Marjorie, asking him to come over as soon as he could, as he had another translation job for him. Both Robbie and Bernard were on tenterhooks as Gilbert read Robbie's valiant attempt at Norwegian writing. What, both men wondered, did the children have to say now?

"Well, Gilbert?" asked Robbie eagerly. "What do they say?"

"Er, it's a bit unclear, but I think I can get the main gist, anyway."

"Go on, man," urged Robbie. "Just tell us."

"All right, I'm going to." Gilbert gave him a scowl as he adjusted his spectacles. "This time the children say that, although they're now safely buried, they still can't rest because their killer hasn't been caught. They say they don't mind for themselves, but they want to avenge their mother's death."

"I see," said Robbie, "I thought it might be something like that. Is that all?"

"More or less."

"So, what happens now?" asked Bernard. "How on earth can we help find the murderer? We only know his first name."

"I could ask the children for a description of him, if you like," ventured Gilbert.

"But how?" asked Robbie. "I'm the only one who can see and hear them. You're not psychic, are you?"

Bernard interrupted again. "Don't be silly, he doesn't have to be. You just write down what Robbie needs to ask them, Gilbert."

Robbie rubbed his chin thoughtfully. "Oh, yes, I see what you mean. But I'll need a lesson in how to pronounce it."

"It's quite easy," said Gilbert. "Now, give me your diary again and I'll write down what you want to ask them."

"Ask if they know the man's full name and for a full description," instructed Robbie. "That should get us somewhere, at least."

The next day, Robbie was in possession of little Halle's description of the murderer, courtesy of Gilbert's translation skills. "So, now we know he's tall with big shoulders, dark hair, a bloated face and slobbery lips," he said triumphantly. "That narrows it down, Bernie, don't you think?"

Bernard was thoughtful. "Yes, it does, but the clincher is the snake tattoo on his arm."

"Of course, I was forgetting!"

"Although we don't know which arm, of course…"

"Don't quibble, old boy. This will be enough to hang the blighter, for sure."

"Well, the police will have to find him first. It's a pity the boy didn't know the man's last name." Bernard's note of caution was getting on Robbie's nerves.

"I know, Bernie, it's a shame. But, you'll see," he said, "Once Gilbert's phones his mother with the description, the police will have to pull their finger out and find him."

Bernard was about to say something else, but Robbie stopped him. "Humour me, old boy. The man will still be in Bergen, I bet, thinking he's safe. After all, he doesn't know that the ghosts of his victims are communicating with a psychic doctor in London, now, does he?"

The vicar of St Stephen's had to admit that Robbie had a point and smiled.

Bergen, January 1949

Gunda had finished cleaning Mrs Hardcastle's apartment at mid-day as usual. She was eager to get going, as she and Baldur were going to the cinema that afternoon. A rare treat.

Berthina's sister was having one of her more lucid days and was sitting in the living room by the fire, wrapped in an eiderdown. Gunda had a lot of time for Liv; she was a gentle soul, with a world of misery reflected in the large pool of her pale blue eyes. She could understand why Berthina didn't want to put her in a home. It would break both their hearts.

She was in the kitchen, putting away the breakfast dishes, as Berthina entered. "Have you finished, dear?" she asked her.

"Yes, Mrs Hardcastle. I've given the hall floor a thorough polishing like you asked. It's as shiny as a new pin now. But be careful you or your sister don't slip on it."

"Yes, thank you, Gunda. I'll make sure. Here's your wages for the month and a little extra as a post-Christmas bonus."

She handed her sixteen krone, which Gunda pocketed gratefully. They would be able to afford the best seats today, she thought, as well as some sweets and maybe an ice cream. They were going to see a Sonja Henie film, and she was really looking forward to it. She loved the blonde ice skating star and wasn't surprised that she had been snapped up by Hollywood.

"I hope you don't mind," she said, "I've asked Baldur to pick me up from here as the cinema's just around the corner."

"Of course I don't mind," said Berthina, "I'd like to meet him anyway. And, as Liv's up today, maybe she could meet him too?"

"Yes, why not?" smiled Gunda. She was proud to be seen with Baldur who, these days, had developed a better dress sense and was shaving more often than he used to. She could take him anywhere now. He was a big, imposing man, and she was glad when women turned to look at him. He wasn't very handsome, it was true, but he had a full head of black hair and looked quite dashing when he made the effort.

The doorbell rang and Gunda ran to answer it. Baldur stood there, looking slightly uncomfortable in his best suit. She could see the stiff shirt collar was chafing his neck, but he looked very well. She wasn't ashamed to introduce him to anybody.

"Come in, darling," she said. "Mrs Hardcastle wants to meet you."

Baldur wasn't enthusiastic. "We'll be late for the big picture," he protested. "Besides, my boots are covered in snow. You don't want me to spoil this nice, polished floor, do you?"

Just then, Berthina came to the door. "Just take them off, Mr – er?"

"Hanssen," he told her.

"Very nice to meet you, Mr Hanssen," she said, shaking his hand. She noticed it was a big, workman's

273

hand, layers of dirt thick inside the nails. "Come and meet my sister," she said, leading him to the living room.

"If you don't mind, we really ought to be going," said Baldur, looking anxiously at Gunda for support. "We'll miss the start of the film otherwise."

"Nonsense," said Berthina. "It will only take a minute. Liv doesn't get out much these days and doesn't meet many people."

Baldur smiled uneasily. "Sure," he replied gruffly, obviously resigned to be shown off.

Berthina opened the living room door and Liv looked up from the novel she was reading. Her eyes travelled over to Baldur, looming in the doorway. She pulled the eiderdown close around her and screamed.

London, February 1949

The cold January turned into an even colder February, as Bernard and Robbie went about their daily routines, waiting impatiently for news from Bergen. The Christmas tree had been planted in the churchyard by Gilbert, at Robbie's request. Mrs Harper had been more pleased than anyone that the tree had been removed from the hall, as she was able now to gather up all the pine needles, once and for all.

But it wasn't only news from Bergen that Bernard and Robbie eagerly awaited. They were still expecting a letter from much nearer home. Dorothy had promised to write, but so far, she hadn't put pen to paper or, if she had, it hadn't found its way from Exeter to the London Borough of Wandsworth. Mrs Harper had been as good as her word and interrogated Charlie the postman thoroughly, even insisting he empty his sack in front of her, but no letter was hidden in its depths.

So, life dragged on for Bernard and Robbie until the third week of February, when Gilbert arrived at the vicarage with a smile on his face. They were both in the study, as it was nine o'clock in the evening, and Robbie's visits were more or less nightly now. It was Robbie who jumped up and pounced on him first as he came through the door. "Well, Gilbert? What's the news, old boy?"

The plumber continued to smile. "Well, it's quite interesting actually," he told them. "Can I sit down? My feet are killing me."

"Of course," said Bernard. "Fetch Gilbert a drink, Robbie."

Gilbert sat down next to the fire and removed his snow-sodden gloves. "It's bitter out," he observed.

"Come on," urged Robbie impatiently, as he handed him a glass of whisky. "What's the news?"

"Well, here's my mum's letter," said Gilbert, taking it out of his pocket. "It's in Norwegian, so I'll read it to you, shall I?"

Robbie tutted impatiently. "Of course, man. Get on with it."

Gilbert cleared his throat as he slowly unfolded the pages and began to read. "My dear Gilbert," he began, then stopped. "I won't read it all, just the bits that will interest you."

"Yes, yes. Carry on." Robbie was having difficulty containing his impatience.

Gilbert cleared his throat again. "She thanks me for the description of Baldur, and then says: 'I think my cleaner, Gunda, may be living with him, as we speak. His name is Baldur Hanssen, and your description fits him to a tee. I don't know about the snake tattoo though – I'm going to ask Gunda if he has one when I get the chance. I should have asked her already, but I don't know how to without giving her cause for suspicion. I don't want to alarm her, either. If she thinks she's living with a killer, she may give the game away and he'll just run off before he can be caught. Alternatively, he might try to harm her if he thinks she'll tell the police. It's a terribly difficult situation'."

Gilbert paused and looked at the two other men. Bernard and Robbie were practically falling over themselves in excitement.

"Yes, it's good news, isn't it?" smiled Gilbert. "But wait, there's more. She goes on to say: 'It is possible that Aunt Liv may have witnessed the murder of the children. You may remember I've mentioned before how she sometimes goes out in the middle of the night and walks for miles until a kind policeman brings her home. So it is possible she could have seen those poor children being killed, although I doubt it. However, the funny thing is, when Baldur called for Gunda last week, I introduced him to Liv and she screamed. She said he was the murderer – not in front of Gunda – but after they had left. I made an excuse to them, that she wasn't well – they knew she was suffering from dementia anyway, so I don't think they thought too much about it. But I had a terrible time with her when they had gone. She kept crying and screaming, so I had to call the doctor. He sedated her, so that was all right. The next day she didn't remember anything about it, so I couldn't go to the police. Not that her evidence would be admissible, of course, even if she did remember. I'll write again as soon as I have any more news'."

Robbie was the first to speak as Gilbert folded up his mother's letter and put it in his pocket. "Did I hear you correctly? Did your mother say that your aunt actually *witnessed* the murder?"

"That's what she says, yes," replied Gilbert. "You can get an independent translation if you like," he added, offering the letter to the doctor.

"Nay, man, no need for that. But this becomes more and more bizarre. So many coincidences!"

"Coincidence or not," put in Bernard, "it would seem that we have a positive identification of the actual killer at last: Gilbert's mother's cleaner's husband."

Robbie stared at Bernard. "By Jove, you're right! We just need to find out whether he's got a snake tattoo on his arm, then we've got him."

Gilbert smiled, proud to be the bearer of such positive news. He hadn't smiled so much in years.

After Gilbert had left, still smiling, Robbie sat on with Bernard for a while, discussing the possibilities open to them. It seemed that this Baldur Hanssen was the villain of the piece, according to Gilbert's mother, at least. The only trouble was, there seemed to be no way of proving it, as the only witnesses were two ghosts and a woman with dementia.

Bergen, March 1949

Gunda arrived at Berthina Hardcastle's apartment on Monday morning at nine o'clock as usual and proceeded to make a pot of tea before starting work. Berthina was sitting at the kitchen table making out a shopping list, as her cleaner bustled about with kettle and cups.

When the tea was poured, and the usual pleasantries out of the way, the older woman coughed nervously and stirred more sugar into her cup than was good for her.

"I thought you only took two spoonfuls," observed Gunda, smiling. "You've put at least four in there."

"Oops!" said Berthina. "I wasn't thinking." She tried to dredge some of the sweetness out, making a sugary mess in her saucer.

"Shall I start with the living room, or is your sister in there today?"

"No, she's still in bed. So, yes, please start in the living room." There was a brief silence before Berthina spoke again. "How's your – er – husband these days? Has he plenty of work?"

"He's – fine," came the hesitant reply.

Berthina noticed a wary look come into her cleaner's eyes. "But he's been laid off since last week and getting a bit bored. He hopes to get back to work next month, though, all being well."

"Er, I suppose that makes him annoyed – having nothing to do." Berthina said this as a statement, rather than a question.

Gunda shrugged. "Sometimes, I suppose."

"Gunda, please tell me to mind my own business, if you like," she said, "but has he – has he ever laid a finger on you?"

She bridled at once. "How dare you! What gives you the right to suggest such a thing? You keep making these insinuations, and I don't know why. I thought you were happy for me that I'd got a boyfriend."

Some boyfriend, thought Berthina. "Of course I'm happy for you, dear. It's just that, well, having met him, he seems the type that could get violent, that's all. He's a big man and if he ever hit you, he'd hurt you badly, I should think."

Suddenly Gunda burst into tears. "But why should you think that he'd hit me? I just don't know how you knew, that's all," she spluttered, fishing for her hanky in her apron pocket.

Berthina rushed around the table to put her arm around her. "Oh, I'm so sorry," she said. "I never meant to upset you. So – he *has* hit you, then?"

Gunda mopped at her eyes and tried to pull herself together. "Once or twice – yes," she confessed. "But only because he gets frustrated with having no work."

"That's no excuse to take it out on you."

"No, I know it isn't." Gunda blew her nose. "Sometimes he seems to get angry over nothing. Like he wants to pick a fight."

Berthina could see her cleaner was ready to open up to her at last. But it was a long way from suggesting that Baldur was the murderer of the Dahl family. A very long way. How was she going to find out about that tattoo? Then Gunda broached the subject herself.

"To tell you the truth, Mrs Hardcastle, I'm worried about him. I've never said this to anyone, but I'm not sure I really trust him. I mean, I don't really know what he's capable of."

"What do you mean, exactly?"

"Well," Gunda put her hanky away and sipped at her fast-cooling tea. "It's to do with that awful Dahl massacre. I was reading the newspaper, and I mentioned to him that the bodies of those poor farm children had been found. I thought he'd be pleased to hear it, like I was."

"Yes?" Berthina poured her some more tea.

"Well, instead of being pleased, he seemed to get upset and – well, that's all, really." She paused.

Berthina didn't say anything, but just waited. She felt sure Gunda was going to tell her more. She mustn't break the spell now.

"He – he didn't hit me then, if that's what you're thinking," Gunda said at last. "But what he said worried me more than if he'd just hit me. I still can't quite get it out of my head."

"Well – what did he say?"

"Oh, nothing much. Just that the children must have been buried very deep for the police to have taken so long in finding them."

"Why did that bother you?" Berthina was disappointed. It seemed like a very innocuous, not to say reasonable, thing to say in the circumstances.

"It's just that I'd told him that the children's bodies had been *found* in the wood – not that they had been *buried*."

"Oh, yes, I see," said Berthina slowly. "But I suppose it was a logical assumption to make, don't you think?"

"I suppose so," said Gunda grudgingly. "But there was something in his eyes that worried me. I can't really explain it."

Berthina began to think her task wasn't going to be so difficult after all. She jumped right in. "Gunda, does Baldur have a tattoo on his arm?"

Gunda stared at her. "Er – a tattoo?"

"Yes – of a snake."

"A snake?" Gunda looked thoughtful. "Yes, he's got a tattoo – on his left arm. But it's of a dragon, not a snake."

London, March 1949

It had been three months since Dorothy had returned home to Exeter, and Bernard had begun to think he would never hear from her again. Then, one cold, windy March morning, Mrs Harper arrived in his study with the post, and she was smiling.

"'Ere's the post, Vicar," she said, putting it down on the desk. "And your prayers 'ave been answered at last."

"What do you mean, Mrs Aitch?"

"There's one with an Exeter postmark. Now who do we know in that part of the world?" Her eyes were twinkling mischievously.

Bernard's heart gave a leap. "Give it to me, please, Mrs Aitch," he said eagerly, trying to snatch it from her grasp. "You know full well it's from Dorothy Plunkett."

"Really?" she said in mock surprise. "Well, who'd 'ave thought it?"

Bernard opened the letter as soon as Mrs Harper had gone about her business. The reason for Dorothy's communication soon became clear as he read. Her mother had died, and she was now having to console and look after her father. He sighed. There seemed very little chance she would be visiting him soon. Her letter concluded:

> *I know we didn't part on very good terms, Bernard, dear. You made your feelings clear to me then and I still respect them, but I would*

love to hear all the news from Wandsworth sometime. I miss you.

Your loving friend,

Dorothy

He had tears in his eyes as he finished reading her letter. The main reason she had written now was to tell him about her mother's death, of course, but she had touched on their own parting. He would write to her at once, offering his condolences. He would also try to hint that she had been wrong about his true feelings for her, even though he would find it hard to find the right words. At least, it would be easier to express himself in writing than face to face. All would be well between them yet.

As he rummaged around in his desk drawer for some writing paper, he heard the front door bell ring. A few seconds later, Robbie was in the room, prancing around in delight.

"I've had a letter from Dorothy, Bernie," he cried, flourishing it at him.

"Really?" he replied. "Well, so have I. And I don't know why you're smiling, Robbie. After all, her mother's just died."

Robbie was sombre at once and sat down. "Sorry, Bernie. How insensitive you must think me. I only meant I was happy to hear from her at last."

"Yes, me too," smiled Bernard. "What does she say in yours?"

They swopped letters. Bernard skipped the sad news about her mother, eager to see any sign of the affection she had shown him in his own letter. He read her closing words:

I shall continue to stay here with father for as long as he needs me, of course, but I want to remain in touch with you and would welcome your news.

Love, Dorothy

Bernard was secretly pleased. Her letter to Robbie was warm and friendly enough, but she hadn't gone into her own feelings like she had with him. And she'd signed herself, 'love, Dorothy', which was much more casual than 'you're loving friend'. On the whole, Bernard was well satisfied.

Bergen, March 1949

Baldur Hanssen sat in the local inn, sipping his lager and staring morosely into space. Having no work irked him and he felt like a caged tiger, sitting around all day waiting for he knew not what. Added to this, Gunda was becoming more and more distant with him. She was behaving towards him like Marianne had done, and this was adding to his misery. Well, he thought grimly, he hadn't stood any nonsense from Marianne, and he wasn't going to stand any from her, either.

Gunda had been fond of him at first, he was sure. He couldn't understand why things had changed, although he had a sneaking feeling it was when they'd discussed the discovery of the Dahl children's bodies. He'd made a big mistake, saying they had been 'buried', and had regretted it ever since. Still, it had been a reasonable assumption, and he'd thought he'd convinced her. After all, what else would you do with a couple of dead bodies in a wood? Hang them from a tree for anyone to find?

But he knew the seed of suspicion had been sown, and she had grown more and more wary of him as the days passed. It had become a vicious circle. The warier she became, the more cause he had to be angry and hit her.

He sighed and took a long draught of his lager. He had to make it last. He couldn't afford a second pint these days.

What was he going to do about Gunda? He had even asked her to marry him but, when once she would have accepted without hesitation, she had more or less recoiled at the suggestion. She was sleeping on the very edge of their double bed now, too. He still wanted her, but he drew the line at taking her by force. There was no love in that.

And now there was something else to worry about. That morning, she had intimated that she would like him to leave. It was her house, so she had every right to tell him to go. But where was he to go? Back to living in one room until he found someone else? The prospect didn't thrill him. Besides, he was comfortable where he was. He didn't want to go anywhere else. He would have to drum this fact into her stupid head. If she didn't like it, there were ways of making her like it.

Then there was the very real fear that she thought he might be a murderer. Yes, since that day when he'd blundered over the Dahl children's discovery, the thought had been at the back of his mind all the time. What if she went to the police?

Whatever happened, he would have to stop her doing that.

Exeter, March 1949

Dorothy Plunkett sighed as she looked out of the window at the early spring daffodils and the postman trotting up the path. Was this all there was to be from now on? she wondered. Her life here in Exeter wasn't exactly one long social whirl. Not that she would have had the heart, even if it was. Burying her mother had ripped the heart out of her.

She remembered her cloistered childhood. Her mother had always been there for her and her sister; they had wanted for nothing. Her father had always been a more shadowy figure when she was growing up, but she recalled how pleased she and Emily were when he read them a bedtime story or took them to the park to play on the swings. He had been very handsome then, and they had worshipped him. Dorothy loved him so much and was glad to devote herself to looking after him now that his dear wife had gone. She prayed he would be spared to her for a few more years at least.

But what was there to look forward to? Practically every day she had sat at the living room window, looking out for the postman, hoping he would bring her a letter from Bernard, but she had waited in vain. She had wanted to write to him as soon as she had arrived back in Exeter, but her female pride had stood in the way. Wasn't it the man who should make the running?

It was the sad death of her darling mother that had given her the excuse she needed to write to him. Now, she felt sure, Bernard would have to write back, if only to tell her he was sorry for her loss. She had also written to Robbie because she owed him that. He was a good friend, probably a better one than Bernard would ever be. But she loved Bernard, and she wished with every fibre of her being that she didn't.

She ran to the door at the sound of the clatter of the letter box and picked up the post lying on the coconut matting.

"Is that the post?" her father called querulously from the kitchen, where he was making the breakfast.

"Yes, Dad," she called back. "Only bills, I'm afraid." But it wasn't only bills. There was one handwritten letter postmarked 'SW'. She prayed it was from Bernard and not Robbie. She tore open the envelope. Her prayers had been answered at last.

My dear Dorothy,

I was very sorry to hear that your mother has passed away, but at least her suffering is ended now and you can begin to rebuild your life. I hope your father continues well and that you have no concerns about his health at the moment. You need time to yourself, my dear.

Robbie sends his love too, and will write to you separately, no doubt. We are making progress on the fate of those poor Norwegian children and have got a positive identification of the killer – we think. I'll let you know as soon as we have more news.

I would love to come and visit you one day, or maybe you can come and stay here when you can get away. Maybe we can go to the theatre or have a meal. I'm sure Robbie would love to join us, too. We'll make a night of it and, hopefully, cheer you up in these dark days.

So, until we meet again, may God bless you.

Your loving friend,

Bernard

He had signed himself off in the same way she had. She had thought long and hard about how to end her letter to him: she didn't want to appear too forward but, at the same time, she didn't want to give him the impression that she didn't have feelings for him. Now he had replied back in the same fashion: that, surely, was a good sign, except the rest of the letter gave the lie to it. He couldn't have been more formal if he'd tried.

Tears were starting to form in her eyes, as her father called out that the breakfast was ready. As usual, it would be a plate of sizzling bacon and eggs, no mouthful of which she would be able to eat now.

London, April 1949

"Hi, Bernie," said Robbie, as he swept into the vicarage study one bright spring morning. "I've just got news from Gilbert – it's not good, I'm afraid."

"Come and sit down, Robbie," said Bernard. He was seated by his study fire, which was burning fitfully as the April weather, although bright, was still bitterly cold.

"It appears, according to Gilbert's mother, that her cleaner's husband is not the man." Robbie sat down, putting his hands on his knees and staring into the fire with a morose expression on his face.

"Not the man?"

"No. Not the man. He's got a tattoo, all right. On his left arm, apparently," Robbie continued.

"Well then! Why do you think he's not the man?" asked Bernard, puzzled.

"Because the bloody man's tattoo is of a *dragon*, not a snake."

Bernard's puzzled frown cleared and was replaced almost at once by a wide smile. "Balderdash!" he exclaimed.

Robbie looked shocked. He had never heard his friend speak with such vehemence before. "What do you mean?" he asked.

"Why on earth can't you see it?"

"See what, man?"

"To the eyes of a child," Bernard started to explain slowly, "a dragon could look very much like a snake. Especially if they didn't get a close look at it."

Robbie's eyes widened. "By Jove, Bernie, you're right! What an idiot I am." He laughed happily. "So the cleaner's husband is very much in the frame again."

"I should say so," said Bernard.

"We have him at last," said Robbie, grinning.

But Bernard's smile had faded now. "But we're no further forward, really," he said. "We don't have a single witness that can verify he's the killer. No court of law will be able to convict him on the evidence, knowing how it was arrived at."

"Bugger!" was all Robbie could say. He didn't even apologise for it, and Bernard didn't blame him.

Bergen, April 1949

Baldur was now back at his lumberjack trade. Work had picked up again and he was out of the way for most of the day, for which Gunda was very thankful. The more she got to know the man who had moved in with her so promptly, the more she disliked and distrusted him. Still, at least he wasn't a murderer. Apparently, the police were looking for someone with a snake tattoo on his arm, and Baldur's was definitely a dragon. A windy, slimy-looking one, it's true, but at least it had legs and was blowing fire out of its nostrils. Definitely a dragon.

They were both sitting at breakfast, and Baldur was leaning his elbows on the table, with his sleeves rolled up. She now had the opportunity to study the tattoo at close quarters, while he was engrossed in his newspaper and not paying her the slightest attention.

Since Berthina had asked her about the snake tattoo, she had been more worried than ever. When she had asked her why did she want to know, Berthina's reply had been vague, and it hadn't satisfied her at all. However, Gunda had got the very real impression that her employer knew more about the Dahl murders than she was letting on. Still, Baldur's tattoo wasn't a snake, so that was all right.

It was definitely a dragon. She screwed up her eyes and looked at it from various angles. It couldn't be mistaken for a serpent, could it? If you only got a quick glance at it, perhaps it could. Its body was long and snake-like, and certainly a child could easily mistake it for either. Suddenly she was filled with fear. She was now more certain than of anything she had ever been in her life that the man sitting there at the breakfast table, *her* breakfast table in *her* house, was a cold-blooded killer.

She leapt up and grabbed his empty plate. "Have you finished?" she asked abruptly. "I need to get on. I have to go to Mrs Hardcastle's this morning."

"All right," he grumbled, folding up his paper. "Give me a chance."

At the kitchen sink, she held on to the taps and thought furiously. I want him out of my house *now*! she screamed silently. *Now*! He came up behind her and put his arms round her waist, slowly raising his big hairy hands up to her breasts. She slapped them away. "Don't!" she cried. "Can't you see I'm trying to wash up?"

"You never seem to want to have any fun these days," he muttered, putting his hands back on her breasts with more force this time.

"Just let go or I'll scream the place down," she yelled, grabbing a knife from the draining board.

"Okay, okay!" said Baldur stepping back quickly. "Put that down, you stupid woman, before someone gets hurt."

"Look, Baldur," she said, as he backed off. She rested the knife back on the draining board, keeping it still within her grasp. "This isn't working."

"What, the knife? Does it need sharpening?"

"Don't make out you don't know what I mean," she said, more calmly than she felt. "I mean our relationship isn't working. I want you to leave my house. Today, please."

Baldur glared at her but didn't reply. The hard glint in his eyes was enough. If looks could kill …

"Did you hear what I said?" She moved her fingers towards the knife.

"I heard you," he said in a low, threatening tone. "Oh yes, I heard you, all right."

"Well, then, please, Baldur, I'm sorry, but I really want you to go."

"And where am I to go, pray?" he asked, still menacingly. She noticed he was clenching and unclenching his fists.

"That's up to you. Maybe some other stupid woman will take you on, if you're lucky," she said with brave sarcasm. "I just want you out of my house."

"But I like it *here*," he said, moving a pace towards her.

"I can't help that," she said quietly. Her hand was on the knife now. "I don't want you here. You make me nervous. You hit me sometimes. I'm not sure I can trust you. Please, Baldur, don't cause any trouble. Just go."

"Why should I cause any trouble?" he asked. "It's you who's causing the trouble. I don't want to go. I want to stay, and I'm going to stay. Got it?"

Gunda was panicking now. She had been living with an extremely dangerous man for almost six months, and she trembled at the thought of what might have happened to her; still might, she suddenly realised. She had to get rid of him somehow: now, at once.

She took a deep inward breath and told herself to calm down. Should she just leave it for now, go to work as usual, then call the police? Mrs Hardcastle had a phone, she was sure she would let her use it, especially in the circumstances.

Berthina was worried about her, and it was clear that she suspected Baldur was the murderer of the Dahl family. She had suspected it herself, and now she was sure it was true. How her employer knew about the tattoo was a mystery, but there was no doubt she had got the information from somewhere. And the reaction of her sister, Liv, to Baldur's appearance couldn't be easily brushed aside, either, even if the poor woman was suffering from dementia.

Gunda started to gather up her things, ready to depart for work. There was nothing else to be done. Soon, she hoped, Baldur Hanssen would be under lock and key. As she made to leave the kitchen, however, he barred her way. "Where do you think you're going?" he asked, raising a dark, bushy eyebrow.

"To work, of course, where else?" She was now thoroughly frightened as she tried to ease past him.

He pushed her roughly back. "No, you're not, missy. There's no way I'm going to let you out of this flat now. What's to stop you going to go to the police?"

"Why would I do that?" she bluffed, wondering if she was going to be able to hold on to her breakfast much longer. It was going to come out of her, one way or the other.

"You know, don't you?" he challenged.

"Know what? What are you talking about?"

"About my killing Marianne Dahl and the children. You've known for a long time."

"Well, if I didn't know before, I do now," she spat at him.

She felt a warm sensation run down her legs, as she realised she wasn't going to get out of the flat alive.

Mrs Hardcastle was worried. It was well after ten o'clock, and there was no sign of Gunda. It was not like her to be so late. Ever since her cleaner had confided in her, she had been worried. It was the tattoo that had finally done it. Snake, dragon: there was very little difference, especially to the eyes of a small child. If Gunda had convinced herself they were different, then she was a fool.

Suddenly, there was a loud ring on the doorbell, as if somebody was leaning with the full force of their body upon it. "All right," she called. "Don't press so hard, you'll break it."

Opening the door, she saw a flustered-looking, red-faced Baldur Hanssen standing there.

"Oh, hello," she said, squaring up to him. Even if she was intimidated by him, she wasn't going to show it. "I was expecting Gunda today. Is she not coming? Is she ill?"

"No, Mrs Hardcastle," he said softly. "She won't be coming as she had to go home to her mother. She's not well and the doctor's told her it's serious."

"Oh, dear," said Berthina, not believing one word of it. "I'm sorry to hear that. Give her my best wishes."

"I will," he said and turned to go. "Oh, by the way, she won't be coming back to work here anymore."

"Oh? Why not?"

"Because I'm working now and making enough money for both of us. I've told her she doesn't need to work anymore. It's a pittance, anyway," he added accusingly.

"I'm sorry you feel I don't pay her enough," said Berthina with feeling. "She has never complained."

"Well, she wouldn't, she's too soft," declared Baldur. "Anyway, you won't be seeing her again, so I'll take what she's owed now."

"You won't," said Mrs Hardcastle determinedly. "I won't accept her resignation either, until I hear it from her own lips."

Baldur looked as if he was about to hit her, then he was all smiles. "Quite right, Mrs Hardcastle. I'll get her to come and see you when she gets back."

"You do that," said Berthina, closing the door firmly on him. She leaned against it and realised she was sweating. She had never felt afraid of anybody in her life until now. Well, maybe a few Nazis, but not a single individual like that. He was an evil man, it oozed out of every pore.

∾

Baldur stared at Mrs Hardcastle's closed front door and grinned. He took the stairs, not waiting for the lift, realising he had a spring in his step and that a metaphorical weight had been lifted from his shoulders. He was looking forward to work today. The weather was bright and dry, perfect for being outdoors, chopping trees.

That's right, he told himself. Do everything as usual; that way no suspicions will be aroused. He congratulated himself on dealing with Mrs Hardcastle. He could have threatened her for the money but had stopped himself just in time. It wouldn't do for her to get suspicious of him now. Now that things were looking up again. He had a job and a nice home. *His* home now. Gunda would have no need of it again.

London, April 1949

Robbie told Bernard he was mad. He told him that several times a day, ever since his friend had confessed to him that he was unsure of his feelings for Dorothy.

"You might as well be dead, man," declared Robbie that Sunday after dinner.

It had been a particularly tasty roast beef that day, courtesy of Mrs Harper. The Yorkshire pudding had melted in their mouths and the jam roly poly that followed had seemingly been sent from heaven, not Mrs Harper's kitchen. Bernard and Robbie had been swapping Sunday dinners now for several months – one week it was Lucy Carter's turn to feed the two of them, the next Nancy Harper's. They both knew whose cooking they preferred, though.

"But you don't understand, Robbie," Bernard protested, lighting his pipe. "I know I should welcome her with open arms, but it's not that easy for me. You see, I've been hurt before. Sophie ..."

"Oh yes, yes," said Robbie impatiently. "I know all about that. But you can't go on living in the past. Why let one unhappy love affair taint you for the rest of your life?"

"It's easy for you to say. Besides, even if I wanted to be with her, she's not here, is she?"

"So what? Exeter's hardly Outer Mongolia, is it? You don't need a sled and a team of huskies to get there."

"I know, Robbie, I know. It's just that ..."

300

"Here we go! Excuses, excuses. Don't you want to be happy?"

"But I *am* happy," said Bernard, "very happy. I've got all I need here. And you yourself envy me Mrs Harper. What more does a man need?"

"But don't you ever feel the need of a woman?"

Bernard reddened with embarrassment. He knew what Robbie was getting at. The lure of the flesh hadn't really been an issue with him since Sophie, and he still didn't feel that way about Dorothy. Perhaps he never would feel that way again about any woman.

"I – I can't say I miss that side of things, Robbie," he confessed. "I don't think I need a woman in the same way most men do."

Robbie sighed. "Perhaps you don't," he smiled. "You know your own mind best, old boy. But it does seem a shame when a lovely lady like Dorothy is pining for you and you can't reciprocate. I'd give anything to be in your shoes."

"It's a conundrum," said Bernard. "I wish there was something I could say or do, Robbie. I wish Dorothy preferred you. It would be best all round."

Robbie didn't reply, and the pair remained silent for a while, sucking their pipes, each deep in their own private thoughts. After a while, Robbie broke the silence with a sigh.

"Changing the subject, Bernie, I suppose we'll never be able to get that man convicted. It looks like the children will go on haunting that blasted tree forever."

"We tried our best," said Bernard. "You, especially, couldn't have done more. You mustn't blame yourself if that man gets away with it."

Just then Mrs Harper knocked on the study door and, as was her wont, entered without waiting for permission.

"Is it too much to ask you to knock?" asked Bernard.

"Sorry, I'm sure," she said, not sounding sorry at all.

"Well, what is it?"

"I've just 'ad Gilbert on the phone and 'e asked me to pass on a message to you. But, if you don't want to 'ear it…" Mrs Harper sounded offended.

"Of course we want to hear it, Mrs Aitch. Just tell us," Bernard wasn't in a placatory mood.

"'E said 'e'd had a telephone call from his mum last night, which must 'ave cost a pretty penny all the way from Norway. Mind you, she can afford it. 'Er 'usband left 'er well off, so Marjorie told me. Did you know, she..."

Robbie interrupted her impatiently. "Mrs Harper, as much as the state of Mrs Hardcastle's finances may be of interest to you, they aren't to me or Bernard. What did Gilbert say she told him?"

"Oh, er – yes, let me think. Something about 'er cleaner 'aving gone to look after 'er sick mother, and that she wouldn't be coming back to work for 'er anymore. Mrs 'Ardcastle, that is, not 'er mother."

"Well, what of it? Her cleaner's private life is no concern of ours, is it?" snapped Robbie.

"Well, that's what *I* said. But apparently she remembered afterwards that 'er cleaner's mum 'ad died a year ago."

Robbie looked at Bernard at hearing this. "Did her cleaner tell Mrs Hardcastle that she was going away?" asked Bernard.

"That's just it. It was this Baldur told 'er, apparently."

"Oh," said Robbie. "That casts a completely different light on matters. So, when did Gilbert's mother say this happened?"

"It would 'ave been only the day before yesterday. She was so worried, though, she decided to call Gilbert, rather than write to 'im, what with 'ow long it takes these days and what with Charlie losing things all the time."

"Anything else?" asked Robbie.

"No, that's all, I think. Gilbert said 'e'd pop round later, if you like."

"No need to bother him," said Robbie. "But thank him for me, won't you?"

"Yes, Doc. I'll do that."

Mrs Harper slipped quietly out of the room and left the two men staring at each other in dismay.

"How about a telegram to the Bergen police?" suggested Bernard.

"I'm sure Mrs Hardcastle would have contacted the police herself," Robbie pointed out.

"Oh, yes, of course she would," replied Bernard.

Just then, there was a polite tap on the door. Both men were surprised when Mrs Harper did not enter straightaway.

"Come in, Mrs Aitch," called Bernard, trying not to laugh.

She remained outside, however.

"Mrs Aitch? Come in."

"Is it all right if I come in?" came her disembodied voice.

Bernard sighed, annoyed now. "Okay, Mrs Aitch, you've made your point. Please do come in."

She obeyed at last, and stood before him, quietly waiting.

"Yes, Mrs Aitch? What is it?"

"I was just waiting, like. I didn't want to interrupt you."

"What is it, Mrs Aitch?" yelled Bernard, exasperated.

"Just that I forgot to tell you, Gilbert said 'is mum 'ad called the police and they'd gone round to question this bloke ..."

"Good, good," beamed Robbie. "Did Gilbert say what came of it?"

"Er, well, let me think," said Mrs Harper, obviously enjoying herself. She could see the two men were desperate to hear the rest of Gilbert's news, but she wasn't in any hurry to dispense it. "Oh yes," she continued slowly. "The police said they were perfectly satisfied that Gilbert's mum's cleaner 'ad gone visiting, and they 'ad no reason to probe any further."

"Idiots! What about the fact that she had gone to look after her sick mother – so sick, in fact, she'd been dead for a year!" Robbie was pacing up and down now.

"Well, that's what Gilbert said. Apparently, this Baldur bloke, or whatever 'is name is, told them 'e'd made a mistake. It was 'er aunt, not 'er mother, she'd gone to see."

"And they just took his word for it? What a shower the Bergen police are," declared Robbie. "They obviously don't like work! They're going to let him get away with it."

"I suppose it's difficult to prove anything," said Bernard, trying to calm him down. Unsuccessfully.

"Nuts!" said Robbie succinctly. "They could at least get a name and address of where she's supposed to have gone. They could follow that up, at least."

"Maybe Baldur doesn't know himself. It wouldn't be that unusual," said Bernard. "Or maybe he told the police that she'd left him, and he'd just told Mrs Hardcastle that she was looking after a sick relative to save face. It's hard to prove, you have to admit."

"It's time the police took this seriously," growled Robbie. "A woman and two children – possibly *two* women – have met their deaths at his hands and they're not lifting a finger."

"I know it looks that way, Robbie, but look at it from their point of view. It's not much to go on, is it?"

"Poppycock! The murders only happened last year. What difference does it make anyway? Our police never stopped looking for Jack the Ripper, even though they had little to go on."

"They never found him, though, did they?" Bernard pointed out.

৵

The weather had turned unseasonably warm during the last week of April. Sick of sitting at his study desk writing sermons, condolence letters and other parish correspondence, Bernard decided to take advantage of the pleasant sunshine and set off for the park. He meandered along its winding paths, lost in thought. Robbie was still hassling him to get in touch with Dorothy again, but he hadn't done so, and wondered now if he ever would. He wanted to see her again more than anything in the world, but every time he'd picked up the phone to call her or a pen to write to her, he'd bottled it. Just what was stopping him? Fear of rejection, he supposed. After Sophie, he knew he couldn't take it.

He sighed as he seated himself on an empty park bench and watched the ducks splashing about in the pond. They were content, at least. Their fluffy, feathery lives were all mapped out for them and they were just happy to quack and fight for the breadcrumbs that people threw to them. It must be great to be a duck, he thought. They didn't even mind when it rained. In fact, they enjoyed it.

He was worried about Robbie's obsession with the Dahl murder case; he had become too involved. He had done everything humanly possible, but it hadn't been enough. His friend would just have to come to terms with it, sooner or later. He couldn't go on knocking his head against a brick wall. If only little Halle Dahl hadn't been a ghost, or Gilbert's Aunt Liv hadn't been gaga.

The sun was pouring down now. The bitter cold of only the previous week was a distant memory. It was even hotter than he'd known it in June. The world seemed topsy-turvy these days. Suddenly he felt a presence beside him and, without turning his head, knew just exactly who it was.

"Hello again," said Diabol. "I expect you thought you'd seen the last of me, eh?"

"Not really. All bad pennies turn up again in the end," said Bernard philosophically. "Who are you after this time?"

"I'll tell you in a minute." Diabol grinned impishly. "Do you notice anything different about me?"

Bernard studied him carefully. Same little weird coloured eyes and tufted hair. "No," he replied. "You look just as repellent as ever."

This was obviously taken as a compliment. "Nice of you to say so," he said. "But look closely at my head."

Bernard didn't really want to look closely at any part of him; the sight turned his stomach, but he did as he was bid. "Er – there seems to be a couple of little lumps just above your ears," he remarked. "I don't remember seeing them before."

"You've got it! They're my horns – I've got them at last. Aren't you going to congratulate me?"

"Congratulations," said Bernard unenthusiastically. "I'm very happy for you. Now, please, can you go away and leave me alone? I want to think."

"They're only tiny now," said Diabol, ignoring Bernard's request. "But as I get more experience, they'll grow. I can't wait."

"Good for you. Now, goodbye."

"Don't you want to know what I can do, now I've got my horns?"

"Not particularly." Bernard sighed. The little red-eyed, jerky-elbowed, tufty-haired runt wasn't going to leave him alone; in fact, he seemed very much attached to him. He closed his eyes in exasperation.

Suddenly a warm, soft female voice spoke into his ear. "Hello Bernard. How are you? Long time no see."

Could it be? How come Dorothy was there? He opened his eyes and there she was. There was no sign of Diabol, just this beautiful woman, dressed in pale green, smiling sweetly at him. "Dorothy! It's lovely to see you. I didn't know you were in London. You should have telephoned to let me know."

"No, Bernard. I'm not here – I'm still in Devon, but I would love to come and see you sometime – if you want me too."

"Of course I do, Dorothy. I'd love to see you, anytime." He turned to kiss her on the cheek but felt the rough parchment skin of Diabol instead. Dorothy had gone. She had never been there in the first place.

"See? That's what I can do."

Bernard glared at him. "Do what?"

"Summon up the people you love most in all the world – even if they're dead – as long as they went down below, of course. I've no power getting people from upstairs, I'm afraid."

Bernard wondered why he was having this conversation at all. "How do you know about Dorothy?" he asked, curious in spite of himself.

Diabol tapped the side of his weird, pointy nose. "I have my methods. My powers are much greater now I've got my horns. Besides, you made quite a fuss when I told you last time that I was about to take her from you, remember?"

Bernard smiled. He didn't know why, but he almost liked him, even though he was so repugnant.

"Hello, Bernard. Remember me?"

Bernard swallowed and went hot all over. Sophie? He'd never forget the sound of her voice. She was sitting beside him now. "How are you keeping?"

"Sophie, is it really you?" She looked lovelier than he remembered, more mature perhaps, but all the better for it. Then he saw the wedding ring on her finger.

"Yes, it's really me. I think a lot about you. I really loved you, you know."

"Then why did you leave me like that?"

"I promise, Bernard, one day you'll find out. One day we'll meet again – oh, not for many years, but one day. Then I'll tell you everything."

Suddenly Diabol was back and Sophie had gone. Bernard was in tears. "How could you do that to me?" he cried. "How could you be so cruel?"

"Well, I'm not exactly on the side of the angels, you know," he pointed out, jerking his elbows. "Now, to the real reason I'm here."

"I'm not interested in the reason, real or otherwise. You've completely upset me. I can't think straight. Go away." Bernard wiped his eyes furiously with his hanky and blew his nose noisily, but Diabol stayed where he was, looking at him quizzically.

"Feeling better?" he asked eventually, as Bernard sat quietly, red-eyed, beside him.

"Not really. Look, tell me what you want, then go."

"Okay. I've been given one last escorting job to do and I think you can help me. I need to get this man down below as soon as possible. He's a special case and needs making an example of. The fire and brimstone treatment will be awaiting him with a vengeance. They're really looking forward to it as they haven't had someone so wicked to deal with for a long time. It'll be no picnic for him, I can assure you."

"You enjoy being cruel, don't you? Anyway, what makes you think I can help you find this man for you? I don't know anyone deserving fire and brimstone. God, it's not Robbie is it?"

Diabol consulted his clipboard. "Robbie? No, it's nobody called Robbie. His name is Baldur, Baldur Hanssen. He lives in Bergen in Norway. I understand you know him?"

"I've never met him," said Bernard, suddenly perking up. He felt himself grinning inwardly. "But I know the name."

"Well, do you know where I can find him?"

"If it's the Baldur Hanssen I think you mean, and it's by no means certain, knowing you." He paused, grinning outwardly now.

Baldur looked hurt. "Go on, if it is? I'm sure I've got the name right this time."

"Very well, then," said Bernard, still grinning. "Then I think I can help you."

Printed in Great Britain
by Amazon